"Hey, Adam," Abe called from the car. "What's the problem?"

I walked back to the Mustang. I didn't want to make a public broadcast of my next move. "They're not going to open the gate," I said. "I'm going over the wall."

"That wall's a mother," Jerry said. "Let me check out that gate."

I heard the barking of dogs approaching the wall. These were not the friendly woofs of the family lapdogs. "What have you got in mind?"

"Easy, man. I just hot-wire the box and we're in. No sweat."

"If you can do it fast, go for it."

Jerry dragged his long frame out of the back seat, pushing Abe's face against the windowshield in the process. "Won't take more than a pair of seconds."

He walked to the post where the gate controls were mounted, picked up a bowling-ball-sized rock and smashed it against the intercom. The shiny steel cover, dented and mangled, swung by a single screw. He plunged his arm into the rectangular hole in the brickwork, yanked out a tangled nest of wires, and twisted the ends of two of them together.

The gate slowly rolled back.

"Nice job," I said to Jerry as he climbed back into the car. "You're a real artist. No one will ever know we've been here."

"Thanks."

HIS TECHNIQUE COULD USE A LITTLE WORK . . .

PRAISE FOR RICK HANSON'S SPARE PARTS

"A very funny first novel!"

—*Playboy*

"With dialogue reminiscent of Robert Crais and characters as quirky as Carl Hiaasen, Hanson has a winner of a debut here!"

—*Once Upon a Crime*

"Free-flowing prose, offbeat humor, an enticing protagonist, and an engaging love affair combine well in this auspicious and entertaining debut!"

—*Library Journal*

"Hanson generates a high energy tale that will leave readers eager for a sequel."

—*Publishers Weekly*

"A brash, friendly, eager-to-please first novel whose cast of comic types makes it as good-natured and mysterious as a rerun of *Get Smart!*"

—*Kirkus Reviews*

"This zany mystery is irresistible!"

—*Rendezvous*

"It's something of a trapeze act to mix humor and crime, capers and comedy. Do it right, it looks effortless. Do it wrong and fall to your death. Rick Hanson proves a deft acrobat, swinging from thrills to laughter with the greatest of ease."

—*Albuquerque Journal*

MORTAL REMAINS

RICK HANSON

PINNACLE BOOKS
KENSINGTON PUBLISHING CORP.

PINNACLE BOOKS are published by

Kensington Publishing Corp.
850 Third Avenue
New York, NY 10022

First Hardcover Printing: June, 1995
First Pinnacle Printing: June, 1996
10 9 8 7 6 5 4 3 2 1

Printed in the United States of America

For Kay.
You made my life more than I ever believed it could be.

Chapter One

The pin was out of the grenade. I gripped the lethal steel ball so tightly I feared it would jump from my muddy fist like a bar of wet soap. Rivers of sweat spilled from my brow and burned my eyes. A Huey-sized mosquito buzzed into my ear and started a blood siphon. The urge to slap away the giant insect was maddening, but the slightest movement would betray our position. And they were too many for . . .

"Adam!"

"Huh?"

"Did you hear me?" Alison asked.

I stabbed a finger into my ear, but the mosquito was gone. I wiped my forehead with a gingham napkin, which had been wadded so tightly in my fist, it retained the shape of my grip like a piece of checkered modeling clay. I strained to remember what she'd said.

Her green eyes narrowed slightly. "Adam McCleet, you haven't heard a word, have you?"

"Hell, yeah. Sure, I have."

She hoisted herself onto the teak bulwark that surrounded the cockpit of *Raptor*, a thirty-foot sloop that I'd borrowed from my friend, Reeves Washington. "So? What did I say?"

"Something about money, wasn't it?" It seemed as good a guess as any.

"No, Adam. We were not talking about money." She crossed her legs and her bathrobe gaped open, offering a distracting view of long, graceful legs. "You never listen to me anymore."

Alison Brooks was not fond of being ignored. We'd planned a day of sailing and I wanted a happy crew. I detected a hint of mutiny in her tone. Lifting my empty coffee mug, I pretended to sip, thoughtfully, stalling as long as I could, but I knew I was kidding myself. She expected an answer and, beautiful as she looked, she didn't look like she planned on letting go until she had one.

I took another guess. "Were we talking about sex?"

"Vietnam, Adam." Alison stood and began clearing the remains of our on-board breakfast, two paper plates sparsely scattered with bagel crumbs. "I said, do you think about Vietnam much?"

"You mean like flashbacks? Steaming jungles, giant insects, ambushes, exploding people, things like that?" I stood, rested my elbows on the boom and gazed beyond the gangway that connected to the floating dock. A rich layer of neon-green grass covered the hillside that sloped from my studio to the shoreline of the Willamette River. "No, Alison, I never think about Vietnam."

I heard a disgusted mutter as she slipped below into the cabin. The fact was, lately I'd spent more time thinking about that part of my life than I cared to admit. Three weeks earlier, my sister, Margot the Malignant, had volunteered me as a candidate to design and sculpt a veterans' memorial of some kind for the Noble Heights town square. The reason she had brought my name up was not that she wanted to help her big brother's career or because she actually believed the critics who said I was one of Oregon's most promising sculptors. Margot asked me because she wanted to earn points with her trendy baby-boomer neighbors who, in the absence of any history of their own, had decided to acknowledge the sixties with a large superficial gesture.

My higher voice told me that I'd be better off with a frontal lobotomy than to get near anything involving Margot. The last time she sucked me into helping her out, I came within a hair's-breadth of losing some fairly essential body parts. However, Alison had been quick to point out that veterans' groups were always struggling to raise funds for memorials. If a bunch of doctors and lawyers in Noble Heights with more disposable income than brains wanted to spend their own money for a statue, I should, as a veteran, be delighted to be the artist.

It did seem like a more valid contribution than tying yellow ribbons in the dogwood tree in my front yard. However, once I got started making the sketches to present to the memorial committee, the exercise had brought back images and emotions nearly forgotten. I had planned to escape, at least for a couple of days, from those memories. That's what the boat was for.

Saturday evening, Alison and I had sailed *Raptor* from its regular mooring, about six miles up river from my place, to my private dock. We'd spent the night on board playing princess and the pirate king. Alison was the princess.

This morning, however, the previous night of sexual abandon yet unparalleled in this century had been forgotten. She stuck her head out of the cabin and gave me her I-mean-business look. "How about war in general? Do you ever think about that?"

The late June sun warmed my face. The boat rocked gently, as a puff of wind carried the scent of lilacs, from the bushes in my yard. I had a light breakfast under my swashbuckle, and I didn't want to dampen my festive mood with a lot of talk about wars.

"Pirate kings only think of buried treasure, tropical islands and bare-breasted beauties with nipples that point toward the sky."

"You're impossible," she said.

"Yar," I replied.

"Oh, all right, Mr. Pirate King," she teased. "I will indulge you. But only if you promise to pay attention when I'm talking."

"Yar," I agreed.

"Yar yourself." She grinned.

Good. She'd kept her sense of humor and the game was still on. I loved her unpredictability. I would have followed her below and had my pirate way with her but we were expecting her younger brother at any minute. I settled for a wet kiss and a quick feel under her robe.

She went below again, and I climbed onto the cabin top and began to strip the blue canvas sail cover from the boom. "What brought this on, Alison? I mean, I don't want to be evasive, but I'd really prefer a lighter topic."

I could hear her rattling around in the cabin beneath me. "I was thinking about Eric."

Eric was Alison's brother and, at age twenty-seven, the baby of the family. "What about him?"

She poked out her head and said, "He's been acting different lately. Edgy, short tempered. Last month he quit his job for no apparent reason. When I asked why, he said his boss was an idiot and he'd rather starve than work for an idiot."

"That's not so unusual," I said, "all my bosses have been idiots, too."

"He was working for my mother."

I kept a straight face. "Are you going to give him a job?"

"Are you implying that I'm an idiot, too?"

"Never," I said. "You, Ms. Brooks, are the highly competent owner of the highly prestigious Brooks Art

Gallery. One of the movers and shakers of Portland. An outstanding woman in the community. A pillar of—"

"Enough of your pirate flattery." She ducked below deck. "To tell the truth, I'd hire Eric in a minute. He's personable and good-looking. He'd be great."

She appeared in the companionway wearing white cotton shorts and a black bikini top. Her auburn hair was tied back and crowned with a white visor. She touched the tip of her fingers to the brim of the visor and made a casual salute. "How do I look?"

Compared to my khaki shorts, no shirt, no-shoes ensemble, she looked overdressed, but very sexy. "Yar," I growled, "yer the classiest mate a gob could hope fer." I leapt, Errol Flynn style, from the cabin top into the cockpit. I pulled her close and planted a bend-over-backward kiss on her lips. She laced her fingers into my hair and relaxed in my arms as if she would be content to stay there all day.

The barking of my neighbor's wolfhound, Binky, distracted us.

"Binky is probably barking at Eric," I said. The huge, scraggly beast apparently thought it was his duty to guard my driveway since he regularly crapped in my yard.

"Post-traumatic stress disorder," she said as I returned her to the upright position.

"Binky? He's a little uptight maybe, but—"

"Not Binky. I think Eric may be having some of the symptoms. Maybe you could feel him out. Share some of your own insights."

I remembered. His Marine reserve unit had been called up for Desert Storm. He'd been wounded in action and had been awarded a number of citations for heroism. Though I'd only met Eric once, he didn't strike me as someone who needed counseling. As far as I was concerned, that was just fine. War stories had long since lost their luster for me. "You think I may have some personal knowledge of PTSD?"

"Hello!" Eric yelled from atop the hill.

We waved to him and he started down the grass-covered embankment.

"Adam, you're one of the only veterans I know, and you don't seem to be in any kind of denial. I was just hoping you could kind of observe him and tell me what you think."

I handed her the folded sail cover. "I don't want to get into your brother's business. But since we're all going to be on the same boat together for several hours, I guess I can't help but observe."

"I love you." She kissed me on the cheek and ducked below to stow the canvas.

Supposedly, it had been Alison's last-minute idea to invite her brother for the day. I wondered if this had been her plan all along. I wondered if my arms and legs would even move if someone else wasn't pulling the strings.

I took up the position of official greeter and watched as Eric strode down the gangway onto the dock. He looked even younger than his age, with his strawberry-blond hair cropped close. He was still in the reserves, but his physical conditioning was above and beyond the call of duty. Though he was only about five feet nine inches tall, his body was covered with thick, well defined muscles.

I resisted an urge to put my shirt on. How much dedication, I wondered, did it take to get in that kind of shape? He looked as if he'd been pumping buildings. All I had on this kid was a few inches in height, a tan, and more chest hair. I figured the advantage could go either way on the extra eighteen years of living.

He smiled like Huck Finn as he stepped onto the dock. "Hey, Adam, it's gonna be a scorcher. But the wind's picking up. Should be a good day for sailing."

I extended a hand to help him make the four-foot step

from the dock up to the boat. But he tossed me his day pack and vaulted into the cockpit.

"It's always a good day for sailin', Eric me lad."

Alison poked her head out of the cabin. "Hi, glad you could make it." I gave her Eric's pack and she disappeared back into the cabin.

"Sorry I'm late," Eric said. "I had an early appointment, then some fool in a Yugo broke down in the fast lane of the freeway. So the idiot cops responded with three patrol cars and two tow trucks and blocked the other three lanes."

"A Yugo, huh?" Eric probably could have picked the dinky vehicle up and single-handedly carried it off the freeway. "You can relax now. There won't be any traffic jams out here."

Eric crouched down and peered into the cabin. "What are you doing down there?"

Alison called back, "I'm stowing stuff. Adam said, if I'm a real good little mate, he'll let me steer the boat." She emerged from the cabin and stepped into the cockpit. "Right, Adam?"

I said she could hold my tiller, but that was last night. "That's right. You're the helmsman."

Alison moved to her station at the classic, knuckle-buster steering wheel and took a wide stance. "Helms-woman, if you don't mind," she corrected.

"So what's the plan?" Eric asked.

"We have a couple of options," I said. "We can sail leisurely up river for a few hours, then turn around and sail back. That'll use up most of the day. Or," I added with considerably more enthusiasm, "we can head down river, about three miles, and join in an open-class sailing regatta. Alison and I already talked it over and decided to leave it up to you."

"A race? I'm up for that." Eric said.

I could see the pirate in his eyes. He'd be good crew. "The race it is, then."

Eric and I took in the lines and the wind did a nice job of pushing *Raptor* away from the dock. Alison held a steady helm while we raised the sails. In a few minutes, we scooted along the Willamette on a close reach for the "Mid-Summer Madness," an open-class regatta. Reeves had already registered and paid the entry fee for the race. Alison and I had been scheduled to be his crew, but he was called away unexpectedly. Which was actually a shame in light of Alison's concerns about Eric. Reeves Washington was a psychiatrist, Chief of Staff, at the Mount Prairie Institute. He specialized in treatment of veterans, and his observations of young Eric would mean something more than my layman's opinion. I made a mental note to pass the buck to Reeves if it seemed that Eric really had a problem, but that was for later. Right now, we were joining a boat race.

The regatta, hosted jointly by several Portland region yacht clubs, had been billed as a low-stress event. More of an excuse for sailors to meet, get drunk and swap lies. A friendly competition, if there was such a thing. I wasn't planning on winning, but I couldn't help sizing up our chances.

Since their late father had been an enthusiast, Alison and her brother were both skilled in the sport of kings. Our primary concern, however, would be the skill level of the crews on the other boats. It would be most embarrassing to return *Raptor* to her owner with a piece of plywood duct-taped over a large hole in her side.

En route, we glanced at a chart of the race course. The configuration was no surprise, one windward mark and one leeward mark. The latter would also serve as both the starting and finish line. Since I could find nothing of any consequence to obsess about, we leaned back and enjoyed the wind, the sun, and the river. Eric stretched out on the cabin top to catch some rays. He couldn't have looked more relaxed. What better therapy for a case of jangled nerves, than a day on the water?

Though I knew Alison expected me to somehow climb inside her brother's head, I had no intention of stirring his adrenaline with the subject of war, or anything remotely related.

Alison was not so inclined. "So, Eric, have you been looking for a new job?"

"I'm going to take some time off. I've got a little saved."

"R and R," she said, looking at me. "Isn't that what you veterans call it? Adam was in the Marine Corps, you know. Vietnam."

"Oh, really?" Eric said. He rolled onto his belly and eyeballed my gut, the gray in my brown hair, and the slouch that had become my permanent posture. "You were in the Corps?"

"Semper Fi," I offered as proof. I pointed out the nesting cormorants at the river's edge, hoping that Alison wouldn't feel obliged to make any other announcements.

She cleared her throat. "As a matter of fact, the man who owns this boat, Reeves Washington, is a veteran. And a psychiatrist."

"Met him," Eric said. "He works at Mount Prairie."

Alison brightened considerably, in spite of the disapproving look I shot in her direction. "You know Reeves?"

Eric flipped over to his back and pulled his Ray-Bans over his eyes. "I know what you're getting at, Sis. You think I'm crazy, disturbed, whacked out with PTSD."

"Why, no," she said. "The thought never crossed my—"

"I already talked to Mom, and I'm getting counseling at Mount Prairie. Everything's under control. I'm dealing with it, okay?"

"Absolutely," I said with heartfelt enthusiasm. Crisis averted. I looked forward to a day of smooth sailing.

After fifteen minutes, we cleared a wide bend in the river and the race course came into view. Not less than sixty sailing vessels, ranging in length from eighteen to forty feet, wove in a chaotic web as each maneuvered for the best position on the starting line.

"Awesome," Eric said.

"Every boat in Oregon must be entered in this race," Alison said as she steered toward a swarm of sails at the south end of the course. "Are you guys sure you want to do this?"

At first glance, it certainly appeared that the Mid-Summer Madness Regatta would not be as casual as previously advertised. Second and third glances led to similar conclusions. I might have been less concerned if the race had been billed as a more serious event. Open-class meant that every novice sailor from Oregon City to Astoria would be doing his best to show up the more experienced Corinthians.

"What do you think, Eric?" I asked.

He studied the cluster of sails. "We don't have to race them all, just the larger boats, in the same class as us. If we hang back at the start, we should be able to stay clear of the pack. By the time we make the windward mark, the beginners will be scattered all over the course and we'll be able to sail our own race."

I looked to Alison, but she just shrugged her shoulders, indicating the decision was mine. "Well," I said, "it's not like we really plan on winning. We're just here for the fun of it, right? If it gets too wacky and we stop having fun, we can always pull out."

After a brief discussion, the three of us agreed that Eric's idea was best for avoiding the starting line collisions that would surely occur as soon as the gun went off. The wind freshened as Alison piloted *Raptor* to the back of the pack and settled into a tight circular pattern with a dozen other boats of our approximate length and displacement. The continuous adjustments to the jib and main sheets required for sailing in circles provided an opportunity to get into synch as a team. Our proximity to the other larger vessels gave us a chance to evaluate the skill level of our competition.

Alison steered the boat and directed the sail adjustment with all the skill of an America's Cup skipper. Eric and I responded instantly and efficiently to her confident commands. We were as good a crew as any in this race, I thought.

With less than five minutes to the start, a black thirty-foot ketch with the name *Rebel* stenciled on her hull joined the pack. The semi-uniformed crew of six men wore backwards bubba caps of different colors with different logos, ranging from "Caterpillar" to "Sox." But they all wore Confederate gray T-shirts with black lettering that said, "Blow Me," and each one of them clutched a tall can of Olympia beer.

Rebel's skipper, a large, round man with a sunburned bald head and a conspicuous layer of zinc-oxide smeared on his nose and lips, reminded me of Dennis Conner with a thyroid problem. "Trim, you bunch of beer-guzzling nose-pickers!" He screamed at his hapless, one-handed crew.

I watched with vested interest as they pulled to within twenty feet of us and matched our speed. "Keep an eye on this bozo," I cautioned.

"Nice boat," he yelled toward us.

"Thanks," Alison replied with a smile and a wave.

"What do you call her?"

"*Raptor*," Eric called back.

"Rupture?" The fat man hollered. "Good name."

The nose-pickers howled, whistled and barked. "That's a good one, Jack."

Alison cast a disgusted look in my direction. "He's got a lot of nerve."

A Confederate flag, flying above the American flag in *Rebel*'s rigging, was an excellent clue as to the kind of people we were dealing with. "Ignore them. Every race has got to have at least one boat full of inbred assholes."

"What do you call that tub of yours?" Eric yelled. "Rubble?"

"Eric," Alison chastised like a big sister. "Just ignore them."

"Jack," one nose-picker yelled, "the muscle-head called us rubble."

Captain Jack cursed his drunken crew and steered the black ketch to within ten feet of us. "Nice tits on that skipper of yours," he bellowed. "She can pull my halyard anytime."

All five of the beer-guzzling nose-pickers moved to the starboard rail and resumed barking and howling.

Eric puffed up like a blowfish. His face was a bright red. "That's my sister, you fuckin' jerks!"

I tried to think of some dignified nautical terminology that would best express my concerns for the safety of my crew and my friend's boat. "Stand off, asshole!" I yelled.

That was the best I could come up with on short notice, but I promised myself I'd have a man-to-man chat with *Rebel*'s skipper after the race.

Alison, however, seemed to have a more immediate plan of action in mind. "Ready about." She spoke quietly enough so *Rebel*'s crew would not hear.

Eric and I prepared to tack. I understood, as I was sure Eric did, that Alison would fake a turn to the left. *Rebel*'s crew would fall all over each other to get to their stations in time to avoid a collision. At the last second we'd resume our previous course and have a good laugh at their expense. "Be careful," I whispered.

Alison eased the helm to the left. When the jib began to luff she yelled, "Helms a lee." A clear signal to anyone within earshot that we were turning to a starboard tack.

Jack belched a string of obscenities and the nose-pickers responded with a Chinese fire drill. One of them stubbed his toe on a turning block and hopped around on one foot until he fell from the cabin top into the cockpit. A man on the port side tried to haul the jib across but the starboard sheet was wrapped around the ankles of one of his mates who was pulled off his feet with a squeal. If Captain Jack had not grabbed the man by the throat as he fell, he might have lost him overboard. The jib back filled and *Rebel* stalled into the wind.

About the time I thought Alison would turn back to the right so that Eric and I could trim the sails for our original heading, I heard an explosion. The starting cannon. I had forgotten all about the race but Alison apparently had not.

"Trim," she ordered as she continued the turn. "We're going for the line."

Eric adjusted the jib sheet, and the big forward sail filled at once with a loud pop.

As we crossed *Rebel*'s course, our bows only missed colliding by a few feet. But the black boat still had some forward motion of her own and looked as if it would crash into our stern.

"Starboard!" I yelled. It was a reminder to *Rebel*'s crew that ours was the stand-on course and that they should yield the right of way. But the nose-pickers were in such a state of chaos I was certain a collision was imminent. I watched with dread as the distance between *Rebel*'s bow and the side of our hull closed rapidly. Captain Jack hollered, "Bear off, you stupid bitch."

I heard Alison's curt response, then her voice took on a tone of alarm. "Eric, don't," she yelled.

By the time I looked to see what it was that Alison didn't want her brother to do, Eric had jumped to *Rebel*'s foredeck, thrown one of the nose-pickers overboard and was wrestling with two more.

Chapter Two

I had a quick decision to make. Leave Eric to battle the *Rebel* forces alone? Or abandon Alison on *Raptor*?

Though I had complete confidence in Alison's nautical abilities, *Raptor* was a thirty-foot sloop. Under full sail, single-handing would be a chore.

Eric, on the other hand, had efficiently engaged the enemy. He'd pitched one crewman overboard and grappled with two others who were using the Velcro method of combat whereby they attached themselves to Eric's flailing arms and attempted to restrain him from his main goal. Which appeared to be killing Captain Jack.

"Let me go, you assholes!" Eric flung free from one of them and the other clung to his left leg, anchoring him until his buddy could grab an arm. "Let go!" Eric pointed aft. "I want him!"

Captain Jack ducked behind the wheel. "Keep him away from me. He's fuckin' crazy."

Alison made my decision for me. "Adam, help him!"

There was only one way onto the *Rebel*. I hurled myself into space. To the casual observer, I'm sure the leap looked absolutely spectacular, but as soon as my feet left the deck, I realized there wasn't enough spring in my forty-five-year-old legs to cover the distance. I was about to embarrass myself in a grand fashion. My arms stretched, and I grabbed a lifeline stanchion near *Rebel*'s bow. Though not exactly on board, at least I was attached to *Rebel*.

One of the crewmen who wasn't already fastened to Eric's biceps noticed me. "Here comes another one. Get him!"

I made a great target. With both hands, I clung to the upright stainless steel stanchion while my body hung over the side. My legs and ass dangled in the cold waters of the Willamette like two hundred pounds of salmon bait.

The half-drunk *Rebel* crewman with a bubba cap that said Coors staggered toward me. I tried to reason with him, "Help me aboard. I want to stop him."

"Ain't no way."

He pried at my fingers.

Hanging on was enough of an effort, but now I had to pull my legs out of the water and swing them onto the bulwark with Coors plucking at my fingers.

I got one leg up.

Coors tried to bite into my palm at the base of my thumb and tasted callouses like leather. Because of my sculpting, my hands and forearms are the strongest part of my body. I exchanged my grasp on the stanchion for a grip on the waistband of Coors' boxer trunks.

"Leggo, you pervert!" He stumbled backward with his shorts around his knees.

I hauled myself the rest of the way onboard.

Eric had managed to shake the two limpets overboard. Nothing stood between him and Captain Jack but Coors and me. And one more guy who poked his head out of the cabin, shrieked and retreated again.

I was still trying to be reasonable. "I'm here to help."

Coors yanked up his shorts and lunged at me. Some bubbas never learn. I stepped aside and he flew overboard and into the drink.

Eric had closed the distance between himself and Captain Jack. They were playing peek-a-boo around the mizzen mast.

"Eric!" I shouted. "That's enough, goddammit. Let's go."

Captain Jack spewed a steady stream of profanities. Interspersed were pleas for help. "Get him away from me."

"Eric!" I got close enough to grab his arm. He whirled, ready to knock me on my ass. The veins on his powerful neck stood out. His lips pulled back from his teeth in a snarl. His eyes were glassy and ice cold. I'd seen that expression before in the faces of men who were about to kill or be killed.

There would be no reasoning with Eric Brooks. He was gone. Pure aggression consumed his brain.

But how the hell was I going to subdue this young body-builder?

He shook off my grasp easily and swung back around to glare at Captain Jack.

I got behind Eric. His muscle-bound arms stuck out from his rib cage like handles. I hooked my arms over his and locked his elbows behind his back. Enraged, Eric struggled violently. Holding on was like riding a Brahama bull, but I knew I'd have to hang on for more than eight seconds.

I attempted to be the voice of reason. "Jesus Christ, get a grip. Calm down. Holy shit. Stop, goddammit."

Out of the corner of my eye, I saw Captain Jack approaching. The guy was so damned stupid that he'd passed up his chance to jump overboard and swim for shore. The *Rebel* captain had a heavy steel winch handle in his fist.

"No!" I yelled at Jack. "Get the hell out of here."

He lifted the handle over his head and swiped at Eric. I managed to yank Eric out of the way and took the full force of the blow on my shoulder. Pain shot through me, but I didn't lose my grip.

Jack was more accurate the second time. He struck Eric on the left temple, and I felt him go limp in my arms. I allowed his muscular body to slump to the deck.

"Jesus Christ," I whispered. I stared at Jack who was breathing hard.

"He was crazy," Jack said. "He was gonna kill me."

I nodded. If we hadn't stopped him, Eric would have killed this asshole. He was a Marine in top shape with recent training. He knew how to maim, mutilate and dismember.

"Maybe, next time," I said, "you'll think twice before you shoot off your mouth."

I heard Alison yelling and looked over to the *Raptor*. The sails were down and heaped on the deck like so much dirty laundry. The four *Rebel* crewmen she'd plucked from the river huddled, dripping and shivering, on the foredeck. She'd started the auxilliary diesel and eased up beside *Rebel*. "Is Eric all right?"

That depended on your definition of all right. He was still breathing, groaning a little and beginning to regain consciousness. The laceration on his left temple bled heavily but not fatally. I yelled to Alison, "We should get him to a hospital." Then, I turned to Captain Jack, "I'd advise you to get your sorry ass out of sight. Go below."

"You can't tell me what to do. This is my fuckin' boat."

Some people never learn. I was tempted to let nature take its course and leave Captain Jack to Eric. The world would probably be a better place. But Eric was Alison's brother, and I felt responsible. "If you don't go below," I said, "I'll kill you myself."

At that moment, Eric surged to his feet. Though unsteady, he balanced on his muscular legs. The blood from his wound trickled down the side of his face and ran a steady stream down his neck and onto his chest where it mixed with sweat. In spite of his weakened condition, he looked lethal. Captain Jack took my advice. He ducked out of sight.

"Eric, are you okay?"

Both hands clamped against the sides of his head as if he were trying to hold his skull together. He wobbled on his feet, staggered to the bulwark and puked over the side.

Though the sight of Eric coughing up his toenails wasn't exactly pleasant, I was relieved. The homicidal rage had passed. He was himself again.

I stepped up beside him. Rested my hand on his shoulder. "Let's get you to a doctor."

"I want to go to Mount Prairie. My doctor is Grimhaur."

Mount Prairie wasn't the closest medical facility, but Alison and I agreed that the best person for Eric to see was his shrink. The head wound came from a glancing blow. The damage was gory but superficial. The rage went deep as the marrow of Eric's bones.

After we'd gotten the business with the boats straightened out and Alison had worked her charm on the *Rebel* crewmen, Captain Jack felt so bad about clonking her brother that he offered us the keys to his vehicle so we could get Eric to a doctor.

The bubba motif carried through in Captain Jack's bigfoot truck, a Toyota pickup with wheels off a jitney earthmover. No less than three emptied six-packs littered the floor. Sunflower seed shells overflowed the ashtray. I climbed behind the steering wheel which was wrapped in pink rabbit fur. Alison and Eric were beside me.

"A manly vehicle," I said.

"If you say so, Adam."

She was annoyed with me. In some bizarre twist of female logic, this whole thing had become my fault. She cooed over poor injured Eric, her psychopathic brother, while she snapped at me. It occurred to me that perhaps Alison and I had been together too long. This relationship was nearly two years old. Familiarity, as far as I know, breeds complacency, then contempt.

The engine started with a predictable roar, and the radio blared a wailing country-western ballad. "Cool," I noted. "Speakers on the outside."

Alison clicked the radio off. "Stop screwing around. Eric is seriously injured."

She hadn't paid any attention to the large purple bruise which had enveloped my entire shoulder or the bite mark on my hand. But I was too macho to mention it.

The bubba-mobile pulled conspicuously away from the parking lot behind the docks and through the forest toward Mount Prairie. I was not totally averse to driving noticeable vehicles. My own car was a perfectly tweaked '67 red Mustang, but the truck was absurd and I didn't like the stares from pedestrians. In order to get to Mount Prairie Institute, we had to drive through Noble Heights village where my sister Margot and her cronies lived and flourished. The combined annual income of the residents could have paid off the national debt, but they chose to surround themselves with rustic, Norman Rockwell-ish Americana.

The town square was, in fact, a square in the center of the only commerce in this mainly residential area. All the storefronts were wood with neatly painted trim and flower boxes. It was the kind of place where the residents bought hammers and nails at Ye Olde Hardware Boutique.

The bubba-mobile clashed badly with the Porsches and shiny minivans. So did we. I was still without shirt and shoes, couldn't even get served at an urban 7-Eleven. Alison looked sexy and wonderful as always. Though she'd patched up Eric's wound and stopped the bleeding, he still looked like a train-wreck victim.

I drove slowly, trying to blend in as the citizens of Noble Heights gawked disapprovingly and wondered if their attorneys could arrange roadblocks. Alison noticed the hostility, too. "I can't believe they allowed Mount Prairie to build here," she said.

"They didn't," I informed her. I knew a lot about the Institute because Reeves worked there. "Mount Prairie was here first. The mansion belonged to the Noble family, the people who originally owned all this land."

"And they donated the property?"

"It's one of those hundred-year-lease things. Reeves told me that Mount Prairie was founded in the late 1940s when two of the Noble brothers came home from World War II with major shell shock."

"PTSD," she said.

"Right. That's what the shrinks called it back then. After Korea, the term was battle fatigue. Anyway, the Noble family had it bad, and they founded Mount Prairie. Then, the township sprang up around it and now people like Margot spend half their waking hours bitching and moaning about how that nasty psychiatric facility is driving down the property value."

"Margot wouldn't do that."

Try as I might, I could not convince Alison that although my sister looked like a stylish woman of the nineties, her appearance was a clever disguise. Margot had been through three husbands and number four, a mild-mannered orthodontist, had just taken off for an alternative lifestyle in Boulder, Colorado. Not that Margot was a wolf in sheep's clothing. She was an alien, more horrible than the creature that followed Sigourney Weaver all over the galaxy. Right now, she was more voracious than usual because she was looking for another victim, husband number five.

I followed the route I'd driven a couple of times when I dropped Reeves off. Past the Noble Heights Country Club golf course and up a two-lane road to the gates of Mount Prairie.

Never before had I gone inside the facilities, and I wasn't anxious to start now. Hospitals, particularly those inhabited by mentally unstable people, made me nervous. And there was that smell. Even in an upscale place like this, the smell of antiseptic and disinfectant reminded me of needles and pain.

I parked in front of the main building, the former Noble mansion, probably built in the late 1800s. The white, wood-frame structure loomed three stories tall with a gabled, slate-blue roof. A wide covered porch surrounded the front. The multipaned windows sparkled in the afternoon sunlight. Pink and purple flowers filled the beds on either side of the entrance.

"Very gracious," Alison said approvingly.

"That's the idea," I explained. "This isn't a state hospital. It's private. According to Reeves, the people who come here pay large bucks for treatment."

She turned to Eric, "Can you afford this?"

"It's V.A. approved," he murmured weakly as he climbed out of the truck. "They got some kind of grant for PTSD."

Though he was able to mount the four wide steps leading to the porch by himself, Alison and I stood on either side, ready to catch Eric if he stumbled. Right now, he looked more exhausted than anything else. Homicidal rages will do that.

A young nurse in a pale peach uniform and sensible white shoes stood at the door to greet us. "I'm sorry," she said, "but you can't stop here."

"This is a hospital," I pointed out. "And we have an injured man here."

"We're not an emergency care facility."

"He's been seeing Dr. Grimhaur."

Her manner changed immediately. "Oh, well then, please come in. He's not seriously injured, is he?"

"He's got a pretty bad bump on the noggin." I figured Alison and I had better go along with Eric so we could tell Grimhaur what had happened. "Is the doctor in?"

"I'm not sure." Her eyebrows twisted in concern. "It is Sunday, you know."

"Grimhaur," Eric said softly. "I want to see him."

"Now, now," the little nurse said consolingly as she nudged me out of the way and walked beside Eric. "I'm sure someone else can help." To Alison, she added, "We have seven psychiatrists on staff full-time. But on Sunday—"

"Can you call Grimhaur?" Alison asked.

"Oh, I can't! Bother the doctor on a Sunday?"

"This is important," Alison said. I could tell that she was trying not to say her brother had flipped out and become a raving madman. "I would appreciate it if you'd call the doctor."

"Oh, gosh, I don't know."

The sight of two small women on either side of Eric, fussing around him, was ridiculous. He had recovered enough to walk on his own. If he'd wanted, he could have picked both of them up, carried them over his head and jogged around the facility. But he played along. Maybe I was jealous.

I came straight to the point. "Listen, Nurse. We need Grimhaur. Our boy here just went berserk."

"Had an episode?" she questioned.

"Sure, if that's what you call boarding a thirty-foot ketch and mauling the crew."

"Oh, dear." Inside the mansion, she pointed to a burgundy-colored Victorian sofa just inside the entrance. "Sit here."

The perky little nurse ran behind the walnut veneer counter in the center of the front foyer and picked up her telephone. As soon as I sat on the wing chair beside the sofa, I felt the first twang of a headache in the back of my brain. All I had wanted today was sailing with the wind in my face and Alison at my side. Instead, I was here, smothering in graciousness.

The little nurse pranced over to us. "We're in luck. The doctor was home, and he'll be right over."

"Does he live nearby?" Alison asked.

The nurse bobbed her head. "Many of our doctors live in Noble Heights."

Convenient, I thought.

"Just wait right here." The nurse looked at Eric with some concern, probably worried that he might bleed on the Oriental carpet. "Will you be all right?"

"I can wait."

We sat in silence, absorbing the classy interior of Mount Prairie. There was gleaming polished wood on the staircase, antique style furniture and a crystal chandelier. The decor was accessorized by green plants and silk flower arrangements.

In my sailing garb, I felt like a slob, and Alison must have thought so too because she grabbed a lab coat from a rack near the door and thrust it toward me. "Put something on, Adam."

The fit was okay. I buttoned up the coat that reached nearly to my knees. Underneath, I was wearing shorts, but that wasn't evident. With my bare legs and feet hanging out, I looked like a flasher. "Perfect," I muttered, "now I fit right in."

Apparently, the doctor thought so, too. He started visibly when he marched in the front door and sighted me. "Whoa," he said, "you're not Eric."

The nurse introduced the man who was dressed only marginally more formally than I in shorts, a cotton shirt and loafers without socks. "This is Dr. Grimhaur."

He pumped my hand vigorously. "And you are?"

"Not crazy," I said. "I'm a friend of Eric's."

I introduced him to Alison who tried to explain the situation as the doctor made strange, unpredictable gestures. He was tall, taller than I am, and his thick black wavy hair added a few inches in height. His eyes darted constantly beneath bushy eyebrows. He wasn't the kind of guy who instilled confidence in me, but Eric seemed to like him.

He directed us toward a hallway to the right. Over his shoulder, he informed the nurse that we'd be in the infirmary. "And I'm going to admit Eric Brooks for a couple of days as an in-patient for observation."

"You can't," she protested. "All in-patients are supposed to be checked in through Nurse Lavin."

"Okay," the doctor said. "Where is she?"

"It's Sunday," she said, throwing her hands up in the air. "It's Nurse Lavin's day off."

"I'll take care of this with Fran later," he promised.

I'd heard about Nurse Fran Lavin. Reeves despised the woman. She ran things at Mount Prairie. No matter what the doctors or the staff thought, the final decision was always up to Nurse Lavin.

Grimhaur escorted Eric through an oak door, marked "Infirmary," and Alison and I were left to wait on a leather bench in the hallway. This part of Mount Prairie looked like a hospital, sterile and white. The only character came from the multipaned windows and a set of French doors halfway down the hall.

I patted Alison's hand reassuringly. Though she did not object, she had that tightness around her eyes that signaled trouble, and I wondered why she bothered to charm all the bubbas and shrinks and nurses of the world while she saved all her gripes for me.

The headache took root behind my eyeballs. I would probably hate myself later for saying anything, but I asked, "Is something wrong?"

"Oh no, Adam. We set out for a lovely day of sailing, my brother had a psychotic episode and attacked five men. Then, you held him while their captain smashed him over the head with a winch handle. What could be wrong?"

I didn't bother to defend myself. I was indefensible. "Good, I'm glad you're not upset because—"

"Of course, I'm upset." Her exquisite hands balled into fists in her lap. "It's not your fault, Adam. I know that."

"Not your fault, either."

"It's just that, at times like this, I feel so . . . alone."

I knew what was coming, and a loud klaxon horn in my brain sounded general quarters. Battle stations! Look alive! This is not a drill!

Alison sighed again. This time, she crossed her legs and I couldn't help but admire her tanned firm thighs and the delicate swell of her calf. "I'm always making these decisions by myself," she said. "I'd like someone to lean on, someone I can always count on to be there."

I made the fatal mistake of looking into her incredible green eyes. "You can count on me," I offered lamely.

"Can I really? We're not married. We're not engaged. We're not even going steady."

"You want to go steady?"

"Shut up, Adam."

We couldn't just sit there with the silence weighing down on us, so I stood up. "Got a little headache. I thought I might ask the nurse for aspirin."

"Sure," she muttered. "Whatever."

I strolled back to the nurses' station, padding along in

my bare feet. The perky nurse was engaged in a phone conversation, so I wandered. My intention was not to get as far away from Alison and her marriage talk as possible. At least, that wasn't my conscious intention. But the thought was there in the back of my head. I'd made it this far in my life without getting married and starting a family, and I really didn't see a need to change the status quo.

Through a set of French doors, I had a view of the rest of the Institute. I pushed the doors open and went outside. The landscaping put my own gardening efforts to shame. Behind the main building, there were petunias, red bougainvillea, irises, every color imaginable. In the center court, a marble fountain spouted like a whale.

Mount Prairie was up on a hill, and the three-story mansion was the high point. From where I stood, I saw four ranch-style structures with white siding and slate-blue rooftops that matched the main building. I meandered along the web of sidewalks, admiring the quiet grounds. I paused by a thick hedge of laurel. I had the sense that I was being watched. The hairs on the back of my neck prickled. I turned slowly, scanning the area, and saw two dark eyes peering through the shrubs.

We stared at each other for a while before I said, "Hello."

He didn't respond.

I came closer, but he didn't run away.

"What's going on?" I asked.

"Ambush," he replied in a whisper. "Be very, very quiet."

I stepped around the shrub quietly as he had requested. I was right beside him now. He wore camouflage fatigues. His wheelchair was festooned with branches of waxy laurel leaves. I asked, "Who are we going to ambush?"

"Nurse Lavin."

"It's her day off," I informed him.

He waved a branch over his head. From out of nowhere, two more soldiers in fatigues appeared. They were quiet, sneaking across the grounds. All three of them were about my age.

The one in the wheelchair said, "Secure the ambush. Mission delayed until further notice."

"Why?" the shorter one demanded. "I really wanted to do it today."

"At ease, soldier."

The two men picked up the racing-style wheelchair and lifted him to the sidewalk where he whipped along ahead of them, tossing his camouflage greenery aside. They'd sparked my interest. It occurred to me that the three of them would make a fitting testimony to the absurdity of war. "Hey, who are you guys?"

The shorter one tossed the introduction over his shoulder, "Abraham, Martin and Jerry . . . The Death Squad."

They kept walking, and I went back inside, wondering who was who.

The little nurse was off the phone and I requested aspirin. "I can't do that," she said. "All medication is strictly monitored."

"I have a headache. I'm not talking morphine here."

Her earlier dithering and cute frustration were no longer in evidence. On the subject of drugs, she was absolutely firm. "Sorry, you'll have to ask the doctor."

I dragged back down the hall to the bench where Alison was sitting. "Do you have any aspirin in your purse?"

She shook her head. "Sorry. Are you okay?"

The bruise on my shoulder ached deeply. The twanging in my head grated at fragile nerve endings like sitting front row at a Garth Brooks concert, and I needed an aspirin. I pointed at the infirmary door. "I'm going in."

"I'll come with you."

Decision made, we nearly jammed ourselves in the doorway trying to enter the infirmary at the same time.

Eric sat on an examining table while Grimhaur looked into his eyes with a doctor tool that looked like a cross between a jeweler's loupe and a miniature telescope.

"I have a drug problem," I said.

Grimhaur's slightly protruding eyes bulged. "Oh? Do you want to tell me about it?"

"I need an aspirin."

"Ah ha." He frowned. "All our medication is secured."

"Could you unsecure it?"

"This way."

I followed Grimhaur, and Alison stood beside her brother, asking how he felt and if he needed anything for his brief stay at Mount Prairie. For somebody who resented making decisions, she was certainly solicitous.

At the rear of the large white room was a stainless steel door. On the wall next to it, at eye level, was the digital pad of a computer lock. Grimhaur punched in four numbers, then twisted the door handle. He entered a room that was small and windowless with a couple of refrigerated units and several cabinets.

"Please stay out there," Grimhaur said as he opened a cabinet above a small sink. "We have to be careful, you understand. If any of the patients got in here, there'd be hell to pay."

He found a green-tinted bottle and tossed it to me. Aspirin. Grimhaur typed a note into a computer beside the door.

While I struggled with the child-proof cap, I asked, "What are you doing?"

"I have to log in every entry to this room. Then we check it against the computer at the door. It's an inventory system." He chuckled. A little bit nervous, I thought. "Can't be too careful in a place like this."

Maybe. But it seemed like a lot of precaution for something so simple.

Chapter Three

The next morning, I picked up Reeves Washington at the marina where he usually moored *Raptor.* Cheerfully, I introduced him to our transportation: the bigfoot truck I still had on loan from Captain Jack.

Reeves circled the monster pickup twice, scowled at me and said, "I suppose there's a Confederate flag in the back."

"You want me to raise the colors on the radio antenna?"

"I want you to get some taste."

"Now, I'm hurt."

"Let me tell you something, Adam. A gentleman of my position and heritage does not ride in a vehicle of this description."

For his heritage, Reeves was black. As for his position, he was a renowned psychiatrist.

"It would be a shame to hitchhike," I said. "Especially since you look so spiffy."

His charcoal-gray suit had been tailored to accommodate his six-foot-four height, his broad shoulders and lean athletic body. His Windsor-knot silk tie was held in place by a diamond tie pin that matched his cufflinks. On his fingers, he wore four heavy gold and diamond rings, two on either hand. I knew he had a similar set of jewelry in rubies and in emeralds. Some people can wear jewelry better than others. Reeves was such a person.

He eyeballed my short-sleeved denim shirt, Levi's and sandals. "I see you dressed appropriately for this . . . truck."

From my back pocket, I produced my own version of a bubba cap. The logo on the front was the insignia for the University of Oregon football team, the Fighting Ducks.

Reeves laughed. "Why do I put up with you?"

"I'm cute?"

We had nothing in common, except that we lived in the same general area, we shared similar political views and, of course, Vietnam. We'd met nearly twenty years ago at a veterans' counseling group and had been friends ever since.

Reluctantly, he climbed up into the passenger's seat, kicked away the beer cans on the floor with his Gucci loafers and settled back on the seat. "I guess this thing is appropriate transportation for the meeting of the Noble Heights Town Square Statue Committee. We should raise eyebrows when we drive through town."

I told him that Alison, Eric and I had already made the inaugural journey past the square. "Indeed, the locals were taken aback."

"And how is the lovely Alison Brooks?"

"Lovely," I said. Like every other male, Reeves adored Alison. Like every other male, he wondered why she was wasting time with a ne'er-do-well like me.

"Have you done more sculptures of her?"

"Not for a while. I'm past my 'nude women riding on sea mammals' period."

"Are you into your war memorial period?"

"Not yet," I admitted. In my small briefcase, I carried five sketches of possible designs for the Noble Heights project. None of them pleased me. But I wasn't willing to devote more of my time until I was sure the memorial statue for the townsquare was a go. "What can I expect at this meeting?"

"Lots of bullshit," Reeves said.

"Is there a psychiatric term for that?"

"Yes, there is. The clinical reference for the behavior of uptight nouveau-riche assholes who have the time and inclination to obsess about statues in their town square is, in fact, bullshit." He batted at the fuzzy dice that hung from the rear-view mirror. "By the way, don't expect me to say much in the meeting."

"Why not?"

"It's bad enough that I am the token black in Noble Heights. Now I'm the token Vietnam vet. The only thing that gives me credibility on this committee is the Dr. in front of my name. I prefer to maintain a low profile."

"Expecting trouble?"

"Not if I keep my mouth shut. Really, Adam, I'd rather talk about Alison."

"I wouldn't. She wants to get married."

Reeves was far too tasteful to burst into raucous guffaws. He merely snickered. "Marriage, huh? That's not a bad idea. How do you feel about that?"

"Don't start trying to get into my skull."

"I already have. Want to hear?"

I gunned the engine to take a pothole, bouncing the truck and unsettling both of us. "Sure. Why not?"

"After you spent two tours in Vietnam, you came back to the States and extended your enlistment for three more years. Not a great time to get married."

"Right." I'd had a couple of semiserious involvements, but the subject of marriage never surfaced.

"Then you entered another high-risk profession." Reeves winced as he said, "Joining the Portland police force."

"I'm with you."

"We don't even have to go into how poorly suited you

were for that profession. After fifteen years you still
hadn't risen above the rank of sergeant."

Though my record with the force was outstanding, I
wasn't known as a cop who could take orders. I wasn't a
team player. "What's the point?"

"High-risk job, Adam. You weren't marriage material.
Then, you did your midlife crisis and became a sculptor,
a successful sculptor."

I nodded. "Fairly successful."

"You've finally settled down. You're more stable now
than you've been in your checkered life. Marriage and
family might be the next logical step, Adam."

"And family?" I yelped. Alison hadn't mentioned family. "No way." I didn't even like kids. The closest I'd
come to taking responsibility for another human being
was my encounters with my sister, Margot, and that was
enough to convince me that family ties were highly over-
rated.

I went on the offensive. "You were married, Reeves.
And divorced. Would you ever do it again?"

"Hell, no."

"But you think it might be a good idea for me?"

He gave me a wide, shit-eating grin and changed the
topic. "Let's talk about my boat."

We stuck to the safety of boats and sailing, a passion
we shared, for the rest of the ride to Mount Prairie. For
some reason, the committee had decided to meet at the
Institute. I asked Reeves why.

"It's convenient for all of them. It's private. And, I suspect, Jonathan Noble will try to take this opportunity to
have a private meeting with me. I've been avoiding the
old man for weeks."

"What does he want to talk about?"

"Property and leases and taxes." Reeves paused.
"Greed. It's occurred to Noble that the property Mount
Prairie occupies is now extremely valuable."

"Brilliant deduction," I said. We were cruising along the back roads leading to the Institute. Half-million-dollar residences were springing up on the hillsides like mushrooms after a heavy rain. "Can he close you down?"

"Not as long as we stick to the terms of our lease. Our obligations are to maintain Mount Prairie as a psychiatric facility and to treat any member of the Noble family for free."

In the parking lot outside the main building, I noticed Margot's new cherry-red Mercedes.

"Amazing," I said. "The license plate doesn't say: Red-hot and Available. But everything else about this car does."

"Margot's car?" Reeves asked.

"Oh, yes. You'll note the convertible top so she can snag unsuspecting males and yank them inside without even opening the door." I warned him, "Watch yourself."

Reeves and I strolled through the entryway where the red-haired nurse behind the counter greeted us genially. I followed him into the large meeting room to the left. The infirmary and more medical facilities were in the opposite wing. This side of the mansion maintained the ambiance that Alison had called gracious. More antique stuff. A marble fireplace. A side table with a silver tea and coffee service. Pastries cut in dainty triangles, tiny china cups and fragile saucers.

Four people sat around a large, dark oak, oval table and Margot stood at the far end of the room between two multipaned windows with heavy fringed curtains. "Finally," she snapped at me. "Can't you ever be on time, Adam?"

Reeves gently corrected her. "We're five minutes early, Margot. And I don't think the rest of the committee is present."

"That's right, Reeves. Take his side." But she gave him a flashy smile, displaying all of her prior husband's excellent orthodontia. "I want you to sit here. Next to me."

Under my breath, I warned, "She's looking for husband number five. Be careful." To Margot, I said, "Where do you want me to sit?"

"Who cares?"

This was the first Noble Heights Town Square Statue Committee meeting I had actually attended. Since it was apparent that Margot didn't consider me important enough to be introduced to the other members, I took it upon myself to do the deed. I turned toward a woman with shining black hair cropped neatly along the jawline of her scrubbed face. I offered my hand. "I'm Adam McCleet."

She lightly grasped my hand with the tips of her delicate fingers. "Raven Parducci," she said, cordial but businesslike.

Though she'd made no cosmetic attempt to embellish her appearance, except for the red enamel on her extraordinarily long fingernails, her olive skin and dark eyes lent her a certain exotic appearance.

An older man—with a walrus mustache and eyebrows that looked like owl's horns—cleared his throat. He was plump but not flabby. He raised one hand in a wave and said, "I'm Jonathan Noble. I know your work, McCleet. Don't understand it."

Raven informed me, "Mr. Noble is an artist himself."

"Really," I said.

"Damn right. Watercolors mostly. Just last month, I had a private show at the Noble Heights Art Guild."

"Really." Just what I needed. An amateur who fancied himself enough of an expert to critique my work. A question loomed heavily in the front of my mind: Is it worth it? Matter of fact, I didn't know what it was worth. We hadn't talked money, yet.

Raven introduced the couple that sat on the opposite side of the table like a pair of Bavarian salt and pepper shakers. "These are the Schmidts."

They rose as one person and simultaneously held out their incredibly clean hands. I shook with the woman first, then the man. His grip was almost a match for his wife's. "You were in Vietnam," he said.

"That's right."

"Our son, William, was in Vietnam. He never came back."

Suddenly, his wife circled around her husband and clasped me in a warm bear hug. "Welcome home, Adam."

Sometimes, I was touched by these personal tributes to the fact that there had been no marching bands and ticker tape parades for the men and women who served in Vietnam. More often, I was embarrassed and not willing to carry the responsibility for lost sons, brothers and husbands.

"Our other son," she said, "was also in the war."

Her husband looked embarrassed as she continued, "He's here. Kurt is here at Mount Prairie, again. Doctor Washington is treating him."

So, that was what Reeves meant when he said the Institute was convenient.

I sat beside Raven. Though she was utterly polite, she appeared to be grinding her rear molars as she frequently checked her Rolex wristwatch. This was a very intense woman. A brief conversation revealed that she was an attorney. That explained her attitude.

Margot fawned over Reeves, making sure he had his selection of tea and sugar cubes and cream and lemon. She went to the door and snapped her fingers at the nurse. "Bring us some more coffee and hot water for tea. This is tepid."

Reeves mumbled an apology to the nurse and said, "Can we get started, Margot?"

"Of course. You probably have important things to do."

She pulled the sliding oak doors closed behind her, and I felt suddenly claustrophobic. The others looked relatively calm, but I was sure none of them had been trapped in a closed space with Margot before.

"Frank Birkenshaw isn't here," she said. "But he'll have to catch up later."

Margot went to an easel at the front of the room and began scribbling figures with black Magic Marker on a large tablet of newsprint. A seven, a six, and a comma followed by six ninety-four and a period and thirty-one. She drew a dollar sign in front of it. "That's seventy-six thousand, six hundred ninety-four dollars and thirty-one cents. The total amount allocated by Town Council for the purpose of building a statue in the town square."

"Does that include materials," I asked crassly.

"Yes-s-s," she hissed at me. Then turned to Reeves and said, "I should think that's sufficient for a decent statue, wouldn't you?"

Before he could answer, she turned back to me. "That's more than enough."

As an artist, I was slightly offended. As a man who has grown accustomed to a certain amount of comfort in my lifestyle, I had to agree with Margot. The figure was three times more than I expected. Not wanting to betray my enthusiasm, I went to the side table near the windows to refill my coffee cup.

Raven moved the meeting along. "Margot, I don't believe there's any problem with the amount. Our concern at this meeting is the subject for the statue. I believe the Schmidts and Dr. Washington prefer a war memorial."

Reeves corrected, "A veterans' memorial."

"I know that," Raven said. "But there are other

suggestions. Mr. Noble and the missing member of this steering committee, Mr. Birkenshaw, wish to commemorate the founders of the community."

"The Nobles," Margot said. "Yes, yes, we've all heard the story. Jonathan Noble's great-grandfather was one of the first settlers in the area and he owned all the land."

"That's right," Noble said. "I see a pioneer statue. A rugged man with a plow or an axe. My grandfather was such a man. When he came here . . ."

While Noble launched his history lesson, I gazed through the multipaned windows. It would have been a great day for sailing. It was July first, midsummer, and the grounds of Mount Prairie were brilliantly sunlit. I watched a couple of young nurses hurry along the sidewalk. A few of the patients were strolling, and I wondered about the Death Squad and what perils lay waiting for Nurse Lavin today.

". . . that was the early nineteen-hundreds. My grandfather was just a tyke . . ."

Noble seemed capable of droning on for hours. I looked out the windows again and saw an incredibly homely man with a bald head and ponytail approaching a barrel-chested blond man. They shook hands, then hugged.

Jonathan Noble concluded. "Such a statue would be a tribute. You know, I've done a little woodcarving myself."

"But what exactly are we commemorating?" asked Mr. Schmidt. "I knew your grandfather. He never let go of a square inch of property for less than twice its value."

"You want to talk about cheap, Schmidt," Noble said. "How much are you paying those Mexican pickers who work in your apple orchards?"

Of course. Schmidt apples. I hadn't made the connection. The couple were a legend in the northwest. They'd started with a small orchard and had grown to become one of the largest producers in the country. George and Martha Schmidt had more money than they could count.

"We take good care of our pickers," Martha said indignantly. "Just ask any one of them."

The impending argument was forestalled by the entrance of the final member of the committee. He made a racket with his choruses of "Hey, how are you?" and "How're you doing?" He was the hugger I'd seen outside and possibly the ugliest human being I had ever met. Up close, his long hair was stringy and greasy. He was short with short arms and legs, almost dwarflike in his bodily proportions. And his head was overlarge with a sickly pasty complexion that contrasted with his long sideburns. When he shook my hand, a vigorous pumping, he introduced himself, "Birkenshaw, Frank Birkenshaw. And you must be the famous Adam McCleet."

"I don't know about famous . . ." I started modestly.

"I've seen your stuff. Don't understand it."

Great! What was so complicated about naked women riding on sea mammals? It was about sex. It was about beautiful women and powerful thrusting sea creatures. What was so complicated about that? I glanced at Reeves. He'd probably have a good psychological explanation about repression. An explanation which didn't apply to Margot. She stood behind Reeves and massaged his shoulders. He looked like he was enjoying himself. I vowed to warn him: Never let Margot that close to your throat.

She lifted both well-manicured hands at once. "All right, people, let's make some decisions. I want my brother, Adam, to do the sculpture. He's a vet, so he ought to have some idea about war. Wouldn't you think?"

The Schmidts nodded complacently.

The opposite side of the table erupted. Friendly Frank Birkenshaw went nuts. "No way, Margot. We aren't going to put up some kind of statue to celebrate war. It's not right, man. It's not nineties. It's not politically correct."

Raven tried to be the voice of sanity. "I suggest that we explore the options before we build yet another bronze statue of soldiers. Or of pioneers."

"But we have to decide," Margot said. "I want the statue, whatever it is, in by the end of summer."

Raven tilted her head and looked toward me. "Perhaps we should hear what Mr. McCleet has in mind."

"Okay, McCleet," Birkenshaw said, "What's it going to be? A naked soldier riding on the back of a canon?"

Noble chimed in, "McCleet's got no ideas. But I do. Now, I've been doing a little experimenting with chain saws. And I could do a crackerjack chain-saw sculpture of my grandfather. He looked a lot like me."

"So did your grandmother," Schmidt put in.

"A wood sculpture for seventy-six thousand dollars?" Margot questioned. "Really, Jonathan!"

Mrs. Schmidt cleared her throat. "I believe we owe it to the boys who served to build a memorial statue. We owe nothing to the pioneers."

"They settled this area," Noble started in again. "My great-grandfather and his wife—"

"He's got a point," Birkenshaw said. "That's our heritage, man."

"Oh, please," Margot said icily. "And I'm sure your opinion is not at all influenced by the fact that you're living—rent free, I believe—in one of the cabins on Jonathan's estate."

"I can't be bought, baby. I do what's right."

Once again, Raven tried to bring order to the proceedings. "Shall we put this issue into the form of a motion?"

Mr. Schmidt said, "I move that the statue in the town-square be a veterans' memorial."

His wife seconded.

Margot took the vote. There were three opposed:
Noble, Raven and Birkenshaw. There were three sup-
porting the motion: The two Schmidts and Reeves. Margot preened. "Well, then, I guess it's up to me, isn't it?"

She strutted around the table, dragging out the sus-
pense needlessly. She perched her butt on the back of a
chair to show Reeves a little of her well-toned thigh. "It's
a difficult decision," she said. "On the one hand, I'm totally in favor of heritage. Adam can tell you that I've always been a family woman. Home and hearth."

Right. As many homes and hearths as one woman
could accumulate in a lifetime.

She was leaning toward Reeves. I had no doubt about
the way the vote was going to go. Still, she prolonged the
tease. "Let me see. Eeny-meeny-miney-mo, catch a—"

"Margot," I interrupted. "Just vote."

"Hold it, man." Birkenshaw was on his feet. "Look
out there. Let the people have their voice."

We obediently turned toward the windows and saw a
small ragtag group marching up the driveway toward the
Institute. It was like a flashback. They wore bellbottoms,
tie-dyed T-shirts and sandals. Several sported headbands
in their graying hair. Sixties holdouts. They carried
crudely lettered signs that said: No More Tributes to
War. Peace Forever. One carried a particularly battered
sign that read, "Hell, no, we won't go."

I found myself smiling at the nostalgic stupidity of it
all. Birkenshaw was right in my face. "You think that's
funny, man?"

"It's hysterical. Where'd you find them?"

"Those are the people, baby. And the people don't
lie."

Outside, they linked hands and began to sing, "Give
Peace a Chance." Scampering among them were several
nurses and orderlies. The whole scene made me long for a

riot helmet and a tear gas canister. I wanted to punch somebody.

Reeves would have called it latent hostility or aggression. He would have told me that I needed to learn to express myself in appropriate ways. But I looked around that meeting room and saw hypocrites, assholes and people who were so rich they didn't need to bother with reality. We weren't talking about veterans or peace or war. We were mouthing self-serving bullshit, to use Reeve's clinical term. The worst part was that I was in it up to my chin, sitting there and considering the commission, thinking that seventy-six thousand dollars and change was enough for a hefty downpayment on a boat of my own.

Birkenshaw jabbed his forefinger in my chest. "You think you deserve respect because you're a vet? Well, I spit on your respect, man."

I wasn't going to get in a shoving match with this asshole, no matter how much he deserved it. I pushed back my chair and went to the front of the room where Margot's easel stood. I tore off the sheet with the dollar sign and crumpled it into a ball. Using the Magic Marker, I drew.

I don't consider myself a genius. My sculptures come from hard work and skill. But there are moments when I am inspired. This was one of those times.

I could feel my hands moving in broad strokes, then feathering lightly, working fast. I had to get it all down before the moment passed. My heart pumped. I was sweating. I heard music in my head, a hard-driving beat that was unlike any song or rhythm I'd ever heard. When I stepped back from the easel, I was breathing hard.

Like everybody else, I stared. The sketch was powerful, strong and non-representational. This wasn't the preliminary design for just another bronze statue of soldiers. This was how I felt about war in the deepest level of my soul. The charging hooves of a stallion. The spokes of a wheelchair. Jungle fronds. Fragments. Shattered bodies and the wings of a dove in flight.

Mrs. Schmidt wept quietly.

I had nothing to add. I set down the Magic Marker and left the room.

Reeves caught up with me outside before I crossed the line of protestors. "Jesus Christ, Adam, I didn't know you had that in you."

"Well, I'm full of surprises."

"Baby, you are good."

I gestured toward the protestors. "What are you going to do about these idiots?"

"The local cops are on their way."

A woman with a weathered face and streaks of gray in her waist-length hair held out a daisy to Reeves. "Peace, brother."

He squashed the flower under the heel of his Gucci shoe. "I am not your brother, lady."

"But we are all brothers and sisters and—"

"No!" Reeves shouted. I saw a flash of the anger he usually kept wrapped tight. The protestors turned toward us as he continued, "Do you people have any idea of the trouble you've created here?"

"This is a bad place," said one of them. "You specialize in treating murderers for stress. If there were no war, there would be no stress."

Reeves spoke in a cold, hard voice. "We specialize in treatment of post-traumatic stress disorder. The people here are victims of rape, abuse and, yes, of war. This is a place of healing."

He turned to me. "Get me away from here, Adam, before I kill that goddamned Birkenshaw."

We must have looked mean because the line of protestors separated to let us pass. In the parking lot, I saw the bigfoot truck. Someone had painted a red peace sign on the shiny black enamel of the driver's side door. "Shit."

Birkenshaw came running up, and his motley crew of protestors gathered behind him. "We're not done with this, McCleet. Not by a long shot, baby."

"You're right about that. Somebody is going to pay for this damage. It's going to need a paint job."

"All that matters to people like you is money. Right?"

I wasn't going to stand here and debate with the Keebler cookie elf. "Let me put it to you in words you understand, Birkenshaw. This ain't cool, man. It is so uncool that unless you pull out your checkbook and write me a cash payment for three hundred bucks, I'm going to break your ridiculous face."

"I don't believe in checkbooks, man."

It figured. "Take up a collection among your disciples."

"I don't pay people like you, people who glorify war." He moved up close. We were chest to chest. He was looking up at me, daring me to hit him. "Go ahead, man. You can't stop yourself."

Raven appeared behind him. "Mr. McCleet, I advise you not to act in haste. I represent Mr. Birkenshaw. If you touch him, I will be forced to file assault charges."

Last straw. This was too much. A powerful primal urge rose in my chest. A violent urge. Time to go.

Smiling genially, I climbed into the cab of the big truck and closed the door. I revved the engine as Reeves walked to the passenger side and climbed in. I was about to pull away when I noticed the smirk on Birkenshaw's face. He thought he'd won. Something snapped.

I motioned for him to move closer, as if I couldn't be heard over the din of the dual exhaust stacks protruding from the bed of the truck.

Birkenshaw cocked a hand behind his ear and squinted.

"Come here," I said, motioning as I raced the engine to drown out the sound of my own voice.

Hesitantly, he stumbled forward. I smiled and urged him closer.

When he stepped within two feet of my door I said, "Your shoe is untied," pointing at his feet.

He obligingly lowered his head for a look and I threw open the door. The center of the peace sign connected with the top of his head with a solid bonk.

He stumbled backward and sat down hard, clasping his head with both hands.

So much for resisting primal urges.

Chapter Four

"You shouldn't have popped him, Adam. They're going to make a lot of trouble for you."

"Maybe."

"Not maybe. Raven Parducci said she'd sue your ass, and that lady does not make idle threats."

As we rumbled away from Mount Prairie, I was relieved to leave the feeble assemblage of protestors behind. I probably should have been ashamed of myself for bouncing Birkenshaw's melon off the door of the Toyota. Actually, I hadn't expected the door to be as rigid as it was, something to do with physics, I thought, smaller surface area than a full-size truck door.

"At any rate, I feel better for seizing the opportunity to humiliate the little freak."

"He was doing a stellar job of that all on his own."

I glanced over at Reeves. A vein in his forehead twitched as he stared straight ahead. He made a growling noise in the back of his throat. I wasn't sure if he was more angry about riding shotgun in the bubba-mobile or about the protesters disrupting the Institute. I decided it was the latter. Captain Jack's truck was a minor annoyance, but the Institute was Reeves's lifework.

This morning, our plan had been to ride together to the meeting, then pick up Reeves's boat at the marina where Alison and I left it yesterday. I could drop off Captain Jack's truck there, and Reeves and I would sail back to the docks where *Raptor* was usually moored. A change in schedule might be indicated.

"So," I said, "you want to go back to Mount Prairie? I can motor upriver by myself."

"I won't go back there. I don't trust myself not to finish off what you started with Birkenshaw. And Noble is going to try to get me alone for an administrative meeting. And the Schmidts are going to ask for a progress report on their son, Kurt, and I'll have to tell them that Kurt needs at least another month as an inpatient."

Sailing sounded like a far better alternative. "What about Raven? Don't you have some kind of problem with her?"

"Not unless she sues me for knowing you."

"She's litigious?"

"No, but her clients are. Half the citizenry of Noble Heights is either suing or being sued. R. Parducci represents just about all of them. Including me."

"Ye Olde Law Practice?"

Reeves laughed. "That wouldn't be so funny if it wasn't true."

"Lucky guess."

In the oversized side-view mirror I noticed a red Mercedes driving erratically behind us. We'd picked up a tail. Margot.

I shifted down for a red traffic light and a right turn at Macadam Avenue, allowing the truck's gears to slow us instead of using the brakes, a habit I'd developed with stick-shift vehicles. But I'd momentarily forgotten what I was driving. When I let out the clutch in first gear, the back wheels locked up as if I had stomped on the brakes. Reeves nearly went through the red tinted window. I checked the mirror in time to see Margot's car skidding sideways with the brakes locked.

"Christ, Adam," Reeves said as he cinched his seat belt tighter.

The truck's gearbox must have been designed for scaling tall buildings. I quickly shifted back to second, turned the corner and headed south, paralleling the Willamette River. I floored the bubba-mobile and we pulled away from the Mercedes with a backfire and a blast of black exhaust.

"Just out of curiosity, Adam, are you trying to kill us?"

I decided not to tell Reeves about our tail. Being a psychiatrist, he'd want to do the rational thing, pull over and see what she wanted. But he didn't know Margot like I did. Rational never worked with her. Best to avoid her whenever possible. "Speaking of killing. What's the deal with the Death Squad at Mount Prairie?"

"Abe, Martin and Jerry? They're my patients. Mostly harmless."

Margot made a move into the left lane and attempted to overtake us. I switched on the radio to drown out the honking from the Mercedes, changed lanes abruptly and cut her off. "Harmless? They were laying in ambush for Nurse Lavin."

Reeves turned the radio from sports talk to a classical station. "They don't like Fran Lavin much," he chuckled. "But that's okay. Neither do I."

"You mean you encourage them to harass the poor woman?" I asked as I switched back to the right lane in time to cut Margot off again. I could see her head sticking out the driver's side window, hair snarling in the fifty-mile-per-hour wind. She was yelling something, but I could only imagine what. "How terribly unshrinklike of you."

"Of course I don't encourage them," Reeves said. "I just don't discourage them. Lavin is the kind of person you love to hate. You know the kind."

"I suppose there are women like that." I swerved across two lanes to thwart another of Margot's attempts to overtake us.

"Goddamn, Adam. Why are you driving like this?"

"I can't seem to get the hang of the steering in this piglet." I ran a yellow light and watched the Mercedes shrink in the rear-view mirror as Margot slowed and stopped for the red. "So . . . are these guys on drugs or what?"

"No," Reeves said. "I don't use drugs."

"Do your clients?"

"You've never taken any of this stuff seriously, have you? From the very beginning, all you had to do was be smug and crack a few jokes and you'd pass as being perfectly stable. Is that it? What do you think is the leading cause of suicide?"

I had inadvertently struck a nerve. Reeves could take a ribbing as well as anyone, but he was dead serious about his profession. "Depression," I answered lamely.

"And where do you think most of that depression comes from?"

Knowing his specialty, I took a wild guess. "Post-traumatic stress."

"Bingo. Over sixty thousand Vietnam vets have killed themselves since coming home. That's about two thousand more than those who died in combat. I'd call that a serious problem, wouldn't you?"

"Absolutely . . . but Nam was over twenty years ago. I'd think everybody would have worked through it by now." I turned left at Nevada, heading toward the river. Margot was nowhere to be seen.

"Adam, I know people. And I know you. You're an intelligent, intuitive human being. Please don't tell me you think that Vietnam was the final great nightmare. What about Beirut, Grenada, Panama, Iraq, Somalia—"

"Well, sure . . ." This wasn't the first time I'd felt intellectually overmatched by Reeves. He had more degrees than a protractor. ". . . I tend to oversimplify."

"Slightly. No one is immune to post-traumatic stress disorder. Every day, in more ways than you or I can possibly imagine, people are victimized, traumatized and driven to self-destruction for reasons they'll never understand without help."

While Reeves talked about adult children and rape trauma and the aftermath of violence, I drummed the steering wheel with my fingertips, checking the mirrors for sign of the red Mercedes. She was gone, and I discovered that, from my lofty vantage point, I could see the legs of the women in the cars we passed. I couldn't see their heads or upper torsos at all, but that was okay. I could imagine any kind of women I liked attached to those legs. Oddly enough, in spite of my fertile imagination, they all wound up looking like Alison.

I heard Reeves ask me a question. "What are you avoiding? With all these jokes, what is it you don't want to look at?"

I shrugged.

"PTSD takes many forms," he said analytically. "It's a serious disorder."

I remembered Eric on the boat. The murderous look in his eye wasn't funny. Not at all. "You're right, Reeves. So, how do you help these people?"

"If you're really that interested in my therapy, I had an article published in last month's *Gray Matters Magazine.*"

"Can you give me the short version?"

"I use many of the standard methods. Group sessions. Role playing. Processing. I've had some success with a modified hypnosis technique which allows the patient to experience and reprocess a traumatic episode with updated logic and coping skills."

"Of course." The only time I'd seen hypnosis was at a

carnival where a guy with a red satin cape made a fat woman cluck like a chicken while she strutted around the stage flapping her arms. "Ladies and gentlemen, The Great Reeves-ini." It was my best Ed Sullivan.

"You're hopeless," he said with a laugh.

"I'm trying to be serious."

"It's more like regressing, remembering the experience. I'll put it in terms you can relate to. You know when you remember those girls in high school and you think, if I only knew then what I know now?"

I had never discussed that particular fantasy with Reeves, but it's a safe bet, if there is a single dream all men share, that's the one. "Oh, yeah."

"Just like that. Want to hear more?"

I nodded. Though I told myself that my interest in PTSD was so that I could understand Eric, a miniscule portion of my brain acknowledged that this might be good for me, too.

"Tell you what," Reeves said, "I'll do better than explanations. I'll show you one of these hypnosis sessions. Be back at Mount Prairie by four o'clock this afternoon."

"Okay. Four o'clock." We bounced into the parking lot of the Creek Rock Marina. "Does Grimhaur use the same method?"

"Why do you want to know about Grimhaur?"

"He's treating Alison's brother." I parked near the marina office and nautical shop. "Is he any good?"

Reeves climbed down from the passenger seat of the bubba-mobile and slammed the door. "It's not professional for me to discuss the methods of another therapist, Adam. Let's just say that a former patient has filed a suit claiming Grimhaur used an experimental drug on him without his permission."

"Did he?"

"I doubt it. He's a little quick with the Rx pad for my

taste, but there's no way he'd administer anything experimental without written consent."

"I get the impression you don't approve of his methods."

"Do you? Why?"

I glared at the big red peace sign before I gently closed the bubba-door. Captain Jack was going to be foaming at the mouth when he saw that mess, and I didn't blame him. Of course, I'd contact my insurance agent and pay for the new paint job, but . . .

"Why?" Reeves repeated. "Why don't you think I approve of Grimhaur?"

"Because there's nothing unethical about telling me what a genius you think a colleague may be. Your silence indicates a low opinion of the man."

"I just don't like his—"

He was interrupted by the screeching of tires as Margot's car skidded into the parking lot and came to a sliding stop next to the truck. She smoothed the snarls from her long black hair as she climbed out of the Mercedes.

"Margot," I said with an appropriate degree of surprise. "Where'd you come from?"

"Shut up, Adam." She brushed past me on a beeline for Reeves.

"Oh, Reeves, I'm so glad I caught up with you." She pulled a gold pen from her purse and held it up. "You left this at the meeting. It looks quite expensive and I didn't want you to worry about it."

Reeves smiled broadly. "That's very thoughtful of you, Margot. But that's not my pen."

As a matter of fact, the pen belonged to George Schmidt. I'd noticed him doodling with it at the meeting. My sister had stolen Schmidt's pen for an excuse to get close to Reeves again. Either that, or she'd stopped at Ye Olde Stationery Store and purchased a two-hundred-dollar pen just like Schmidt's.

"The pen," she said, fluttering her eyelashes shamelessly, "it looks like it should belong to you. It's expensive. Solid gold." She ran her finger down the shaft. "Classy."

"Sorry, Margot." But his attention focused on her glossy lips and the way she slipped her tongue across the gleaming surface of her front teeth.

Delicately, she pointed to the diamond tie pin he wore. "Is that real?"

Reeves nodded. I could see his Adam's apple gulping hard.

I interrupted, "I'm going into the office to drop off the keys for the guy who loaned me the truck."

"Run along," Margot said.

I hesitated. Reeves may have been a brilliant psychiatrist, but I'd wager he'd never come up against the likes of Margot. I couldn't bear to watch her reel him in. "I'll be right back."

"Whatever," Reeves said, moving slightly closer to Margot.

"Hey, Reeves," I tried to sound casual, "want to come with me?"

Margot whirled and shot me a Medusa stare. "Get lost, Adam." She slid her hand down Reeves's sleeve and purred, "Show me your boat. I love sailing."

A blatant lie. She hated all activities beyond shrieking range of her telephone or a shopping mall. But she did have a soft spot for doctors and their credit cards.

As they strolled down the pier, Reeves glanced back over his shoulder and wiggled his eyebrows at me. The poor fool didn't have a prayer.

I trotted into the office, hoping I could take care of business and get back in time to save Reeves from a fate worse than conservatism. But there were two people ahead of me, both with ridiculous bottom scraping and storage problems. I tried to cut in, but the man at the desk shut me off. I grabbed an envelope from the desk, wrote an apology note to Captain Jack about how I would pay for the paint job, stuck his keys inside and wrote his name on the outside in big block letters. I placed it on the desk and raced back to the dock.

Too late! They were already on board the *Raptor*. Reeves had peeled off his suit jacket and tie. He stood at the helm and, as I approached, Margot cast off. She tossed me the keys to her Mercedes. "I'll pick up my car at your place, Adam. Bye-bye."

Not only was I concerned about the clear and present danger to Reeves's apparently happy state of unmarried being, but I was disappointed that we hadn't finished our discussion about Grimhaur. He was about to tell me something when Margot interrupted, and I wanted to know what it was.

All I could do was watch and wave as Margot tottered across the deck in her high heels.

Outside my studio, I took a moment to admire the attractive slope of green grass leading down to the water's edge. The lawn had been Alison's idea. For years, I insisted that I preferred a no-care, xeriscaped look. She'd convinced me to have sod and an automatic sprinkler system installed, and I had to admit that it did look nice.

Binky, the neighbor's dog, preferred the grass, too. He stood beside me with doggy drool cascading over his lower lip like Multnomeh Falls.

We were on our way back to the house when Binky bolted, barking at my driveway.

It was Birkenshaw.

Geez, hadn't the guy taken enough abuse for one day? I sauntered forward with my hands stuffed low in my pockets. Though I didn't want to, I knew I should apologize for bonking his head. I started, "I hope you're okay. I'm sorry I—"

"Fuck you, McCleet."

"Look, I understand you're upset. My friend, Dr. Washington, has pointed out the error of my ways." And the fact that I could be sued. "And I really want to apologize."

"Fuck Washington, too. That son of a bitch. This is all his fault."

Binky and I took a step back, waiting to hear the explanation on this one.

Birkenshaw jabbed his stubby finger at me. "Reeves Washington thinks he knows everything. He's got his big house and his fancy degrees and everybody listens to him like he's the black Messiah or something."

If memory served, Reeves was the only person at the meeting this morning who hadn't said much of anything.

"He thinks he's got the answer," Birkenshaw continued, "with his bullshit trauma treatment for vets. Well, I'll tell you something, man. You weren't the only one who suffered in the sixties."

"Never claimed I was."

"I was there, baby. I was at Kent State. I was at the Pentagon when we stood around it in a circle and made that fucking building levitate. I was at Haight-Asbury, baby."

"With flowers in your hair? Isn't it about time to leave those places. We're creeping up on the twenty-first century."

"You don't leave, man." He tapped the tie-dyed shirt that covered his scrawny chest. "It's here."

"So, what does this have to do with Reeves?"

"He doesn't understand us, man. He forgot where he came from. Know what I mean? Reeves Washington is too uppity."

"Uppity?" I knew what that meant. Uppity black man

in the white man's neighborhood. I understood why Birkenshaw was so cranky all the time. It must have been hard to be a bigot and politically correct at the same time. But I had no sympathy. "Get off my lawn."

"Nice grass, man."

"I think I've got some clippings in the back. You can take a bag with you and smoke it later. Just leave."

"Smoke it?"

He opened his eyes wide. The whites were red, striated with blood vessels. His pupils were tiny black dots. As I stood with Binky and watched, he licked at the white residue in the corners of his mouth. He was stoned to the bone.

I'd seen enough cokeheads in my years on the Portland police force to recognize the symptoms. Birkenshaw hadn't made a quick trip to his doctor to get treatment for the lump on top of his head. He'd prescribed for himself. Coke? Speed? I took a closer look.

"What are you staring at, man?"

"Were you there, in the sixties, with Timothy Leary?"

"Tune in, turn on, drop out. Baby." His forearm raised, ready to flash the peace sign, but he thought better of it.

Birkenshaw was a sad case, in need of major counseling, but he wasn't my problem. "Okay, I apologized. What else do you want from me?"

"A warning, man." He pulled a square of white paper from his hip pocket and unfolded it. It was the sketch I'd made at the meeting, the surprise piece of inspiration that had impressed Reeves and made Mrs. Schmidt cry.

Birkenshaw threatened, "If you do turn this town square statue into a war memorial, you'll regret it." He tore the drawing into several pieces and threw them at my feet.

Binky growled. And so did I.

Birkenshaw took a jittery step backward. He was

sweating heavily. "I mean it. We can make things very bad for you, man."

I nodded toward Margot's Mercedes. "Please don't paint any peace signs on my new car. Oh, please."

I turned and headed back toward the house, resolved to come up with a design for the statue that would stop Frank Birkenshaw's heart.

He kept yelling for a while, then he apparently went away because Binky announced his departure with a woof.

Chapter
Five

I checked my phone messages, heard that Alison planned to visit Eric then come here after doing a few errands. About seven or seven-thirty. In time for dinner. She sounded terse and businesslike, a little icy around the edges. Was she still ticked off at me?

In the kitchen, I perused the refrigerator and drank milk straight from the carton which was probably one of those things I'd have to stop doing if Alison lived with me, or I with her. Was she still thinking about marriage? I shuddered. There was no way we'd be able to work out the details. She had her place. I had mine. We'd be taking each other for granted in no time. One of us would have to give up a home. No way, I decided, no wedding bells.

Surely she realized that. Alison wasn't usually one to hold a grudge. Her coolness on the phone message prob-ably didn't indicate anything more than an appropriate manner for the owner of Brooks Art Gallery, and I knew she'd called from work because I could hear her assistant, Monty, whining in the background about the track light-ing in the front gallery. At the gallery, Alison was effi-cient, tough and cool. Although there were a couple of times when we slipped into her private office, scraped the paperwork off her antique rosewood desk, and . . .

Shaking my head, I erased that fantasy. There was work to be done this afternoon.

In my studio, formerly a three-car garage that I'd enlarged to half again its original size, I set up an easel with a newsprint tablet, attempting to simulate the conditions of the meeting this morning. With a black Magic Marker, I scrawled frantically, hoping to recapture the emotional fire of the moment. I would not stoop to collecting and piecing together the torn scraps of the original sketch. Was it the pounding hooves of stallions or the flared nostrils? Tattered flag or tattered shirttail? Birkenshaw had me thinking with the wrong side of my brain.

An hour and seven crumpled drawings later, I went outside with my binoculars and scanned the downriver horizon, looking for *Raptor*. By now, I thought, Margot should have Reeves lashed to the boom by his ankles, and she would be proudly weighing her biggest catch yet.

Downriver, the white sail with the flaring eagle insignia rounded a bend and came into view. Delicate as a butterfly wing, the *Raptor* fluttered across the sparkling waves.

Through my binoculars, I could see Margot prone on the foredeck. She wore a red string bikini. No visible tan lines. How did the woman do it? Did she carry an all-purpose seduction kit in the trunk of her Mercedes? Reeves leered naively from his station at the helm. I made a mental note to send my best-man tux to the cleaners.

Feeling slightly depressed, I went inside, and for the next couple of hours, sequestered myself in the studio, playing with clay shapes. Around three-fifteen, I set out for Mount Prairie again. Sometime during the afternoon, Margot had apparently come for her Mercedes because it was no longer in my driveway. I checked overhead to make sure Birkenshaw hadn't levitated it.

Driving my own car through Noble Heights was infinitely preferable to the bubba-mobile. The Mustang was the kind of car a man can feel proud to drive. A classic.

I'd owned the '67 Ford for nine years, bought it at an auction when I was still a cop and restored the body and trim myself. The engine work I left to the experts.

Riding in a respectable vehicle, I had a different perception of Noble Heights. The whole development was less than fifteen years old and the town square was brand new. But they were working to make everything look traditional, slapping together brick walls that were already covered with ivy and taking care not to disturb the indigenous trees so that the buildings looked like they'd been here for a hundred years.

Apparently, they yearned for tradition, like monuments to war dead or to pioneers. But the most suitable monument for their town square, a real expression of the Noble Heights consciousness should have been a gigantic, shiny, stainless steel bank vault.

When I parked next to Alison's car at the Institute, all evidence of the protestors was gone. Alison herself sat on a stone bench beneath an oak tree. Her smile seemed friendly enough. So far, so good. When she stood, I saw that her skirt was a good three inches above her well-shaped knees. And her silk blouse was unfastened three buttons to show a hint of cleavage. This might be an okay evening.

Still, I approached her cautiously. "You're the friendliest thing I've seen all day."

"Am I?"

"Other than Binky. He's always friendly. Not that I'm comparing you to a dog." Or to the evil Margot. Or anybody else.

"Thanks, Adam."

Obviously, I'd blown the compliment, so I changed the subject. "How's Eric?"

"He seems fine. I hope that means he's going to be okay. But I'm not real comfortable with his doctor."

"Grimhaur." I remembered that Reeves was going to

tell me something about him. "We can always change Eric to another therapist. Maybe Reeves."

"I suggested that. If I'd known he was coming here to Mount Prairie, I could have directed him to Reeves in the first place. But now, Eric seems attached to Grimhaur. He said he'd already given Grimhaur his history and didn't want to go over that ground again."

From the little Reeves had told me, I thought the purpose of post-trauma therapy was remembering and reprocessing the bad times. If Eric was avoiding it, that might be why he snapped out.

She frowned, "I don't know what to do, Adam. Should I insist that Eric change therapists? Should I trust that he knows what's best for himself? I spent hours wandering around in Ye Olde Strip Mall, thinking about it."

I nodded. Alison often shopped to soothe her mind. "Buy anything?"

"No, I'm not really into the whole L. L. Bean look."

"I've got to go," I said. "Reeves is going to let me watch one of the therapy sessions where he does hypnosis. Why don't you go to my place? When I'm done here, we can have dinner."

"Fine," she said. Her eyelids lowered, and her green eyes took on a sexy glow. She frequently amazed me with these lightning changes of attitude. From concerned sister to seductive siren. She trailed her fingers along the open collar of my cotton shirt. "Before we eat, we might want to work up an appetite."

Sounded promising. "What did you have in mind?"

"We might start with weight-lifting wineglasses," she suggested. "Followed by a quick jog around the bedroom."

This was the Alison I knew and adored. I caught hold of her hand and gave a tug. She melted against me.

I leaned close to her ear and whispered, "We could skip the preliminaries."

"Without a warm-up? I wouldn't want you to tear a groin muscle."

"My groin is fine."

"I know," she said as she pulled away from me. "You go see Reeves, and I'll be waiting for you later." The soothing tone of her voice said, we're okay.

I paused on the porch of the main building and watched her car pull away. I told myself that I'd been carried off by my own ego. It was absurd to think that all the emotions of this highly complex woman revolved around me. Still, I was reasonably certain we weren't finished with the subject of cohabitation.

The nurse at the front counter directed me to the second floor, and I climbed the sweeping oak staircase and faced a large reception area where a woman in a vest and matching skirt who sat behind a semicircular desk with a personal computer and a state of the art telephone console. I introduced myself.

She quickly checked her computerized appointment book. "Yes, Mr. McCleet. The doctor is expecting you."

She pointed to a hallway at her left. In the main reception area, there were four closed doors with four brass nameplates. More doors lined the hallway on either side. All closed, except for the one with a brass placard that said: Reeves Washington, Chief of Staff.

Reeves waved me in.

He was on the phone, so I wandered around the room, trying not to eavesdrop. The office was decorated in the same tasteful Victorian style as the meeting room I'd seen earlier in the day. Among the neatly organized rows of clinical texts lining the built-in bookshelves, the names Clive Cussler, Stephen King and Douglas Adams stood out like hookers at a Catholic Youth rally. Two strange photographs accented the diplomas and awards arranged on either side of a large, paned window. One was of Reeves, as a skinny Marine, holding Sammy Davis, Jr. in his arms. The other was an enlarged snapshot of our early Vietnam veterans group. We all had facial hair of some kind. Reeves had an enormous afro. I barely recognized my old friend and former cop partner, Nick Gabreski, with his walrus mustache. Hell, I barely recognized myself in a mustache and muttonchops.

The surface of Reeves's antique desk was clear except for a silver eagle, a casting I'd made for him to celebrate the day he launched *Raptor*. On the wall opposite the desk, hung an ornately framed, two-by-three-foot mirror. With no etching or beveled edges, the glass looked cheap for its surroundings. A two-way mirror. I touched a corner of the frame to confirm my suspicion, it was firmly affixed to the wall.

He hung up the phone. "Okay, Adam, we've only got a couple of minutes before my patient gets here."

"What do I do?"

"Come with me." He led me back into the hall and opened the door to what appeared to be a broom closet. "This is the observation room."

It was small. Two folding chairs faced the back side of the mirror I'd just inspected in his office.

"We use this area as a learning center. You won't be spying. I've already told the patient that he would be observed. It goes without saying, Adam, that anything you see or hear goes no further than my office. Patient confidentiality extends to you, too."

"Got it." I nodded.

"I mean it. You don't tell anybody, not even Alison."

"Right."

"Because the person I'm working with is Kurt Schmidt. Son of George and Martha."

"The son who survived," I said.

"And there's a lot of guilt about that." Reeves stood at the door of the dark, little room and waited for me to sit. I felt enclosed. "Any questions?"

"Can I get out of here if I want?"

"Sure," he said. "The door is closed but unlocked."

"So, what do I expect?" I asked. "Is Kurt going to get crazy or something?"

"I don't work with anybody who's violent. Kurt had a drug problem when he first came back from Vietnam. He's somewhat addictive. Mainly, he's sad, in mourning. Like I said, there's a lot of survivor's guilt. He might do some weeping, but I can promise you he won't get crazy."

I had another question. "When you're talking to Kurt, can you hear me?"

"Not unless you start yodeling or something. This room is pretty well sound-proofed. But you'll hear us because there are microphones." He started to close the door, then opened it wide and grinned, "By the way, your sister is hotter than a pistol."

"And twice as deadly. Reeves, she'll suck the life out of—"

"Talk at you later." He closed the door.

I watched him reappear in his office and take a seat in front of his desk, facing another chair. He glanced over at the mirror and stuck out his middle finger. *Very professional.*

Then Kurt Schmidt entered. He was a large, barrel-chested man, but gentle-looking with a straight thatch of blond hair that fell across his furrowed brow. He was the guy I'd seen Birkenshaw hugging earlier today.

"How are you feeling today?" Reeves asked.

"I sure didn't care much for those protestors." He sat down. "But I'm okay with it."

"Before you say anything else, Kurt, you remember what I said earlier about being observed. Does that bother you?"

Reeves projected trust and fidelity in his soothing

voice. He might have made a good politician if he hadn't been so honest.

"No." Kurt had a wide farm boy's grin. "Kind of a compliment, ain't it?"

"It is." Reeves nodded. "We're making good progress."

"I know. But I gotta tell you, Doc, sometimes that worries me. Sometimes, I don't wanna leave here. I gotta get back to work for my pop, and just as soon as I'm in those orchards, everybody wants something from me. It's quiet here. I like it."

He drummed the arms of his chair with his fingertips.

"You seem tense," Reeves observed. "Did anything else happen today?"

"Well, my parents were here, and you know how that is. They wanna have me back . . . working. My pop thinks I'm slacking off."

"You're a hard worker, Kurt. You know that."

"Damn right I am. I get out in the orchards with the pickers." He sighed and his shoulders slumped. "But Pop's right. He's always right. My brother, Willy, he's the one who should have been the field boss. He was the smart one. And I'm just . . . oh shit, let's just get on with it."

"Not unless you're ready. We don't have to work with hypnosis if you'd rather talk about your parents."

"Nope. Don't want to." He tilted back his head. But he appeared to be faking relaxation. His massive jaw clenched tight. His eyebrows frowned when he squinted his eyes closed. "Ready when you are, Doc."

"Hold on, Kurt. We don't have to rush."

He shook his head so vigorously that the loose skin below his chin trembled. "I gotta get out of here, Doc. Pop says I gotta work at it."

"You're doing fine. Just fine." Reeves studied him. "Tell me what you had to eat today."

He listed a typical breakfast and lunch. "Why?"

"Any pills?" Reeves asked.

"You mean drugs? You know I don't do that shit no more. Not a chance, Doc. Especially not around here. You keep the stuff locked up too tight." He closed his eyes again. "Let's get going. I wanna be okay."

Reeves spoke in a quiet baritone, taking several minutes telling Kurt to relax his arms, his legs, his chest. "Breathe deeply. I'll count backward from ten. When I reach zero, you will be asleep. And you will remember."

In the dark room, I inhaled and exhaled slowly. The hypnotic suggestion reached through the two-way mirror and touched me. Reeves was good. My arms and legs felt heavy. I was incredibly sleepy.

"That's zero," Reeves said. "When you open your eyes, Kurt, you will be in Vietnam, in Mai Loc village. Open your eyes."

The big blond guy looked about ten years younger. His shoulders straightened. His movements were full of vigor. His blue eyes were wide and staring at something I could not see. "Fire," he said. "Fire. It's in the fields. The rice. The harvest. No food. These people are gonna starve like rats. No food."

"Tell me what you hear."

"Women crying."

"What does it smell like?"

"Sweat. All I can smell is my own sweat. I'm scared."

"Why?"

He gave a loud sob, but his face remained emotionless. "I don't wanna kill anybody. But I gotta. They killed my brother." He wailed. "Willy. Don't leave me here. I can't go home without you."

"Kurt!" Reeves was alert. His voice was hard. He sat up straighter in his chair. "Kurt! You can hear me."

"My mama . . . she's always crying . . . bitch."

Reeves looked concerned. "You're in the village. What do you see?"

"William . . . got all the girls. I got nothing."

"Where are you Kurt?"

"Apple trees. Pink. Spring. Smells like heaven. Me and my girl." His big hands drew into fists. "The bitch dumped me."

"Tell me about Mai Loc," Reeves tried. "The Marines. The fire."

"I'll tell you to go to hell."

Reeves leaned close to him. "When I clap my hands, Kurt, you'll wake, rested and relaxed."

He slapped his hands together right in front of the big guy's face. "Now!" Reeves shouted.

"Bitch," he said. "Bitch."

"Listen to me, Kurt. Wake up. Now!" Reeves clapped his hands again.

Kurt bolted out of his chair. "I'm awake, goddamn you."

"Sit down, Kurt." Reeves voice was emphatic. "Right now."

"Everybody gives me orders." He was pacing, but his movements were uncontrolled. He bumped against a chair, then turned and walked into the desk. He grabbed Reeves's lamp by the neck and threw it to the floor. "I'm sick of it, you hear me?"

"All right, Kurt." Reeves rose slowly from his chair and started for the door. "That's enough for today."

"I'll say when it's enough."

"Calm down, Kurt. Breathe deeply."

I might have been more concerned if Reeves hadn't retained his cool manner.

"I don't take orders from you, boy."

Kurt turned toward the mirror and I saw into his eyes. The pupils were dilated, and his gaze was vacant. I knew something had gone badly wrong. The guy who was supposed to be docile and mourning was gripped by violent rage. I hoped Reeves could control him. He barked out another order, "Sit down, Kurt."

"Fuck you."

The big man threw himself, using his bulk to pin Reeves against his desk. He roared unintelligibly, grabbed Reeves by the shoulders and slammed him up and down like a rag doll.

I was already on my feet when Reeves yelled, "Adam, get help."

I banged against the glass, trying to distract Kurt.

Reeves pushed against the big man's face. "He's stoned, Adam. He's on something."

I jerked open the door to the little room and hollered down the hall to the receptionist. "Get help! Reeves needs help."

"Kurt!" I yelled as I raced into Reeves's office. "Kurt! Stop it!"

He didn't hear me. With his left hand pressed against Reeves's chest, Kurt held him down on the desk. In his meaty right hand, he held the silver eagle statue. Kurt struck hard. The base of the heavy statue crashed against Reeves's forehead. His legs went limp.

Kurt screamed and raised the statue again.

I tried to grab the big man by the elbows, the same way I'd subdued Eric, but Kurt was massive. I could barely reach on either side of his body. He wheeled around and swung the bloody base of the eagle statue, missing my head by inches. His other fist landed a roundhouse punch on my chin. Then he swung back to Reeves and struck another blow against his skull.

I picked up one of the office chairs and smashed it over the big man's back. Where were the orderlies? Jesus Christ, where the hell was somebody who could stop this madman?

Reeves slumped off the edge of the desk. He looked bad.

Kurt wobbled on his feet, but was not distracted. I clubbed him with the chair again.

He fell on Reeves, but he wasn't out. He raised the statue again and hammered Reeves's bloodied face. Reeves offered no resistance. Schmidt was beating a dead man.

I wanted more than just to stop him—I wanted to kill him. "Kurt!" I yelled as I swung the chair.

He deflected the blow with his arm, but the statue dropped from his hand. When he turned toward me, I focused my own rage and bashed him in the face with the return swing. Schmidt groaned and fell to one side, only stunned. I was about to finish him off when three men in white uniforms crashed into the room and swarmed over him.

I threw the chair aside and dropped to my knees beside Reeves. His face was covered in blood that gushed from his badly broken nose and two pockets of exposed bone in his forehead. His eyes were clenched tightly closed, lips pulled back in a painful grimace. His breathing was shallow and labored, but at least he was breathing.

"Reeves," I said, trying to control the feeling of hopeless panic that strangled my own breathing, "can you hear me?"

He opened his eyes, and in them I saw the pain of every blow Kurt Schmidt had issued, but I also saw life. "Adam?" He whispered, then coughed on the blood that ran into his throat.

"I'm right here, buddy. You're going to be okay. Don't try to move." My worst fear was displaced by a shred of hope. He was tougher than I'd given him credit for. When Schmidt had issued that last blow, I was certain Reeves was a goner. Now, he wasn't even unconscious.

The office was suddenly full of people. Other doctors. Two of them pushed me aside. Reeves was surrounded by the white-coated chaos of modern medicine—codes, carts and a stampede of people.

"He's going to be okay," I said. I gave them room to do their work, but I stayed close by. If Reeves needed me, I had to be there.

The receptionist stood in the door, sobbing.

"He'll be okay," I assured her, but she continued to weep into her hands. I had to believe that Reeves would be fine. The alternative was too awful to contemplate.

Orderlies wrestled Schmidt into the hall. I had a vague impression of Grimhaur outside the door. Echoes in the back of my head. How had this happened? Why hadn't I moved to help Reeves as soon as Schmidt got out of his chair?

I heard the words, "He's dead. It's over, people. Call the code."

"What? Hell, no," I objected, pushing aside one of the white-coats. "He was just talking to me."

"Who the hell are you?"

I picked up Reeves's hand. His fingers were limp. God-dammit, that couldn't be. "Reeves," I said softly, "Come on, man."

His eyes were still open, but they stared blankly. The life in them was gone. A sudden quake of anguish shook me into the reality that I had fought so hard to deny. Reeves was dead.

I wiped at the tears that streamed down my face. The room was still. Not even the sound of breathing intruded on Reeves Washington's final sleep.

I touched his cheek, caked with blood. I closed his eyes.

Chapter Six

Reeves Washington was dead, and the murderer wasn't Kurt Schmidt. That illogical thought hammered in my brain as I slowly rose to my feet and stepped away from Reeves. Though he'd inflicted the fatal injuries, he wasn't responsible. He'd been a load of high explosives, no less deadly than a terrorist's pipe bomb, carefully placed and timed for maximum impact.

Someone had given him a drug of some kind. Reeves had known it, and so did I. Schmidt had been used as a murder weapon. They'd somehow filled him with a deadly, unstoppable rage.

I will know the truth, I promised myself as I turned away from Reeves's body, someone will pay.

When I stepped into the hallway outside Reeves's office, Dr. Grimhaur touched my arm. "Are you all right?" he asked.

Hell, no. I wasn't all right. My friend was dead. "I'm okay."

"Let's put some ice on that jaw," he said. "It's beginning to swell."

"Perfect, my chin and my shoulder can swell into one big, happy injury."

"Come with me," Grimhaur urged. "You're Adam

McCleet, aren't you?" He stroked his chin. "Yes, we met yesterday. You had a headache."

"Still do."

"Eric has spoken of you. He sincerely admires you."

Again, he touched my arm, wanting to remove me from the scene. I shrugged away. "Where's Kurt?"

"He was subdued by the orderlies."

"Sedated?" I asked.

"Yes, of course."

I remembered how long it had taken to unlock the drug supply. "You're pretty quick with the syringe, aren't you?"

"I was downstairs. One of the nurses said a patient was violent. I prepared myself." He sounded defensive. "Listen, Mr. McCleet, my only concern at the moment is that you are physically all right."

"Afraid I might sue the Institute?" Reeves had told me about Grimhaur's impending malpractice suit. "I suppose you'll be the new chief of staff . . . now that Reeves is dead?"

He gave me a shocked look, his head jerking back like a woodpecker. "This is not an appropriate time to discuss such a matter."

"It's a motive," I said.

"Motive? What are you saying? I was under the impression that Reeves was attacked and killed by his patient."

"That's right. I was in the room behind the two-way mirror. I saw the whole mess."

"Then you know it was an . . . an accident. Of sorts."

"Oh no, doc. Reeves's murder was premeditated."

I strode away from him, down the hall to the reception area where one of the nurses was tending to the nearly hysterical secretary. I felt slightly hysterical myself, but I made a conscious effort to maintain some composure. Losing my cool would not rack up credibility points when I explained my theory to the police. I couldn't show them a shred of evidence to cause them to look beyond the obvious, but somehow I had to convince them. They would have to investigate.

When the ambulance and the cop cars arrived, I repeated that phrase at least two dozen times. But nobody paid me any particular attention. They told me I was distraught—whatever the hell that means. They told me I was in shock. Though they agreed to run tests on Kurt's blood, they told me I was crazy.

They told me to accept Reeves's death. I told them to kiss my ass and wandered outside.

I was sitting on the porch steps under the veranda, and I spotted Nick Gabreski, my former partner on the Portland PD. What was he doing here? Nick was in Missing Persons, not Homicide.

His big face rumpled in a frown. It was the end of the day, and his eyes were tired. He slumped down beside me.

"I heard about it on the radio," he said. "Reeves is dead."

"Murdered," I corrected.

"Dead is dead, Adam. Let it go."

Though Nick's voice was a low growl, a result of a gunshot wound to the throat, I heard every word with painful clarity. Bad news always sounded different coming from a friend. The resonance stayed with me and echoed in the empty places.

"What happened?" he asked.

"You're not investigating?"

"I'm off duty right now."

"Come over to my place," I offered. Alison was there. I'd forgotten all about her. "Let's go."

Nick got back in his car and followed me on the route that was rapidly becoming second-nature to me.

Alison greeted me at the front door. I could tell by her

expression that she'd already heard about Reeves. "Eric called," she said. "Adam, I'm so sorry."

"Me, too." I gestured toward Nick's car, pulling into my driveway. "Nick's here."

"I'll make coffee."

While she headed into the kitchen, Nick lumbered heavily through the door and trudged toward the sofa. I remained standing, not moving, inert until my brain could process the fact that Reeves Washington was dead. A familiar numbness paralyzed my legs and arms. I'd been through this exercise more times than I cared to remember. Often, Nick had been there.

We both started working on the Portland PD at about the same time and had been partners. Nick had stayed with the force and was now a lieutenant. We also shared a common background. Vietnam. Once a month, on the second Tuesday, we'd gone to a support group. Reeves was there. He called us the Yuppy Vets group.

"God damn it," I said.

"What happened?" Nick asked. "All I heard was that one of his patients snapped out during a session and attacked him."

"I saw it happen. I was there."

"Jesus Christ, I can't believe it. Reeves is . . ." He corrected himself, ". . . was a good man, a good friend. I remember . . ."

The low gravelly voice mumbled softly, but I didn't hear the words. I had slipped into a separate reality.

We were on the street, Nick and me, near Columbia Park. To the south, beyond the cranes and ship stacks at Swan Island, we could see the skyline of the city, lit up like a Christmas tree for the night. But it was August and the light rain had raised the humidity to one hundred percent. I'd sweat through my uniform. We'd been in pursuit of a suspect, a fast black kid in sneakers who'd fled like the wind off the river.

I gulped for breath, wanting to believe the kid was gone but I was sensing the presence of danger.

Nick went to the black and white to call in our report. A liquor store holdup, no one injured, armed suspect fled on foot. Send backup.

I heard a sound, a rustling in the brick-lined alley between two closely spaced buildings. "Did you hear that, Nick?"

"Hear what?"

"Probably nothing. I'll check it out."

I unholstered my revolver. Everything suddenly felt more serious with the weight of the Smith and Wesson .38 pressed in my hand. I walked slowly and cautiously into the dark, holding my flashlight above my head to shorten the length of the shadows it cast. The reflection from a streetlight glistened on the wet asphalt, but the recesses of the alley were draped in blackness.

The noise came again. It sounded like breathing. From behind a stack of shipping pallets. I braced, legs apart, right arm extended, aiming my weapon toward the sound. "Police! Come out with your hands up. Now!"

The silence filled my head to the point that I flinched at the sound of my own voice when I yelled again. Identified myself. It was probably a small animal, but I couldn't leave until I was sure. I edged forward a few more steps and yelled again.

The kid jumped out and faced me. I could see the gun in his hand. The light from my torch splashed across his face. He looked like Reeves.

I squeezed the trigger and the silence exploded with a deafening horror that . . .

* * *

"Adam?" I heard Alison's gentle voice. "Adam, would you like coffee?"

My eyes refocused and I saw her and Nick. I made a clumsy gesture and knocked the steaming mug of coffee from her hand. The black liquid spread across my hardwood floor. "No problem," I said, "I'll clean it up."

She followed me into the kitchen. "Are you okay?"

"I'd like something stronger than coffee."

"Well, you could have just said so." Her voice was gentle and understanding. Her arms closed around me for a reassuring hug. "I understand. It's okay."

I appreciated the comfort in her voice and in her arms, but everything wasn't okay. Reeves was dead. I checked my watch. Six hours ago we were bouncing across town in a ridiculous black pickup with a peace sign painted on the door. Six hours ago, we were laughing.

"Where were you?" she asked. "For a minute there, I thought you'd left us."

It might have been a flashback. If Reeves had been alive, I might have called and told him about it and acknowledged that he was right about post-traumatic stress. There was plenty of stress to go around, even without the sixties. More than enough for everyone. More violence. More victims. More ways than he or I could possibly imagine . . .

"Adam?"

"I'll be all right."

Her eyes questioned, but she said, "I know you will."

I wasn't sure if I deserved her confidence.

I grabbed a new bottle of Wild Turkey, two tumblers and paper towels. Alison took the towels and offered to clean up. I didn't argue.

I opened the bottle and set it on the coffee table, a thick slab of oak planks bound together at either end by heavy iron straps, once a hatch-cover on an old lumber ship. I poured a couple of shots and slid one across the varnish toward my friend. "He was murdered, Nick. The patient who snapped out was stoned, crazy stoned."

"Part of his therapy?"

"No. None of Reeves's patients were on drugs. Somebody doped this guy. He was a time bomb waiting to go off."

Nick slammed back the whiskey, grimaced and helped himself to another. "You think somebody dosed him? Purposely set him up to kill Reeves?"

"That's what I think."

Alison knelt on the floor, swabbing at the coffee. "There are strange things going on over there. I'm getting my brother out. First thing tomorrow."

"What if he doesn't want to go?" I asked.

"I can't leave him there. It's too dangerous. In fact, I'm going to call Mount Prairie and see if Eric is okay. I'll use the phone in the bedroom."

I acknowledged with a nod.

Nick sipped from his shot glass and gave a puzzled look.

"Her brother," I said. "He's an in-patient at the Institute. Post-traumatic stress disorder. He was in Desert Storm."

"And the guy who killed Reeves?"

"Same problems. Different war."

I hated that the killer was a Vietnam vet, and that Reeves's murder might be reduced to one more incident blamed on the horror of Vietnam, another example to fuel the phony moral outrage of people like Frank Birkenshaw. Quietly, I said, "The guy who killed him, Kurt Schmidt, wasn't responsible."

"Of course not. He's crazy." Nick rubbed his eyes. "You know the stuff, Adam. The post-traumatic stress disorder shit. The flashback shit. The general whacked-out vet shit."

"But why now? After twenty years, why would this guy snap out right now?"

"Reeves was putting him in touch with stuff that had been simmering the whole time, then it exploded."

Nick sipped carefully at his drink and so did I, allowing the alcohol to trickle down my throat and burn away the pain and regret. I sensed there was something he wasn't telling me, but I was too impatient to wait. "Why were you there?" I asked.

"You mean, at Mount Prairie?" Nick stood and carried his drink to the moss-rock fireplace. "I was coming to see Reeves."

"Yeah? I saw Reeves today, and he didn't mention that you two were getting together for anything."

He grumbled, "I didn't know Reeves had to clear his social schedule through you."

Nick and I had been friends for a long time. I took a guess at what had been going on. "This wasn't social. You were seeing Reeves in his professional capacity?"

"Good guess." He set his drink down to study a burnished silver eagle on the mantle, about six inches in height, on a heavy base of polished green agate. The mate to it was in a police property room by now. The murder weapon.

"A couple of months ago," Nick said. "I got together with Reeves to play golf, and we started talking. My oldest son enlisted in the Marines, you know."

"I remember." Nick had eight children and the most understanding wife in the world.

He continued, "I guess the fact that my kid was in boot camp opened up some old stuff for me. Ramona said I was being a pain in the ass, hassling the other kids about where they were going and what they were doing, being too protective. After I talked with Reeves, I made an appointment. I've been seeing him once a week."

"Been doing any good?"

"I don't know. Reeves did this hypnosis stuff."

"With flashbacks?"

"Yeah. I'd go under, then we'd talk about things that happened. You remember when you shot that kid, over by Columbia Park?"

"Vividly."

"Well, that came up. It wasn't always Vietnam. Stress situations. Traumatic episodes, he called it."

"How'd you feel afterward?"

"Sometimes good, sometimes drained. But never violent."

"Not like the guy who killed him," I said.

"Right. The flashbacks would really get me worked up, but Reeves could always pull me out of the hypnosis if it got too intense. Just like that." He snapped his fingers. "Adam, he didn't treat anybody who was prone to violence. He screened his patients before he started therapy. No drugs. No extreme crazies."

"What about Abe, Marty and Jerry?"

"The Death Squad." In spite of the seriousness of our conversation, Nick smirked. "Quite a scam those three have going. They act like loons and the V.A. pays their room and board. For the rest of their natural lives."

"You don't think they're dangerous?"

"I doubt they could live on the outside." He rubbed at his eyes, again. "Sometimes I wonder if any of us can. I mean, what's so great about functioning in society and being a responsible citizen?"

"My sentiments exactly."

"Too bad we can't all be gentlemen of leisure with beautiful girlfriends and houses on the beach. Shit, Adam, how'd you get so lucky? You're never bothered by any of the shit from your past, are you?"

"Never." Except for a few minutes ago. Except for the other day on the boat with Alison. "I am the picture of sanity."

Nick laughed. "Bullshit. We're all crazy. We're all bozos on this bus. It's just that some of us don't wear orange fright wigs and oversized shoes. But every last one of us is rabid-ass-nuts."

That was as philosophical a speech as I'd ever heard Nick utter, and I realized how deeply Reeves's death had affected him. He winced and swiped at the corners of his eyes. "Gotta get home," he said, "Ramona's fixing dinner. Life goes on."

He looked at me with moist eyes and held out his glass. "To Reeves," he said, and tossed back the last of his whiskey. I responded in kind, then rose to see Nick to the door.

"We'll talk later. Say bye to Alison. I hope her brother will be okay."

When he was gone, I went into the bedroom where she lay stiffly on the king-sized, forest-green silk comforter she'd given me to replace the Indian horseblanket that scratched her delicate skin. She said, "I want Eric out of there."

"What's wrong?"

"They wouldn't let me talk to him. Grimhaur isn't there, and the nurse said the patients were agitated and not allowed to speak with anyone."

Unfamiliar as I was with the inner workings of any hospital, especially a psychiatric institute, this seemed weird to me. Why shouldn't the family be allowed to converse with the patients? Was there something to hide?

"Nick said that Reeves never treated patients who were violent." I went to the sliding glass doors, opened them and went out onto the deck. On the moonlit river below me, a tugboat passed. Its lights reflected off the wake. A few hours earlier, Reeves had stood on the deck of the *Raptor* with a broad smile plastered across his face. He wasn't in a high-risk profession. Psychiatrists shouldn't be taken by surprise by bizarre quirks of human behavior.

Alison stood beside me. I felt her nearness, smelled her perfume, heard her lightly sighing. When I glanced down at her, I saw the shimmer of moisture on her cheeks. I reached up and wiped below her eyes with my thumb.

She didn't have to say that she would miss Reeves. We didn't need to engage in lengthy epitaphs for our friend. Not now, when the hurt was still too fresh for mourning.

I held her chin in my hand and kissed her hard, seeking the life-affirming warmth of her passion. And Alison responded. Her mouth was hot. Her tongue thrust past my teeth.

She was still crying, clinging to me and sobbing. I held her tightly, trying to absorb her pain. She was crying for both of us.

I carried her into the bedroom and placed her on the forest-green silk. Her auburn hair splashed across the pillow.

"Can I get you something?" I asked. "Tea?"

"You, Adam. I want you." She sat up and tore her blouse off over her head, unfastened her bra. "I want you now."

She coiled her hand around the back of my neck and pulled me down onto the bed. Furiously, she ripped at my shirt and the buttons broke away.

I threw the shirt aside and in seconds our clothes lay strewn in disarray on the hardwood floor. I pushed her down and her back arched as I stroked her firm, heaving breasts. I tasted her nipples, hardening between my fingertips. She trembled under my touch like an animal driven wild by fear and passion. The fires of grief were our foreplay; only lust would quench the flames.

I silenced her whimpers with my mouth and entered her hard and fast. She dug her fingernails into the fleshy part of my butt and pulled me further inside her, grinding. I thrust hard and furious as she writhed and screamed beneath me until our passions were spent.

We fell away from each other limp and exhausted. In the dark, she reached across the bed and took my hand. We lay there listening to the sounds of the night.

Chapter Seven

When dew washed the air and sunlight glistened off the backs of hummingbirds whirring at ruby feeders, Alison and I circled the asphalt drive to Mount Prairie's front entrance. The meticulously groomed landscaping, spreading graciously toward the Noble Heights Country Club golf course, betrayed no hint of the previous night's horror. The sights, sounds and smells of the summer morning lifted my spirits, but in my chest a certain heaviness constricted my breathing.

All this serene, sensory stimulation was completely wasted on Alison. Having been denied access to her brother last night, she'd started working on her 'tude as soon as she awoke. By the time I parked the Mustang outside the Institute, she'd built up a full head of steam.

"I'm taking him out of here," she muttered. "I'd like to see any damned nurse try to stop me."

I mumbled encouragement.

"He's my little brother. I have every right to look out for his well-being."

"He's a grown man," I pointed out. "What if he doesn't want to leave? Maybe he thinks Grimhaur is helping him."

"Grimhaur is a geek."

"I wouldn't argue with that."

"Adam, I'm positive that he's doing some kind of drug stuff with Eric. Grimhaur denies it, says that Eric only gets vitamins." Her tone was matter-of-fact. "I know my brother. There's not a shred of meanness in him. I've known him all his life, and he's never attacked anyone, provoked or otherwise."

Though Alison's assessment of her brother's emotional state may have been biased, I knew that the uncontrollable burst of rage we'd seen in Eric had been identical to the murderous fury I'd witnessed in Kurt Schmidt. I also knew that the two men had three things in common. War, sadness and Mount Prairie. "Reeves mentioned something about Grimhaur and drugs. Somebody's suing the geek."

"I knew it," she said.

"Reeves was about to tell me something else about Grimhaur."

"What?"

A shadow of despair dimmed the storybook morning. "We'll never know."

I opened my door and started to climb out of the car, but Alison caught me by the sleeve. "This might seem like a strange request, Adam, but I'd rather you didn't come with me."

"Strange," I said. "Why not?"

"To be frank, you don't deal well with authority figures."

There was a certain amount of truth to her accusation. Still, she'd put me on the defense. "What do you mean?"

"Remember the Olympic Roosevelt in Seattle? You convinced hotel security that you were a Secret Service agent. And then there was the time a cop stopped you for speeding and you told him you were a surgeon on your way to do an emergency mastectomy on the governor."

"I got a police escort to the hospital."

"But we weren't going to the hospital."

"But I didn't get a ticket."

"Stay in the car. I'd rather do this my way. Simple and direct, if you don't mind."

As if I could stop her. When Alison Brooks made up her mind to do something, she was a force to be reckoned with. She strode up the walk and ascended the steps. Her long, burnished red hair flew behind her like a banner of righteous indignation. This was not a woman to be crossed, but I wasn't about to stay in the car like a neglected child.

I climbed out from behind the steering wheel and took a deep breath of Mount Prairie air. I wanted to ask some questions. It had occurred to me that the inhabitants of this place might be more forthcoming if they thought I belonged here. I reached into the back seat and took out the doctor's jacket I'd borrowed the first time I was here. I slipped it on over my black polo shirt and set out to explore the grounds.

Halfway around the first building on the north side, I saw a sapling arched over the sidewalk so that the top branches almost touched the ground on the other side. A length of yellow polypropylene rope stretched from the branches to a slipknot tied around a stick and ended in an open noose, arranged in the center of the sidewalk. A sign with an arrow pointing to the noose read: "Nurse Lavin, Step Here."

I approached the snare with interest and heard a hushed whispering from the shrubs nearby. Either Wile E. Coyote was on the loose or this was the work of the Death Squad.

"Hey," one of them called to me in a low voice. "Hey, you!"

I turned to see the guy in the wheelchair, apparently the brains of this outfit.

"Don't step there," he said.

"Thanks for the warning."

"It's for the bitch," he confided.

"Nurse Lavin?"

"You guessed it, man. She killed somebody last night."

This was interesting. Insane, but interesting. "So you want to kill her?"

"No, we just want to send her for a little trip across the compound. If we'd wanted to kill her, she'd be dead."

Reeves had said he was treating these three guys. They weren't exactly a testimonial to his skill as a psychiatrist, but they might know something. I tried to be reasonable. "What happened last night?"

The other two crept out from their hiding place between the shrubbery and the building. All three spoke at once.

"Lavin hated Doc Washington. She killed him. She's a master of disguise. Bad, evil woman."

"She dressed up to look like Kurt Schmidt and she beat him to death."

"Yeah, we got to get out of here. We got to escape before she gets us, too."

I held up my hand. "Wait!" I looked at the guy in the wheelchair. "You're Abe, right?"

He nodded.

"Abe, you tell me."

"First, identify yourself."

"Adam," I said. "Adam McCleet."

"How do I know you're not lying?"

When I held out my wallet to show him my driver's license, he grabbed it out of my hand. Quickly, he sorted through the contents and extracted my library card. Holding it up to show the others Abe announced, "He's okay."

"Here's what happened. Doc Washington was talking to his patient, same as always, but Kurt Schmidt, he went nuts. We were watching outside his office window. The doc hated when we did that."

"Isn't that window on the second floor?" I asked.

Abe shot me a look of incredulity. "Surveillance is vital. No one ever said it was easy."

"So, you witnessed the whole thing?"

"No, but we saw Kurt when they took him away. His face was red, and the veins were bulging out in his neck. His eyes were crazy. The Incredible Hulk, man. Just like the Hulk."

"So, you didn't see the whole thing."

"Well," Abe scratched the day-old growth of whiskers on his cheek. "Probably . . . not really. Sometimes it's hard to tell. You know?"

I was beginning to know. "Pretty violent guy, this Schmidt."

The three conferred and the taller one, who identified himself as Jerry, shook his head. "No way, Jose. Kurt Schmidt is a groovy kind of guy. Mellow yellow."

The short blond one, Marty, pointed at my white coat and asked, "Are you a doc?"

"No, I just like to dress up like one."

"Sure, I can dig it." Marty bobbed his head. "We had a guy here who liked to dress up like his sister."

"Now, that was spooky," Abe said.

Jerry spoke up. "Hey, phony doc, can you sign us out of here?"

"How would I do that?"

"Happens all the time. Docs come in from the V.A. and they sign forms and patients leave." He pulled a notepad from the pocket of his fatigue uniform. "Here's our full names, ranks and serial numbers."

"Don't give him that," Abe cautioned. "He might be one of Lavin's spies."

"Hey," I feigned hurt.

"No way, man," Marty said. "Lavin's snitches always wear polyester. This guy's right-on."

"Yeah, I guess you're okay."

"You guys don't really think Lavin killed Reeves, do you?"

They huddled to confer, and Abe in the wheelchair spoke again. "We don't know. But we don't like what's going on here. That was the third time in a month that somebody snapped out. But nobody's been hurt before."

I heard raised voices coming from an open window of the main building and I recognized Alison's dulcet tones. She was shouting, "You can't throw me out of here! I demand to see Grimhaur."

The Death Squad inched toward the disturbance. I took the more overt route, heading around to the front of the building. I waved to Abe, Marty and Jerry. "See you, soon." I meant it. I wanted to hear more about the other two incidents.

"We'll get packed," Abe assured me.

I found Alison storming down the front steps. "I can't believe it," she huffed. "That bitch of a nurse won't let me take Eric out of here. She won't even let me see him because Grimhaur isn't in."

"Want to try my way?" I offered.

She looked warily at my white coat. "It won't work. Not even you can trick Nurse Lavin."

"Oh, ye of little faith. I'm great at this undercover stuff. Frank Serpico has got nothing on me. I'll have her eating out of my hand."

"Be sure you count your fingers," Alison called after me as I walked through the double doors of the main building.

I formulated my plan as I strode confidently toward the front desk, footsteps echoing through the corridors. It might be easier to spring four patients than one. Nurse Lavin would be so delighted at the prospect of getting the

Death Squad out of her hair, she'd probably throw in Eric as a token of her appreciation.

A severe-looking woman with purple cat-eye glasses stood behind the counter making marks on a clipboard. She was tall, almost my height, with broad, square shoulders and hard angular features to her face. Her hair was permed into tight curls and bleached blond—a do-it-yourself job if ever I'd seen one—I could tell she bleached by the coarse, dark brown hairs on her upper lip. She looked tough, but I'd seen tougher.

"May I help you?" She asked, glaring over the top of her clipboard. Her voice was husky, with a hint of an Eastern European accent.

With great honesty, I said, "I was a friend of Reeves Washington."

Her composure wavered a bit, but she recovered quickly and offered the perfunctory sympathy. "A terrible tragedy."

"Yes," I agreed. "But that's not why I'm here. What's your name, Nurse?"

"Lavin. Fran Lavin."

"I'm Doctor Sterling from the Veterans' Administration," I said with a rising degree of pompousness. "Doctor Lionel Sterling, perhaps you've heard of my work in anorexia."

"No," she said.

"An entire issue of . . ." I remembered the name of the shrink magazine Reeves had published in. ". . . *Gray Matters* was devoted to my therapy. You haven't read it? Shame on you, Nurse Lavin. You ought to keep current in your field."

"We don't see much anorexia here."

"Are you sure?" I leaned across the counter and matched her hostile glare with one of my own. "Is that an opinion? Are you offering your own diagnosis?"

"Certainly not. I read the charts."

"And so shall I." I stepped briskly around the counter to her side, rattling off the full names for Abe, Marty and Jerry. "And Eric Brooks."

She started to object, but I raised one hand. "If you don't mind, Nurse, I am in a hurry."

Using her middle finger, she pushed her glasses up on her nose. It was a not-so-subtle way to flip me off. "Absolutely not. These charts are strictly confidential."

"Oh, please, I don't have time for your petty, self-involved hostility." I glanced at my wristwatch. "I'm due in Washington this afternoon for a group session with the Joint Chiefs of Staff."

"I don't believe you."

"You don't believe the leaders of our fine country deserve psychiatric counseling?"

"I don't believe they need it."

She was tough, all right, a bit naive about government, but definitely no pushover. Intimidation wasn't going to work with her. So, I changed tactics. Flattery, I hoped, would get me what I wanted. I chuckled genially. "You're very clever, Fran. Very bright, indeed. It's so unusual to find a woman who is both intelligent and devastatingly attractive. I salute you."

"Dr. Sterling, what are you talking about?"

"You were clever enough to see through my little white lie. Of course, I'm not treating the Joint Chiefs. Although, between you and me, a few of them could use some help with their eating disorders and tendencies toward anal-retentive behavior. My mission this afternoon is providing psychiatric profiles of leaders in South American countries." For good measure, I added, "And Canada."

"Why?"

I whispered, "Invasion."

"We're invading Canada?"

Her piggy little eyes widened. Her large mouth gaped

open. And I said, "God, you're beautiful when you're surprised. You're not married, are you?"

"Well, no. But—"

"And you live alone with your cat. Lucky pussy."

"Lucky guess," she snapped.

This woman was hard as obsidian. But I sensed a weakening. Dealing with her was like sculpting in stone. I had to be aware of the flaws not immediately apparent to the human eye. And Lavin was susceptible to flattery. The corner of her hairy upper lip twitched as if she actually wanted to smile.

"Forgive me," I said, "I've been too forward. I will try to maintain my professional distance, a task that will be difficult when all I truly want to do is to take you into my arms and taste the nectar of your ruby lips."

Her lower jaw dropped lower, revealing some excellent bridgework. I pressed on. "Take pity on me, Fran. I may be a world-renowned psychiatrist, but I'm still only a man."

"Well, I—"

"Don't speak. The sound of your voice drives me mad, I tell you, mad. I shan't be able to hold myself back." *Shan't?* I'd never used the word in my life. Damn, I was good at this. "Give me the charts."

She reached into the files and pulled out four folders. I took them from her and read Eric's room number. Room eight. Building C. I also quickly noted that Grimhaur diagnosed Eric with slight PTSD, low self-esteem and borderline Oedipal tendencies. "Not a risk to himself or others." No drug therapy indicated. After a scribble about Eric's minor head injury, Grimhaur added a recommendation of release from in-patient care and a once-a-week group therapy. Eric seemed to be pretty much okay.

The charts for Abe, Marty and Jerry included one line each: "No drugs. See general files."

If these guys had been in treatment for twenty years, the files had to be encyclopedic.

I handed the charts back to Nurse Lavin. "Thank you, Fran. From the bottom of my heart."

"You're welcome, Doctor."

"Building C is that way?" I pointed in the direction of Grimhaur's office.

She appeared stunned. "Yes, Doctor."

I hurried away.

As soon as I rounded the corner beyond her line of sight, I ran to Eric's room, slowing my pace whenever I came in sight of staff. I closed the door to Room Eight behind me. Eric was sitting on his bed, fully dressed in walking shorts and a T-shirt, staring out the window.

"Hey, Adam, what's up?"

"Your sister wants you out of here. Put on shoes, and let's go."

He didn't argue. Stuck his feet into loafers and we headed down the hall and out onto the grounds via a side door.

"Did Grimhaur release me?" Eric asked.

"No, kid. You've been sprung by Doctor Sterling. Which is why we're not leaving by the front door."

I led him on the side route, around the domain of Fran Lavin.

As we approached the parking lot, I was surprised to see the Death Squad crammed into the back of my Mustang. Though I had no qualms about releasing Eric, these three were quite another matter. "Alison?" I pointed to them and they waved cheerfully. "Why?"

"They told me you sent them. They used your name."

Abe stuck his head out the window. "Hey, Adam, we don't have time for bullshit. I humbly suggest we saddle-up and haul ass."

He was right. "Later," I promised, "we'll sort this out." Our only obstacle in leaving Mount Prairie was transporting six full-grown adults into a '67 Mustang. It was like packing Wilt Chamberlin into Woody Allen's boxer shorts. I had a feeling my car was bulging at the seams. Alison sat on Eric's lap while the Death Squad took turns leaning between the bucket seats to check out her thighs.

"Man," Marty said with astonishment as we rounded the first turn that allowed a full view of Portland, "it's amazing how much Saigon has grown since last time we were out."

"Don't be stupid," Abe said. "It's called Ho Chi Mihn City."

Alison rolled her eyes. "It's called Portland."

"Portland, huh?" Jerry said. "Is that north or south of the DMZ?"

Alison's eyes registered total astonishment. She started to correct them, but I held up my hand. I knew she didn't subscribe to the "we're all Bozos on this bus philosophy" to the extent that dealing with Abe and company required. Verbal communication with the Death Squad would be all but impossible for her.

"We're south," I said, checking Jerry's reflection in the rear-view mirror. "Way south. Most of the area has been designated semisecure. Minimal enemy activity, occasional small-arms fire."

Jerry nodded once. His eyes never changed expression. I'd seen the look before, the thousand-meter stare. But I caught the slightest hint of a twitch at the corner of his lips. I suspected he was not acknowledging his understanding of my situation report so much as his appreciation of the fact that I could play the game.

We didn't talk much after that, at least Alison didn't until we were half a mile from my place and she said, "Adam, that smoke looks like it's coming from your house."

Her observation instantly whipped the Death Squad

into a frenzy of chatter and speculation. Mortars, rockets, sneak attack, low-level bombing. Marty said, "If his hooch burnt down, we're not going to have a place to crash tonight." The squad silenced and ducked into a conference huddle.

True, at first glance a cloud of black smoke to the southeast, near the river, did appear to be coming from my house. "No," I said, "That smoke's coming from at least a block south."

Eric and Alison disagreed vehemently with my assessment, much to their credit. As we turned down my street, I could clearly see the smoke was indeed coming from the back of my house. I gunned the Mustang, and a few seconds later we skidded to a stop in front of my driveway.

Leaving my five passengers to unpack themselves, I jumped out of the car and ran to unlock my front door. Once inside, I hurried cautiously toward the kitchen, the most likely place for a fire, I thought. A heavy odor of kerosene permeated the air but no real smoke, and no fire in the kitchen. But through the window over the sink, I could see flames in the backyard. As I pulled the back door open, thick, oily smoke filled my lungs. Stumbling and coughing, I felt my way along the back of the house for the faucet where I'd left the garden hose attached. In my blinded state, I had no idea if I was walking straight into the fire. I hoped that I would feel the heat in time to stop myself.

I stumbled over something that crumbled under my weight, very much like a cheap aluminum lawn chair. As I fell, my forehead bounced off a rigid metal object. Eureka, I thought. Just before I blacked out, I found the faucet.

Chapter Eight

An hour later, I stood on the dock with Alison. One of the firefighters had strapped a large swatch of gauze to my forehead. But it would take a lot more than that to repair my formerly emerald-green back lawn. The thick smoke and flames had come from a humungous peace sign. About thirty feet in diameter. About ten gallons of stinking kerosene.

When the cops who accompanied the fire company asked if I knew who might have done it, I told them about my run-in with Frank Birkenshaw. They nodded, made a note and I knew that was pretty much the end of it. Even if they got around to questioning the little creep, he'd simply deny any knowledge of the whole incident, and the investigation would end right there. As usual, if I wanted answers I'd have to get them myself. That was just fine. I needed an excuse to talk to Birkenshaw anyway. I wanted to know about his relationship with Kurt Schmidt.

From the dock, Alison and I watched as the fire trucks, with sirens at full blast, careened over the remains of my yard. The sections that hadn't been burned or singed had been driven over or sprayed with megaforce hoses. On the plus side, only two of my pine trees had been axed by overenthusiastic firemen before I directed their attention to the blaze that had pretty much petered out to nothing more than smoke and smoldering Kentucky bluegrass. They'd gazed longingly at the rear door of the house, axes at the ready, but I promised that there was no more fire. "Thank you very much," I had said. "You can leave now."

I might have found a smidgen of gratitude in my heart if one of the firemen had actually rescued me from suffocating in a state of stupor, but I'd had to do that one myself. Though, if pressed, I'd have to admit that I'd been awakened by their sirens, and had managed to stumble out of the blinding smoke by following the sound of their chain saw cutting down my Russian olive tree.

They wanted to take me to the hospital in the ambulance, with the siren and flashing lights running, and they were clearly dying to use mouth-to-mouth on Alison. Only after repeated assurances that we would see our own doctors immediately were we able to convince them that their duty was done. We waved good-bye.

"I'm glad they're gone," I said.

"Me, too."

"Wonder how long it will take for the xeriscaping to kick in?"

"Should we have told the police we have three escaped lunatics in the house?"

"Four," I corrected.

"Not Eric. You can't possibly put my brother in the same category with those three."

"He was in the same hospital." I was still working on a way to tell her that Eric's sudden burst of uncontrollable rage that day on the boat had been basically identical to Schmidt's emotional state when he clubbed our friend to death. Reeves had lowered his guard, and it cost him his life. I wouldn't allow the same thing to happen to Alison.

"Eric's all right," she said. "He's just tired. A little run-down. A little . . ." Her calm expression crumpled. She drew a ragged breath. "God, Adam, I sound like a text-book example of a co-dependent in the throes of denial. I know better than this. I know better than to ignore the elephant in the kitchen."

"You got to keep an eye on those pachyderms," I said, having no clue as to what she meant. Alison usually didn't resort to psychobabble.

"The elephant," she explained, "is a metaphor for a raging problem, like alcoholism, that the co-dependents ignore while they focus on other, less threatening, things."

When I glanced at her, she avoided direct eye contact. "What's going on with you?"

"Nothing." Her delicate hands drew into fists. "There I go again, ignoring the problem."

"What problem?" I was beginning to feel stupid.

"Nothing."

"Okay." I put my arm around her shoulders and she leaned against me as we walked up the gangway toward my house. "You don't want to talk about it right now. Let's just acknowledge that there is a problem, and we'll deal with it when you're ready. How about that?"

She held my arm closely with both hands as we picked our way around the muck that was my backyard, trying to avoid the soggiest spots. "Thank you for understanding."

I had witnessed the murder of a close friend. I was probably going to be seriously sued for bruising Birkenshaw's ugly little noggin. In my house were three delusional nutballs, and the jury was still out on Alison's brother, Eric. The peace Nazis, probably lead by Birkenshaw himself, had declared war on my lawn. And I was about to sell out to the Noble Heights memorial committee for seventy-six grand to do a project that I wasn't sure I believed in. I understood nothing, but the concept of ignoring any new problems until I could figure out ways to deal with the rapidly mounting backlog of old ones appealed to me.

The heel of Alison's shoe made a sucking noise as she pulled her foot from a particularly squishy patch of mud near the back of the house. "I don't understand," she said. "Where do these people find the nerve to attack your lawn in broad daylight? I'd always assumed that people who do this kind of thing strike at night wearing white sheets and pointed hoods."

Tie-dyed shirts and pointed heads in this case, I thought. "Actually, it's the safest time, very nineties. I don't have many neighbors and most of them work during the day. Usually it's just me and Binky. They only had to ring the doorbell to know I wasn't home."

"Are you sure you know who did this, Adam?"

"I know," I said, using the mangled patio chair to scrape the mud from the sole of my loafer. I didn't bother telling her that I planned to have a chat with Frank Birkenshaw. She had enough to worry about.

Eric sat in the living room, flipping through the pages of my latest *National Geographic.*

"Where are the boys?" I asked.

He nodded toward the kitchen door. "Your studio."

I shook my head, which was beginning to ache severely under the sloppy bandage. "There is no way this can work. They've got to go back to Mount Prairie."

I picked up the phone to call Margot, an exercise I hated in the best of times. Waiting for her to answer, a shiver of dread crept through me, a sick feeling of anticipation that might otherwise only be experienced immediately prior to driving a blunt nail into one's own ear. But I needed to know Birkenshaw's address.

"Are you all right?" Alison cooed over her brother. "How are you feeling?"

"I'm okay." Eric shrugged his heavily muscled shoulders.

Margot's phone rang for the third time. In my head, I began to compose a succinct message for her answering machine.

"I'm taking you home with me," Alison said. "We're going to find a doctor who can do you some good."

"I like Grimhaur."

Margot's housekeeper answered on the fourth ring. She informed me that Margot was indisposed right now because she was in mourning. Of course, Reeves's death would provide a grand stage for Margot to wax dramatic. In disgust, I muttered, "Have her call me. Soon."

While Alison and Eric argued civilly about the merits of Grimhaur as a shrink, I went through the kitchen and opened the rear door to my studio.

Predictably, the Squad had turned the place into command central. Abe had found a map of Portland and spread it out on my drafting table. He was busily drawing lines and arrows with a broad-tipped grease pencil. In his other hand, he held the telephone. "Hey, Adam," he called out. "How do I call Paris? I need to check on the peace talks."

Jerry dug noisily through a flat-bin of metal scrap, sheets of brass, copper and tin. He'd already bent and shaped two large rectangular pieces of tin and fitted them into the window casings, transforming the light, airy studio into a bunker.

In a corner at the rear of the studio, Marty leaned back in a director's chair stroking his chin, his feet comfortably propped on the corner of a cluttered work bench, studying the sketch I'd been working on a day earlier.

I feared for my works-in-progress. "What the hell are you guys doing in here?"

"Battle plan," Abe said. "We have to establish a perimeter, primary and secondary lines of defense. And we'll need an LZ." He poked at the map with his index finger. "This looks like the best location."

I looked over his shoulder at the spot he'd indicated. "That's the Portland Zoo." About ten miles from my house. In fact, none of the black marks he'd scribbled on the map were anywhere near my house, but I wasn't in the mood to teach geography. "Perfect," I said, "they'll never expect an air-cavalry assault."

A loud clatter drew my attention to Jerry, who was dragging a three-foot-square sheet of stainless steel from the scrap bin. "Hey, be careful with that stuff."

"I'm cool," Jerry said. He stared at the bandage on my head. "How's that head wound?"

"No problem." I sounded like Alison, ignoring the three elephants who had taken up residence in my studio.

"Let me take a look," he said.

I took a quick step back as Jerry approached. My survival instincts were becoming more acute with each new contusion. "Don't touch me," I warned.

"I was a medic," he said, quietly. "I can fix anything."

I remembered that there was something behind the craziness, the trauma that Reeves referred to. I had seen the medics in Vietnam, ignoring their own safety, as all of hell's worst exploded around them, trying to save the lives of others while the rest of us only worried about ourselves. Twenty years ago, I would have trusted him with my life. "Later, Jerry. Okay? I really am not in pain."

He shrugged and went back to his scraps.

Abe whipped up next to me, doing an impressive wheelie with his chair. "Good thing we're here, Adam. You need help."

"No, Abe. You guys are going back to Mount Prairie. I don't need your—"

"Look, man, you just had a major assault on your perimeter. This time, they burnt your ground cover. Next time, they might burn your whole freakin' hooch down."

He had a point. "No," I said, as much to myself as to him. "I can't be here all the time to keep an eye on you guys. Besides, I've got no place for you to stay. No barracks. Only one bedroom."

Abe said, "Jerry'll take care of that. He's our scrounge."

I flashed a mental image of Jerry sneaking out, in full camouflage, to steal patio chairs from my neighbors. "No," I repeated.

Marty waved to me. "Hey, Adam, come here for a sec."

"Now what?"

He pointed to the sketch I'd been working on, and to my lumpish attempt to mold a clay model for the proposed sculpture. "Are you an artist or something?"

Or something. "A sculptor."

"This is okay stuff, but kind of old-fashioned. Kind of Rodin. Kind of Brancusi. Kind of cliché."

Everybody was a critic. "Got any ideas?"

"Well, I assume you're attempting to depict the horror of battle and the despair of mortality while symbolizing hope and courage with these dove wings over here."

He sounded like the art critic for the *Oregonian*. "Yeah?" I said cleverly.

He picked up the marker and reached toward the tablet. "Do you mind if I modify this sketch?"

"Be my guest. It wasn't working anyway."

He added a few strokes, some shading and a smooth shell-like structure that would surround the whole piece. "I knew you were a sculptor," he admitted. "Soon as I came in here, I knew. Doc Washington used to talk about you. I always wanted to meet someone who made a real living doing real art."

"It's not easy."

"Takes a lot of training?" he asked.

"A lot of luck," I said. "Where'd you learn about art?"

"Twenty years of arts, crafts and occupational therapy in one hospital or another. I know clay and casting. Jerry taught me welding and brazing."

Abe had silently inched up behind me. "You need us, Adam."

I was about to review all the reasons why they had to go back to the Institute when I remembered what Reeves had said about how much he liked having them around. "Let me ask you guys a question."

"Shoot," Abe said.

I looked seriously into the eyes of each of them, trying to send the message that if any of them ever visited planet Earth, this would be a good time to do so. "Have any of you ever experienced a violent or psychotic episode? You know, like uncontrollable rage where you actually had to be restrained?"

"You mean like trying to drive my wheelchair over Nurse Lavin's toes?" Abe asked.

"Like flashbacks," I said. "You know what I'm talking about."

Abe said, "No." The other two echoed his response, and Abe explained, "We're not violent. Not of real danger to ourselves or to anyone else. Doc Washington didn't treat anybody who was violent."

"Except Kurt Schmidt," I said.

"He wasn't like that," Abe said.

"But I saw him kill Reeves." Half to myself, I added, "It had to be drugs."

"No drugs. Not on our wing. Grimhaur is the only shrink at Mount Prairie who uses drugs."

"What about a raid on the drug cabinet," I suggested, "Maybe Schmidt got hold of something."

"Not with Lavin holding the keys," Abe said. "I'm going to give you a piece of advice. Adam, this is straight poop. Don't try to make sense of Doc Washington's death. Everybody dies. You gotta shake it off. You know, nothin' but a meatball."

"He's right," Marty said. "Shit happens."

Jerry nodded sagely. "Ain't no use to sit and wonder why, babe."

Surrounded by these three, with their wise but crazy eyes following my every move, I felt a strange kind of comfort. Reeves had liked them, too.

Abe repeated, "You need us."

Maybe he was right. Maybe I'd just picked up three assistants and a first line of defense against Birkenshaw and the Friends of Political Correctness. "Okay," I said. "You can stay. On a trial basis. Any of you guys gets weirder than you already are, I'll ship you straight back to Lavin."

When the telephone near the drafting table rang, Abe whizzed across the wood floors and answered, "Adam McCleet's residence. May I say who is calling?"

He whipped the phone away from his ear and glared at it with the sort of revulsion even the crazed saved for snakes, spiders and Margot.

"It's for you," Abe said.

I took the receiver. "Hi, Margot. Listen, I need an address and a phone number for—"

"You're a pig, Adam. How dare you intrude on my grief." She heaved a sigh that roared through the phone wires at gale force. "Reeves and I were extremely close. We were going to be married."

Normally, I don't argue with my sister. It's a futile exercise because she always manages to bludgeon me into submission with her whining and outright hostility. But her phony mourning was too much for me to take. Reeves deserved a more dignified and thoughtful send-off. "Shut up, Margot."

"Never talk to me like that."

"Reeves Washington was a good man. He's leaving behind an ex-wife, two kids and a lot of patients who will miss him a hell of a lot more than you. Stop thinking about yourself for sixty seconds."

"I cared about him."

"No doubt. But if you show up at his funeral, draped in widow's weeds and wailing like a—"

"Oh, speaking of funerals, I spoke to Reeves's ex on the phone. What's her name?"

"Felicia."

"Yes, that's it. She said the funeral is tomorrow at the Noble Heights United Methodist Church. Ten in the morning. Don't you think she's rushing it a little?"

Maybe, I thought, but that was Felicia's business. She was a strong woman, with a mind of her own. "I'm sure she has her reasons, Margot. I wish you wouldn't bother her."

"You never approved of Reeves and I," she accused.

"Until yesterday afternoon, there was no such thing as Reeves and you. Now, give me Frank Birkenshaw's address and phone number, and we won't have to talk to each other anymore."

"Why do you want Frank's number?"

"He burned a giant peace sign in my backyard."

"You're out of your mind," she said in a sisterly display of sensitivity. "Birkenshaw isn't one of my favorite people, but he *is* from Noble Heights."

Which, in her mind, absolved him of any wrongdoing. I remembered from the meeting that Birkenshaw lived with Jonathan Noble. "Where does Noble live?"

"None of your business. Don't you dare come over here and embarrass me. I have a standing in this community."

I'd figure it out on my own. "Bye, Margot."

"Never speak to me again about Reeves's tragic accident."

"It wasn't an accident," I said. "He was killed."

"Of course, it was an accident. One of those violent men he worked with had a psychotic episode."

"But he didn't work with violent patients." Schmidt hadn't just slipped through the net. "He was murdered." The more I heard myself say it, the more I believed it.

Margot, ever the supportive sibling said, "You're a hopeless idiot, Adam," and hung up.

I set down the phone and turned to the Squad. "Here are the ground rules: Don't leave the house. Don't touch any of the artwork in the other room. Don't answer the phone. If you see anybody outside, call the cops. Got it?"

Abe looked at the other two, then grinned at me. "If I was you, Adam, I wouldn't expect too much."

Marty smirked. "We are nuts, you know."

I left them in the studio and returned to the house where Eric had settled into a magazine article and Alison was making him a sandwich. She motioned for me to join her in the kitchen and whispered, "He doesn't want to come with me. He wants to go back to Grimhaur."

"He's a big boy. It's his decision."

"Thanks, Adam." Eric's broad shoulders filled the kitchen doorway. "I'm not saying Grimhaur is the best shrink in the world, but I don't have time to be going in and out of mental hospitals and I don't want to retell all this stuff to somebody else."

"How long have you been seeing Grimhaur?" I asked.

"About a month. After I quit working for Mom, I figured I needed to talk to somebody. I went to the V.A., and they referred me to Mount Prairie. The first time I went to see him, I almost cracked. Told him everything I could remember. Cried like a baby."

Alison made a soft, murmuring sound.

"After the second time," Eric said, "Grimhaur himself told me that he thought I was pretty much okay, that I had a good handle on my problems. This wasn't going to be a big deal. A few occasional visits, and I'd be on my way." He frowned. Eric had the face of an all-American kid, freckles and all.

"Then what happened?" I asked.

"I snapped out."

"This was before the time on the *Raptor,*" I clarified.

"About a week and a half ago. I didn't hurt anybody."

"Oh, God." Alison looked like she might burst into tears. "Why didn't you tell me?"

He shrugged. "It was kind of embarrassing. I just got frustrated. Know what I mean? It was late, probably eleven o'clock at night, and I went to an automatic teller machine. The damn thing ate my card. I kept punching the fucking buttons, but it told me I used the wrong code. I don't remember going back to my car, but I must have because I had my tire iron and I was hammering away at the computer screen."

I forced myself to keep a straight face. "You beat up an ATM machine?"

"Yeah. But it all turned out okay. I arranged to pay for the damage from my savings account and the bank dropped the charges."

"And when you told Grimhaur?"

"He scheduled me for twice-a-week sessions."

While Alison escorted him to the kitchen table and plied her little brother with sandwiches and milk, I thought about drugs again. Eric seemed like a mild-mannered kid, easy-going. I could understand why he quit his job with Alison's mother, and I could understand why anybody might want to assault one of those smug machines. If I hadn't witnessed the force of his rage on the *Raptor,* I might have dismissed the whole thing.

"Eric, do you use any drugs." I looked at his muscles. "Steroids, maybe?"

"No way, man. This body is a temple. I've seen too many people fucked up on drugs. I'm totally organic."

"And when you went to Mount Prairie. Did Grimhaur prescribe any kind of medication?"

"B-12 shots. That's it." He took a mouthful of sandwich and chewed. "Vitamin B-12."

But there was something unnatural about Eric's psycho episodes. "Did you know Kurt Schmidt?"

"The guy who killed Reeves? Yeah, I met him. He was on the other wing, but he used to work out and we hung around in the exercise room together. For an old guy, he was in great shape. Real quiet. Good sense of humor. He was like me. Not a long-term patient. He'd only been at the institute for a month or so."

"Do you know why he was an in-patient?"

"He was depressed. Bummed. Said it was a midlife crisis thing that started last year around Christmas time. Said he kept thinking about Vietnam. Not having flashbacks, but thinking about it. He started seeing Reeves then, and Reeves suggested he spend some full-time at Mount Prairie while he got his shit together. Kurt said he was planning to go home within the month, but I don't think he was looking forward to it."

"And he wasn't on drugs," I said. "None of Reeves's patients were on drug therapy."

"That's enough," Alison said. "I'm taking Eric home with me. I know of a few psychiatrists who might be good for him. But, of course, it's his decision."

"Thanks, Sis. I appreciate that."

Alison didn't notice the sarcasm in his voice. She turned to me. "I'll be in touch." She nodded toward the studio. "Will you be okay with those three . . . guys? Can you get them back to Mount Prairie?"

"Actually, they're going to stay with me. Just for a little while."

"I guess that's your decision, too."

The sarcasm in her tone was not wasted on me. At that moment, I wasn't sure whose decision it was. None the less, I felt compelled to justify myself. "They're going to help me with the Noble Heights piece." I watched her eyes for a hint of approval. Finding none, I added, "It's a therapeutic kind of thing. An idea that Reeves and I were kicking around."

She fluttered around Eric, trying not to rush him but anxious to be on her way.

Since she obviously hadn't heard a word of the fabrication, I let it drop. I stared out into my scorched backyard. My number one order of business was Birkenshaw.

Finding him wasn't a problem. If he lived with Jonathan Noble, though I'd never actually been there, I had a pretty good idea of the approximate location to start looking in.

I closed the door behind Alison and Eric, then I returned to the studio. I wasn't quite comfortable with the whole concept of leaving the Death Squad in my house without a keeper of some kind.

"Let's go, guys."

"Where?" Abe questioned.

"LZ Noble."

Chapter
Nine

When I opened the front door, with the Squad following close at my heels, I heard Alison's delicate soprano raised in a loud, fairly profane shout.

"Move that thing," she yelled. "What the hell do you think you're doing, you obnoxious, ridiculous—"

I pulled the door closed and faced the Squad. "Stay here."

"You need our help," said Abe, the stalwart leader.

"I mean it. Stay here."

The Squad continued to protest, but when I added, "That's an order," they fell silent.

When I stepped onto the front porch, I could see that Alison's car was blocked in the driveway by the big-wheeled bubba-mobile. Captain Jack sat in the driver's seat, his face as red as the crude peace sign that still scarred his door.

Alison flung herself off the porch and stormed toward him. She looked like a hummingbird attacking a rhino. "What the hell are you doing?" she yelled. "Move that absurd machine or I'll—"

I caught up with her before she physically assaulted the truck. She whipped around and faced me. Several decibels lower, she said to me, "Can you believe this guy? He won't move his truck. He's deliberately goading Eric."

I waved to Captain Jack, and he rewarded me with a middle finger in front of his murderous scowl. "Actually, I think he's here to see me."

"Why?"

"The truck."

"You offered to pay for the new paint job, didn't you?"

"Yeah, but—"

"He's being unreasonable."

I didn't bother to explain to her that men like Jack considered their trucks to be sacred, regarded with far more reverence than their jobs, their beer, their wives and several nonessential body parts. "Let me handle this. You go back to the car and wait with Eric."

"Oh, no. I'm tired of being the quiet little woman. He's a pig, and I intend to tell him so."

"He was nice enough to lend us his truck when we really needed it, and I brought the damn thing back trashed. You can understand why he'd be a little upset."

"Upset enough to burn a peace sign into your lawn?"

The thought had crossed my mind, but a peace sign didn't seem like Jack's style, and it wasn't really the desecration of my gardening that I was worried about. The only good use for the destruction in my backyard was that it provided me with an excuse to get in Birkenshaw's face and find out more about his connection with Kurt Schmidt.

"You think he did it?" Alison asked.

"Don't say anything, okay? Let's see some of that famous Alison Brooks charm."

She stuck with me like a furious little shadow as I approached the truck. "Hey, Jack, I'm really sorry about the graffiti. You got my note, didn't you? I've already called my insurance company and you're covered."

"Fuck your insurance, McCleet," he grunted.

Alison may have been on to something with her pig theory. "Okay," I said. "Do we have a problem?"

"Hell, yeh. We got a problem. I put a shitload of work into this vehicle. I love this hunk of iron, and I'm gonna need more than money before I can sleep with myself again, you smartass yuppie liberal."

I was stung. Jack hated me for being a liberal. Birkenshaw and his gang hated me because I wasn't liberal enough. Still, I tried to be reasonable. "So, what do you want?"

"I want twenty-five hundred bucks."

Money may not have been enough, but it was certainly at the top of his list. "Isn't that a bit steep for a door? The whole thing can't be more than six square feet."

"This here is a custom paint job, boy. They'll never match the color."

"It's black," I said.

"They gotta paint the whole truck." He thrust his arm out the window, a sheet of yellow paper wadded in his plump fingers. "Here's the estimate."

I reached up and took the paper. "How hard can it be to match black paint?" I gestured toward Alison as I glanced over the hand scribbling on the official Daddy Bud's Custom Paint and Body Shop estimate form. "She has a master's degree in fine art. Tell him how to match black, Alison."

"Certainly." She cleared her throat like a guest lecturer at a school for the intellectually deprived. "Mix equal parts of the primary *pig*-ments."

"There you go," I said, stuffing the paper into a hip pocket of my Levi's. "It doesn't get any simpler than that. Tell Daddy Bud to bill my insurance company."

"I'm not waitin' on a damn insurance check. I mean to collect every dollar of it from you, right now."

I tried to speak in his native tongue. "Here's the problem, old horse. My dearly departed daddy used to always say sometimes, he'd say, 'Son, never give cash to a moron. He'll just do something stupid with it.' " My bubba-speak was rusty.

"Then I'll take it out of your hide and use your eyeballs for change."

"That's so stupid," Alison put in. "You can't solve anything with your fists."

"I want some goddamned payback," he said.

"Maybe you already got your payback when you burned my yard."

"What if I did?"

"Did you?"

"What are you going to do if I did?"

"Did you?"

The speed at which our level of communication deteriorated was mind boggling. I could feel I.Q. points tearing away.

"Okay," Alison said, "I've had it. Either you move or I'm calling the police."

"Oh, sure," he said. "When that loony attacked me and my boat, you were all smiles and apologies. Now the shoe's on the other hoof and the first thing you want to do is call the cops."

Throughout the bickering and snarling, Eric had remained calmly in the passenger seat of Alison's car with his seat belt fastened. Now, the door creaked open and Eric emerged. Captain Jack recognized him immediately. "Shit. You got your bodyguard."

Clearly, he was terrified. He gunned the engine and snarled at me. "I'm not going to forget this. I'll be back."

His giant tires kicked up gravel as they spun in reverse.

"Shit," I said.

"Ditto," Alison said. "Can you believe that guy? I'm sure he's the one who burned your yard."

I doubted that Jack was the culprit. He wouldn't have

stuck his red neck out while the scent of kerosene still lingered on the air.

"Adam," Eric said, stepping up beside his sister, "I'm really sorry about all the trouble I caused."

When I looked into Eric's eyes, I could not detect the slightest hint of the rage we'd seen on Jack's boat. He was far calmer than either Alison or I. Resting my hand on his thick shoulder I said, "Don't worry about it, buddy. Rest up. Let Alison take care of you for a couple days. You'll feel better in no time."

"I feel fine. Really."

"Of course you do," Alison said, taking her brother by the hand and leading him back to her car. "Let's go home."

As they pulled away, I waved and watched till they were out of sight, all the time wondering what had made the difference in Eric's mind between today, when he'd remained so cool, and Sunday, when he'd snapped like a tightly coiled spring. Captain Jack was certainly no less obnoxious or insulting. Could two days at Mount Prairie have been so tranquil?

The rage I'd seen in Kurt Schmidt's eyes flashed in my head. Tranquillity? I doubted that Eric's current mood had much to do with Mount Prairie and his shrink, the good doctor Grimhaur. Instead, I thought I was probably seeing Eric in his natural state of heavily muscled calm. So, why had he gone nuts on the boat?

Turning to go back to the house and rally the Squad, I stumbled over Binky. He'd been standing close behind me smelling my butt, one of his favorite things to do on a hot day. "Get out of the way, you worthless cur. Where the hell were you when somebody torched the yard? Seems like you'd have protected your bathroom."

Binky gave a single muffled woof, then turned to show me a red peace sign spray-painted over the coarse gray hair on his left side.

"They got you too, huh? Who was it, boy?"

Binky's woof sounded more intelligent this time. I felt like I was living a scene from an old episode of Lassie as I watched the big dog run to his own yard and nose around in the bushes. In a few seconds, he emerged with something in his mouth and jumped around, growling and shaking his head as if he were reenacting his struggle with the vandals.

"What is it, Binky? Bring it here, boy."

He loped back and laid the object at my feet. "Arf," he said.

I took that to mean, here's a dirty rag, soaked with dog slobber. "Good boy, Binky," I patted him on the head as I bent down to inspect the cloth.

Holding the material gingerly, between the tips of my thumb and index finger, I was less concerned about preserving evidence than I was about getting slimy Binky drool all over my hands. After I shook the dirt from the six-inch-square rag, I realized what my neighbor's brilliant dog had brought me. A torn piece of tie-dyed cotton. Birkenshaw's favorite garb.

There was no need to question Binky at length. He'd told me everything he knew. I fixed him a peanut butter and jelly sandwich, loaded the Squad into the Mustang and headed for the highest of the heights. The estate of Johnathan Noble.

I didn't need the map that Abe had thoughtfully snatched from my desk file. It wasn't just that the map was of southern Italy. I only had to aim the car in the general direction of Mount Prairie, and turn right at the sign that read "J. Noble Rd."

Two lanes of impeccably maintained asphalt led us through a wide greenbelt of lush forest, past the Noble Heights Country Club, across a neatly painted covered bridge spanning Noble Creek, around the north side of shimmering Noble Lake, from where Mount Prairie and the burgeoning village of Noble Heights could be seen on the far side of the golf course.

J. Noble Road ended, or began, at an ornate twelve-foot-high steel security gate, attached to an equally high red brick wall, which extended into the forest and out of sight in either direction. I slowed to a stop and set the parking brake. "This is it."

Abe looked up from his map. "Naples?" His voice lacked the usual tone of self-assurance.

"Noble's," I said, "Wait here."

Abe's face disappeared into the map.

I climbed out of the Mustang and walked to the intercom, which was bolted to the wall on the left side of the gate. The printing on a single black button set into the wall below the face-level speaker grill told me to push. I followed the instructions carefully, and waited a few seconds, wondering if I should speak into the grill. I looked at the Squad, who looked back expectantly. *No help there.* I decided to say something, but I didn't know if I should hold the button in and speak, or if it was one of those push and release kind of things. I turned to the boys and shrugged. "They could have put a little more thought into these instructions."

"What?" A female voice said over the speaker.

The fidelity of the intercom system took me by surprise. It sounded as if the woman were standing beside me. "Hello?" I said into the grill. "Do I need to push this button, or what?"

"Just talk." The voice sounded tired of hearing that question. "What do you want?"

"I'm here to see Mister Noble." I thought I'd start at the top and work my way down to Birkenshaw. "I'm Adam McCleet. He's expecting me."

"You don't have an appointment," The voice said.

"I know . . . But if you'll tell him that Adam McCleet is—"

"If you don't have an appointment, you're not expected," the tired voice explained. "Go away."

"Wait. What I meant to say was that he knows me. And I'm sure he'd like to see me if you'd just tell him I'm here." I waited for a response, but after a minute, I realized the bored lady had gone away. I tried pushing the button several more times, but no luck.

"Hey, Adam," Abe called from the car. "What's the problem?"

I walked back to the Mustang. I didn't want to make a public broadcast of my next move. "They're not going to open the gate," I said. "I'm going over the wall."

"That wall's a mother," Jerry said. "Let me check out that gate."

"Really. Jerry is great with electrical stuff," Abe said.

"Yeah," Marty added.

I was about to reject the idea when I heard the barking of dogs approaching the wall. These were not the friendly woofs of the family lapdogs. These were deep, angry barks with lots of snarling and snapping. "What have you got in mind, Jerry?"

"Easy, man. I just hot-wire the box and we're in. No sweat."

"If you can do it fast . . ." I started to regret my next words as they came out of my mouth. ". . . Go for it."

Jerry dragged his long frame out of the backseat, pushing Abe's face against the windshield in the process. "Won't take more than a pair of seconds."

He walked quickly to the brick post where the intercom was mounted, flashed a glance at the unit then began wandering along the wall with eyes turned toward the ground.

"Do you need some tools?" I asked. "There's a small kit in the trunk, and—"

Jerry picked up a bowling-ball-sized rock and smashed

it against the intercom. Three times. The shiny steel cover, dented and mangled, swung by one screw.

"Never mind." I should have guessed.

He plunged his arm into the exposed rectangular hole in the brickwork and yanked out a tangled nest of wires, twisted the ends of two of them together and asked, "Are you ready?"

The barking of the dogs grew louder, closer. I jumped into the driver's seat and started the engine.

Jerry attached a third wire and made a dash for the car as the gate rolled slowly back.

The dogs, two rottweilers with choppers bared, arrived at the gate ready for lunch. Fortunately for Jerry, they stopped abruptly at the invisible boundary line where the gate had been.

"How come they stopped?" Marty asked.

"Because they're trained not to go off the property," Abe explained. "It wouldn't be cool to have your dogs eating the shorts off the friendly neighborhood joggers. They could get Spandex poisoning."

"Nice job," I said to Jerry as he climbed back into the car. "You're a real artist. No one will ever know we've been here."

"Thanks," he said modestly.

We rolled up the windows and drove slowly past the dogs as they snapped at the tires and chomped on the door handles on either side of the car. When they started gnawing on my back bumper, I stepped on the gas and left them to catch up.

For three miles we followed the winding driveway through more enchanted evergreen forest before we finally caught our first glimpse of Noble's house. The brick-and-stone country-squire mansion stood on an elegantly landscaped twenty-acre clearing in the trees. This place made Mount Prairie Institute, the old family digs, look like a Homes for the Homeless project.

I parked in front of a two-story six-car garage, roughly twice the size of my house. "Wait here," I said as I stepped out of the car. "I mean it. Wait here."

"Sure." The Death Squad nodded its collective head.

I was headed for the front porch when I saw a dwarfish creature leaving the house by a side exit. He was dressed in white, and carrying a tennis racquet. His stubby legs were as white as his starched shorts. A tie-dyed bandanna held his stringy, thinning hair in place. "Hey, Frank!" I yelled.

When Birkenshaw stopped to see who had called him, he looked surprised to see me, but he didn't try to run away. "McCleet? What are you doing here?"

"We need to talk," I said walking toward him. "You know. Kind of clear the air between the two of us."

When I came within arm's reach, we shook hands. His grip was limp and damp, insincere. His eyes were red, dilated and glassed over. He was wasted.

"Clear the air?" Birkenshaw squinted.

"Yes. Clear the smoke away, so to speak." I added a chuckle to set him at ease.

"Smoke?"

"I just want you to know there's no hard feelings. I did a violent thing to you, and you retaliated. I understand. But this is the way wars begin, and I'm as opposed to war as you are. So it just doesn't make sense for us to escalate. You know what I mean?"

"Retaliate? Escalate? What the hell are you talking about, man?" His eyebrows raised until the furrows on his forehead looked like a strip-mining project. "You don't think I had something to do with your friend getting killed?"

I hadn't even thought of a way to bring the subject up. My plan was to keep him talking and off his guard until the opportunity presented itself. Instead, he had caught me off guard with his drug-induced candor.

"Actually," I said, "I was talking about me banging you on the head, and you burning my yard. But, as long as you mentioned it, I was wondering how you knew Kurt Schmidt."

"I don't know anything about your yard." His eyes shifted from side to side. "And what makes you think I know Kurt Schmidt?"

Birkenshaw sounded convincing, but he had the look of a liar and a cheat. He was a politician in rebel's rags. I didn't trust him as far as I could drop-kick him.

"I saw you and another guy together at the Institute. Before the committee meeting. You embraced each other. A casual observer such as myself would have thought that you were good friends."

"I hug a lot of people, man. I didn't have anything to do with him killing Washington."

"Of course you didn't. I saw Reeves get killed, and you weren't there. But if you don't know Schmidt, how did you know that the man you hugged and Reeves's killer are the same person?"

"I didn't." Birkenshaw shifted nervously from one foot to the other. "I just . . . you know . . . assumed." He shrugged his drooping shoulders.

He was lying. I was certain of that. I resisted an overpowering urge to punch the psychedelic stuffing out of him. Birkenshaw was hiding something, and I didn't want to scare him away before I could convince the police to investigate Reeves's death. I decided to ease off on the Kurt Schmidt issue for now.

I reached into my hip pocket and produced the drying swatch of rainbow-colored cloth that Binky had given me. "I found this at my house. After someone burned an oversized peace sign in my lawn. You can understand how I might have thought—"

"Look, man. When you attacked me, you attacked the

people. And when you attack the people you attack the
. . ."

I heard the barking of the dogs again. They were heading this way. I wondered if the Death Squad had stayed
in the car as I'd asked. Birkenshaw was getting speechy.
It was starting to feel like time to leave. The feeling inten-
sified when I saw Jonathan Noble, also dressed in tennis
whites, appear from behind a wall of poplar trees about
fifty yards north of the house. He looked like a snowball
with legs.

"Hey, Frank!" Noble hollered.

Frank Birkenshaw ceased his patented, endless line of
bullshit. He turned toward the tennis court and yelled,
"Be right there, Jonathan. I'm just saying good-bye to
Mr. McCleet." He turned back to me and said, "You
should leave, man. He gets really strung-out about tres-
passers. You know?"

The twelve-foot-high wall around the estate had been
my first clue, but as I watched Birkenshaw's chubby tennis partner pep-step up the path toward us, I had a feeling I was about to get a sample of Sir Noble's wrath.

Noble had covered half the distance when he yelled
again. "Hey, Frank! Go tell Fidel to take those damned
dogs in before they kill somebody. I want to talk to
McCleet."

Birkenshaw looked hurt but, like any good leech, he
didn't argue with his benefactor. "Nice talking to you,
McCleet," he said sarcastically.

"I have security now, Frank," I said. "If you or any of
your people come within a mile of my house, I will cause
physical harm."

"Thanks for the warning," he said, and hurried away
to carry out his orders.

Noble was out of breath by the time he reached me.
We shook hands. "How are you?" I said.

"Old." He panted. "I'm sorry about what happened to

your friend." After a dozen more deep breaths he added, "He was a good man."

"Yes. He was."

"I guess he kind of underestimated how dangerous Schmidt is, though."

"I don't think so."

"What?" His broad chest stopped heaving. "I thought you were there. You saw Kurt Schmidt club Washington to death."

Though the entire incident had been covered in depth by the local media, my name had never been mentioned. "I'm surprised you would know that, Mr. Noble. You must have friends in high places."

Noble smiled. "If you count the President of the United States, I guess I do. But I got that piece of information from Marion Grimhaur."

"Dr. Grimhaur's wife." I assumed.

"Marion is Dr. Grimhaur's name," Noble said patiently.

"Of course." I nodded. "You and Marion are friends."

"We have occasion to speak."

"I suppose Marion will be appointed chief of staff." I wondered how far Noble would go to have a voting member of the Mount Prairie board of directors in his back pocket. How far would he go to reacquire the rights to his precious real estate?

"I suppose." His tone was noncommittal. "Walk with me, McCleet. I want to show you something." He turned and headed east across the lawn, toward a stand of first-growth Douglas fir.

I followed. "Call me Adam."

"I checked you out, Adam."

"Checked me out?"

"That's right. You did two tours in Nam with Fleet Marine Force recon. Tough outfit. You were wounded twice in the line of duty. You'd need a wheelbarrow to carry all your citations for valor, including two Bronze and one Silver Star, which would have been a Congressional Medal of Honor if your company commander hadn't taken half the credit for something you did while he was catching a dose of V.D. at China Beach . . ."

Jonathan Noble's sources were extremely good. I'd never told anyone about the CMH recommendation, not even Nick.

". . . You were a good cop, too," Noble continued. "In spite of your little problem with authority figures, you managed to walk away from the Portland P.D. with consistently high proficiency ratings and another stack of citations for valor. With a history like that, a person might get the idea that you have more balls than brains. But you had the good sense to get out while you were still breathing. In a relatively short period of time, you established yourself as a nationally acclaimed sculptor."

"Why have you gone to all this trouble to find out about my past?"

"I like to know things about the people I'm working with. Gives me the upper hand. I now know that you're a straight shooter, a standup guy. I'm trusting you to do a respectable job of the town square project."

"Thanks." I didn't bother to mention that I had never felt like I needed his trust.

Listening intently to Noble's intelligence report on me, I hadn't paid much attention to the surroundings. When we stopped at a small clearing in the fir trees, I looked up to see a twelve-foot-tall woman with oversized bare breasts and a pioneer dress clinging loosely to her hips. She was carved from one of the ancient trees. Scattered about the clearing were several more giant-sized frontier women in various stages of undress. Noble's chain-saw carvings. It looked like a lumberjack's version of Frederick's of Hollywood.

Noble waved his arms in a gesture that encompassed

the entire open-air gallery. "What do you think?" He asked.

"Gosh," I said, "I don't think I'm really qualified to comment. I'm a mallet and chisel man, mostly. No chainsaw experience at all."

"Like I said, I checked you out. You're qualified, and I'd value your opinion."

I hated critiquing the works of others with the artist present, but I gave it my best shot. I stood back and studied the first piece. I walked around it, trying to get a feel for the message that Noble must have been trying to convey. Though the contours were smooth and the detail was surprisingly precise, considering the medium, the entire piece lacked passion as well as proportion. The two huge spherical breasts with long, pointed nipples mounted squarely in the center looked like beach balls with the inflation stem protruding. They were more than twice the size they should have been, as compared to the torso.

"Very interesting," I said stepping closer to reach up and touch one of the freakish appendages.

"It's my grandmother," Noble said proudly.

"Really," I said, quickly stuffing my hands into my pockets. I should have guessed. Her face was Noble's face without the mustache. "You've done a fine job of projecting her strong matriarchal pioneering spirit."

"Do you really think so?" Noble beamed. "Any suggestions?"

He needed some criticism to validate the compliment. "As you know, art is highly subjective. You shouldn't take any single critique too seriously," I cautioned.

"Of course," he said with a smile. "That's good advice. So, what do you think?"

"To me," I said thoughtfully, "the breasts seem disproportionately large."

A shadow of resentment fell across his face. He walked

to the center of the clearing and picked up his carving tool. A chain saw that had been sitting on a low tree stump. He pulled hard on the starter cord and the saw roared to life. Determination in his eyes, he walked slowly toward me.

"Highly subjective," I yelled over the din of the saw motor.

I scanned the ground for a suitable weapon to defend against a thirty-inch chain-saw blade. Nothing. Only dirt and seed cones from the evergreen trees. I prepared myself to move quickly, should the need arise. When Noble and his smoking saw came within hacking distance of me, I fought the urge to run screaming out of the woods; it wouldn't have been dignified. I stepped to one side, but he did not change course. He proceeded past me to the statue, where upon he began to cut. In less than a minute, both of Grandma Noble's tits lay in the dirt at her feet.

Some people can't take criticism. I wondered if Reeves Washington had ever second-guessed or insulted Jonathan Noble.

The racket of the chain saw continued to ring in my ears for several seconds after he killed the motor and tossed it to the ground.

"You didn't have to do that," I said. "I could have helped you save them."

Noble wiped the sweat from his forehead with the back of his hand. "It's no damn good. I never can get the tits right. When a project turns sour, it's best to end it quickly and move on."

I had used those same words on a number of occasions, but in the context of turning a small forest into so much sawdust because you're too rich to go to the library and check out a book on anatomy, the words took on a new significance. "Did you ever consider practicing on something smaller?"

"This is smaller," Noble said. "When I get good

enough, a Congressman friend of mine is going to fix me
up with a couple of giant redwoods from California." He
squinted at something behind me. "Are those guys with
you?"

I turned in time to see Marty scurry from behind a
bush and dive for the cover of a nearby tree stump. As
soon as Marty had established his new position, Abe appeared from behind a tree and wheeled like a maniac to a
large boulder. I turned back to Noble and saw Jerry
peeking from behind the flat-chested statue.

I shook my head, indicating no. "Yes. They're with
me. Did you know somebody broke your front gate?"

Chapter Ten

Rain might have been more appropriate for the morning of Reeves Washington's funeral. Instead, bright sunlight glinted off the hood ornaments of expensive automobiles as Nick and I walked through the parking lot of Ye Olde United Methodist Church in Noble Heights.

On either side of the walkway leading through the churchyard, songbirds splashed in fountain baths surrounded by bushes of hybrid roses, snow white to blood red. The building, large but traditional, was pristine. White clapboard, peaked stained-glass windows, and a tall three-sided steeple. Organ music, playing a mournful rendition of "Amazing Grace," resounded through the carved open doors leading to the sanctuary.

Though completely surrounded by beauty, I couldn't shake the empty feeling of loss. The music could have been a dirge. All the colors might as well have been gray.

My spirits lifted slightly when we found Alison waiting just inside the double archway.

"You both look very nice," Alison said.

In my best charcoal-gray, double-breasted suit, with my face freshly shaved and my hair neatly combed, I could have passed for a Noble-ite. "You think Reeves would approve?"

"I don't think he could ever disapprove of you two."

Rick Hanson

Alison turned to Nick. "Didn't Ramona come with you?"

"She doesn't do very good at funerals," Nick said. "Since she'd only met Reeves a couple of times . . . you know."

"I understand," Alison said.

So did I. Given a choice of possible ways to spend my late morning hours, a funeral would not be number one. Or number twenty. I hated death ceremonies under any circumstances, and this one especially. It shouldn't have happened. If I'd reacted a few seconds quicker, none of us would have to be here today.

Dr. Marion Grimhaur came up the walk behind us. His usually wild hair, plastered down with industrial strength grooming gel, had the look of high-gloss plastic. He wore a dark semi-pressed four-button suit of summer wool. I introduced him to Nick, and we stood in the sunlight outside the church, shuffling our collective feet and having nothing to say.

From inside the church, the organ switched to "Long and Winding Road." A delicate soprano voice sang the words.

Nick broke the ice. "Going to miss him."

We all concurred.

"He was a good man. A good doctor," Grimhaur added.

"You did have your differences of opinion," I mentioned.

"What?" A spike of shiny hair sprung up at the back of his head. I could almost hear it go, *proing!* "No, not at all. Not really."

"Regarding drug therapy," I elaborated. "You were for it. Reeves was—"

"This isn't the time or the place," Grimhaur said. "Let's leave it at this: I respected Reeves Washington."

Again, we stood in uncomfortable silence as we

watched Raven Parducci pace the distance from the parking lot to the church entryway. When I introduced her to Nick, her dark eyes brightened. "Nick Gabreski? May I have your card?"

He pulled out his police I.D. wallet and flipped out a business card. "Why?"

"You're mentioned in Reeves's last will and testament." She glanced at me. "So are you, Mr. McCleet. I plan to read the will after or during the reception following the funeral since the family is in town. Will you be able to attend?"

I wasn't surprised that Reeves had left a will. But the idea that I might be mentioned in it had never occurred to me. "I'll be there."

"So will I," Nick said.

"Excellent." Her smile was brisk and efficient. Obviously, she was glad that she'd been able to use this occasion—or any occasion—for conducting business.

The organ and the voice switched to "He Ain't Heavy, He's My Brother," and Raven's eyebrows arched. "Unusual choice of music for a funeral, isn't it?"

"Actually," Grimhaur said, "this isn't a funeral. It's a memorial service."

"Yes, of course," she said.

Nick grunted. "Huh? What's the difference?"

Grimhaur was happy to explain. "At a memorial service, there is no casket, no body and no graveside ritual. The purpose of this sort of service is to remember fondly. It's the time set aside for Reeves's friends and family to process their grief."

Nick muttered, "Process, huh."

Grimhaur gestured condescendingly. "Naturally, there are feelings of regret accompanying a sudden death. Also, anger. Shock. Guilt. This memorial ceremony allows the opportunity to express these emotions outwardly."

"And then?" Nick asked.

You weep in private, I thought.

"Once we've shared our grief, we may begin to accept the loss of our friend and colleague. Reeves and I talked about this often. He had lost both parents at an early age, you know. And, as doctors, we have seen our share of death and grief."

"As cops," Nick said, "Adam and I have, too."

The lovely female voice inside drifted into a sentimental version of "Yesterday."

"That's beautiful," Alison said. "Who's singing?"

Raven supplied the answer, "Reeves's daughter. She's very talented. A second year pre-med student at Stanford."

I hadn't seen Reeves's children for at least ten years, not since his marriage had broken up. The daughter, even at age eleven, had been a straight-A student, destined for great things. His son, if I recalled correctly, was a major screw-up.

Alison nudged me toward the door. "We should go inside."

"Right."

Nick and I followed the others into a mostly full church. We were about to be seated by a sympathetically smiling usher when I spotted Margot. She was dressed in black, of course, with a gigantic black hat and a veil that immediately caused me to think of Dracula's bride.

The sight of her reminded me of how much I didn't want to be here. I didn't need anyone telling me how to remember my friend. And I didn't want to deal with my sister's phony grief or Grimhaur's emotional processing or Raven's businesslike reading of the will.

I took a backward step. To Nick, I said, "I'm out of here."

Nick mumbled, "I got your back."

Outside, the songbirds competed with Reeves's daughter and her delicate voice. There was a light breeze, but I was sweating. I aimed in the opposite direction from the parking lot. Nick was right beside me.

"I hate this," he muttered.

We walked along the sidewalk into the heart of Noble Heights. Nick glanced over at Ye Olde Donut Shoppe. "Did you eat yet?"

"Nope." Abe and Jerry had whipped up something for breakfast, but I didn't recognize it so I didn't eat it.

Despite the cutesy name, the donut store offered familiar Formica tabletops and plastic booths. Nick and I got extra large coffees and maple bars. One for me, and four for Nick. We settled down to process in our own way.

In a few minutes, I recapped what little I actually knew about Birkenshaw, Grimhaur, Noble and Kurt Schmidt.

Nick listened with the ears of an experienced investigator, but he watched me through the eyes of a trusted friend.

"The way I see it," I said, "Frank Birkenshaw slipped Kurt Schmidt some kind of drug earlier that day. Kurt took it, flipped out and killed Reeves."

"Why?" Nick asked. "Why would Birkenshaw give Kurt drugs?"

"Money," I said. "Maybe Birkenshaw's a dealer."

"I can check his record easy enough," Nick said. "But I thought Kurt was clean. Isn't that what Reeves told you?"

"Yes, but when Kurt went nuts, and Reeves said, 'He's on something,' he wasn't talking about a vision quest."

When we were partners, Nick and I had done this exercise dozens of times. I'd throw out a theory. He'd shoot it full of holes. Then, I'd start over with Theory Number Two, or Twenty-Two, until we had a scenario we could live with.

The problems with Birkenshaw being a dealer who was supplying Kurt were numerous: Kurt was trying to get out of Mount Prairie, and he knew drugs weren't the way. Also, if Birkenshaw was a dealer, Jonathan Noble would have to be aware of that fact. Which made Nobel into . . . what? "An accessory?" I suggested.

Nick shook his head. "Bad theory, Adam. Even if Birkenshaw had given Kurt drugs, he couldn't have known when he'd take them or when he'd snap out. If you want to make a case for conspiracy to murder Reeves, you've got to have more than a hug to hang it on."

"How about this," I tried a new angle. "Kurt was drugged up by Grimhaur right before his session with Reeves."

"Now you've got something. Why?"

"Grimhaur wanted Reeves dead so he could take his job."

"Head of a nut house? Do people kill for that?"

"What if . . . Noble promised Grimhaur big bucks for taking over Reeves's job?"

"Why?"

"Because," I said, "Noble's getting a dollar a year for property worth millions. Chief of staff is also on the board of directors. He could influence the other board members to abandon the Mount Prairie lease."

"Money, again. Good motive," Nick agreed, as he polished off the third maple bar and licked his fingers. "But Grimhaur's already got bucks."

"We'd be talking about the kind of money Grimhaur could build his own hospital with. Plus, Reeves had something on Grimhaur." I told Nick about the conversation Reeves and I almost had in the parking lot when I dropped him off. "Grimhaur is getting sued for malpractice, and I don't think Reeves would have backed him up."

This was sounding better and better as a theory, but I still wasn't happy with it. "Doesn't explain how Birkenshaw fits in."

"Maybe he doesn't." Nick front-loaded the last maple bar into his mouth and washed it down with a gulp of coffee.

"Then why did he lie about knowing Schmidt?" I asked.

"You're not sure he was lying."

Nick was right, but Birkenshaw had a certain stink that lingered. He was connected somehow.

"Your turn," I said to Nick. "What's happening on the cop end?"

"Not a hell of a lot. They took blood and urine from Schmidt for testing."

"Anything?"

"Too soon to know, but I have a friend in the D.A.'s office. Said she'd call as soon as the results come in."

"She?"

"Just a friend," Nick growled.

I checked my wristwatch. "The funeral ought to be winding up pretty soon."

"Memorial service," Nick corrected. "I'm glad we missed it. I'm not real big on expressing my emotions outwardly."

"Are you up for this reception?" I asked, sliding out of the booth.

"Not really, but . . . I hate to be shallow, but I'm kind of curious about what Reeves left us in his will."

I laughed. "He probably wants you to look after his son."

"Randell?" Nick flinched. "I'd rather take a bullet in the chest. Have you seen that kid lately?"

I hadn't, but that situation would soon be remedied.

At Reeves's house, we were greeted at the door by Fran Lavin, the head nurse at Mount Prairie and nemesis of the Death Squad. I was glad they couldn't see her in

this uniform—a severe black suit with padded shoulders
and large gold buttons that enhanced her Nazi Storm
Trooper bearing. She snarled when she recognized me.
"Well, Dr. Sterling, we meet again."

"Small world," I said.

"You're not so smart," she pointed out with obvious
relish. "Your name isn't Sterling. You're Adam McCleet.
And you're not a doctor, you're only an artist."

She said "only an artist" with the sort of disgust usually reserved for "only a child molester." As if that
wasn't enough, she added, "You were there when Dr.
Washington was killed."

I waited for her to add the obligatory comment, like "it
must have been awful." Instead, she echoed the guilt that
had been ringing in my head. "You could have stopped
him. You could have saved Dr. Washington."

Nick and I moved past her without further comment,
and he headed toward the buffet table in the dining room.
The last thing I felt like doing was eating—unless the
main course was hemlock, so I abandoned Nick to the
buffet and roamed through the crowd that had gathered
in the ultramodern, two-story custom home.

Apparently, everyone else had processed successfully
because they were chatting in a civilized manner. I found
myself mood-swinging from a need to break into loud
mourning and a desire to gather everyone—Frank Birkenshaw, Jonathan Noble, Margo, Dr. Grimhaur, Fran
Lavin, Raven Parducci—in the drawing room, like an
old-time detective, and question them intensely until I
knew which of them had given Kurt Schmidt drugs.

It was a good thing that I spotted Alison in the living
room, sitting on the arm of a Norwegian recliner of oak
and soft, brown leather. Alison was always a good sanity
check. She was talking to Reeves's ex-wife, Felicia
Hobbs-Washington.

I stood for a moment, admiring these two beautiful

women. Alison's auburn hair and delicate tan contrasted with Felicia's coffee-brown complexion and precisely styled black hair. They both wore perfect makeup and an attitude of assured sophistication. Felicia was a news anchorwoman for a network affiliate in Denver, Colorado.

"Hello, Adam." She greeted me in an unaccented, well-modulated voice that made me feel like she should be saying, "details at ten." Instead, she added, "It's been a long time."

"Yes, it has. But the years have been kind to you."

"And you." Her smile was wistful. "I remember when Reeves was running that veterans' group that you and Nick were part of. Every Thursday night. You boys sure were screwed up."

"Still are," I assured her. Turning to Alison I said, "I hope you understand about me and Nick ducking out at the church."

Alison gave me her don't-worry-about-it look as she took my hand. "I do understand."

Felicia gestured toward Alison and said, "Why haven't you married this woman, Adam?"

Et tu, Felicia?

"I mean it, Adam. She's bright, beautiful, understanding and better than anyone I ever expected you to end up with."

"Thank you, I think."

"You need to have children," she continued. "Times like this make me glad I still have my babies to comfort me. Reeves and I had our differences, but he was always a good father."

"I understand your daughter is going to Stanford."

"Rhonda is going to be a doctor," Felicia beamed, "like her father."

"And Randell?"

"Quite the opposite from his sister, I'm afraid. You're going to meet them both right now, Adam. Ms. Parducci wanted to read the will as soon as you and Nick got here."

Felicia was one of those organized women for whom everything falls into place. She took my arm to lead me toward the study.

"Wait for me," I said to Alison.

"I'll be here," she assured, giving my hand an extra squeeze before she let go.

In the study, Raven sat behind Reeves's desk, looking businesslike. Felicia introduced me to Rhonda, the Stanford student with a four-point-O grade point. And Randell, the boy most likely to be slapped at any given moment.

Just as we sat down, Nick strolled in, carrying a plate heaped with frog-eye salad and chicken wings.

Felicia repeated the introductions, for Nick's sake.

"I appreciate your cooperation," Raven began. "This seemed to be a convenient time for all parties."

"Oh yeah." Randell stood and began stalking about the room. "What's up with that? Convenient? Shit! Ain't no difference that my father's dead?"

He was tall, like Reeves, but the resemblance ended there. Randell was dressed in a rapper's version of funeral wear. Black, hooded sweatshirt, baggy black denims and Air Jordans. His head, shaved close, bobbed with every word he said.

"Randell," his mother snapped. "Sit down."

"Yo, I'm standing."

Raven continued, "This is the last will and testament of Reeves Washington. He says: 'I will start with my son, Randell, because it is of him I am most concerned. Randell, I leave you a trust fund in the amount of two hundred thousand dollars, to be administered by Raven Parducci and to be used to pay for your education until you graduate from an accredited four-year college or university. At that time, you will receive the balance of the funds. Only your mind can set you free, son.'

"Oh, man," Randell groaned. "That mean I got to finish high school. What's up with that? Huh? You know what I mean? What's up with that shit?"

He continued to whine while his sister received a similar trust fund, which she accepted graciously as she dabbed at the corners of her moist eyes.

Raven glanced at Nick and read, " 'To my friend, Nick Gabreski, who never has enough time to enjoy himself, I leave two courtside seats for all the Trailblazer home games. The tickets will be delivered to you at the beginning of each basketball season, until we meet again.' "

"Damn," Nick said softly. "I can use that."

" 'And to Adam McCleet, who allowed me into his very special world, and shared his passion for sailing with me.' " Raven read, " 'I leave *Raptor*. Sail her into history, Captain McCleet.' "

I should have felt overjoyed. *Raptor* was a beautiful craft, and I had often envied Reeves for owning her. But a wave of sorrow washed up in my heart as I remembered all the good times we'd had sailing. Laughing. Goddamn, I was going to miss him. I missed him already.

" 'Additionally,' " Raven continued to read, " 'I would ask that Nick and Adam see to the final disposition of my remains, which by now should amount to a neatly packed box of dust. I never learned how to swim so don't dump me into some grand body of water. Beyond that, I would not intrude upon your creativity.' "

I looked at Nick, who was obviously stunned. He'd stopped eating. Reeves had suddenly given the two of us something new to think about as Raven read the rest of the document, a series of bequests to friends and family and ended with, " 'And, Felicia, for those years when I was in med school and you put up with me, the rest is yours. I always loved you.' "

The room was quiet for a moment, then Randell swaggered up to the desk and got in Raven's face. "He can't make me do that."

"You don't have to do anything," she said. "But you don't get the money unless you're in school."

"Uh-uh, I can't get with that."

"Fine," she said. "Be poor."

"You listen to me, bitch—"

"Randell!" His mother stood. "You shut your mouth and sit in that chair before I knock you down."

Randell smirked, "How you gonna do that?"

Nick and I rose as one. "We'll help," I said.

The kid had about four inches on me in height and he used it to look down. "You can't hit me, man. My daddy just gave you a boat."

"Show some respect," Nick advised. "Your father was just murdered."

"Murdered?" Felicia questioned. She was an actual journalist, not just a talking head, and she knew the difference between aggravated assault, manslaughter and murder. "Nick, why would you say—"

"What's up with that shit, man?" Randell said.

"Yes," Raven put in, "What are you suggesting, Mr. Gabreski? According to the district attorney's office, the death of Reeves Washington was manslaughter. Kurt Schmidt is expected to enter an obvious plea of guilty by reason of temporary insanity."

Nick and I could have bobbed our pointed heads obediently and agreed with her, proceeding with our own investigation on the quiet. But I figured it was time to get some shit stirred up, and Raven was the lady to do it. She was the attorney for half of Noble Heights and well-acquainted with Jonathan Noble, Frank Birkenshaw and Marion Grimhaur.

I looked her in the eye and said, "Schmidt was doped.

He never would have attacked Reeves if he hadn't been on something."

"Oh, really? And is that your professional opinion?"

"That's an eye-witness account."

"I'm sure the D.A. will be impressed," she said, gathering up her papers. "I believe we're done here. My office will contact each of you when we have worked through probate."

Nick left the room with the family. At the door, Raven called me back. "A minute of your time, Mr. McCleet."

I turned toward her and closed the door. "Yes?"

"I sincerely hope you are not planning to interfere with the police investigation."

"If somebody doesn't make trouble, there isn't going to be an investigation." We both had remained standing. "Reeves didn't deserve to die."

"No, he did not." She sank down in the chair behind the desk and pressed her fingertips against her temples. "But it happens, doesn't it?"

Reeves's death appeared to have taken its toll on Raven Parducci, too. "How long had you known Reeves?"

"Since childhood." Her dark eyes lifted and stared into mine. "In Vietnam."

"Really?" I was somewhat surprised by her answer, but I tried not to let it show. "Reeves never indicated that he'd known you for more than a couple of years." We'd talked about Raven the day of the committee meeting. Reeves had very little to say about her past or present.

"He wouldn't have," Raven said. "He didn't remember me. I was only eight years old, and he was a grown man. A soldier."

"Would you like to tell me about it?" I pried as delicately as possible.

Her smile spoke of fond memories and melancholy. "The story is long. Perhaps another time."

"I have time," I said.

She sighed. "Unfortunately, I do not. And I have a favor to ask of you."

"If it's about the murder. Nick and I are going to do whatever it takes to get the cops to expand the investigation."

"I'm sure you will. But this is a favor of a more personal nature."

"Ask away."

"You've heard about the Noble Heights Independence Day Parade? It's tomorrow."

I recalled seeing some advertising for a Fourth of July event of some kind, but I hadn't paid much attention. "Yes."

"Reeves was to be one of the parade judges." She sounded apologetic. "Would you consider taking his place on the reviewing stand?"

"I've never judged a parade."

She laughed. "It doesn't matter. Neither have any of the other judges."

"Who are the other judges?"

"Besides myself, your sister Margot, the Schmidts and Marion Grimhaur."

"The Schmidts?" I questioned. "Under the circumstances, I would think you'd be looking for substitutes for them as well."

"Indeed, but they insist. The Schmidts are a proud couple who do not take their commitments lightly."

Should be a fun ride, with almost all of Noble Heights's most outstanding wing-nuts holding the wagon together. "What about Jonathan Noble?" I asked. "Seems like he'd be right in the middle of an event like this."

"He's the Grand Marshall," Raven said. "Can I count on you, Mr. McCleet? To be there, I mean." She batted her dark eyelashes clumsily, and her scrubbed cheeks flushed slightly.

If she was flirting, she wasn't very practiced at the art. But it didn't matter. I'd already made up my mind. Though I didn't relish the idea of coming within sobbing distance of Margot the Morbid two days in a row, I had questions for everyone and the whole affair sounded too juicy to pass up.

"I'd be honored to take Reeves's place."

Chapter Eleven

After Raven left the den, I sat behind Reeves's desk. The position I'd most often seen him take was with his feet up and his swivel chair tilted back, while he was staring up at the ceiling. I positioned myself exactly that way, wishing I could ask questions of a dead man. Like, "Who wanted you out of the way? Was it Grimhaur?"

Reeves hadn't particularly liked the other doc, but he was too much of a gentleman to bad-mouth a colleague directly. Still, he had told me that he and Grimhaur disagreed.

"Enough of a disagreement for murder?" I wanted to ask.

Given that Grimhaur was on trial for malpractice, Reeves would have been in a tense position if he, in fact, disapproved of Grimhaur's treatment. What had he told me? That Grimhaur had administered an experimental drug to a patient without the patient's knowledge. Sounded like malpractice to me.

During my lifetime, like most of my generation, I've had some firsthand experience with a variety of recreational drugs . . . and I'd have to admit to a protracted period of time when I did, in fact, inhale. But in my early years on the police force, I'd witnessed families, friends and whole communities devastated by illegal drugs. If the huffers and the snorters and the shooters were the only victims, it would have been ugly enough. But that was seldom the case.

Reeves also had knowledge of drugs that extended beyond the textbook. He'd grown up in a family where drugs and alcohol were the prime motivators. "The shit is destroying black culture," he'd said during one of our late night discussions on the ills of modern man, "more effectively than the KKK ever dreamed was possible."

I suspected that his clashes with Grimhaur had a sharp, angry edge behind their professional shields. But were those clashes enough to make Grimhaur dope up Kurt Schmidt with something that made him aggressive and send him into a session with Reeves? Wouldn't Kurt have mentioned it? Reeves had asked him, point blank, if he was "on" something, and Kurt's denial sounded honest. All Schmidt had wanted was to get out of Mount Prairie, back to the apple farm.

I tilted forward in Reeves's office chair and slid open the center drawer of his desk. The contents were neat and organized. Expensive pens and standard-issue paper clips. There was a mini-tape recorder. I took it out, rewound the tape, and punched the play button.

Reeves's voice, mechanically distorted, issued forth. "June third . . . get somebody to check on those big orange flowers in the lobby. Possibly triggering hay fever reaction . . ."

Reeves always had spring sniffles.

". . . Lavin's birthday," he said. "Don't let the Death Squad know. They'll booby-trap the cake."

I chuckled.

"Lavin's obsessing on the drug inventory again. Get the aspirin and the B-12 out of there."

I clicked off the tape, recalling my own battle with the nurse at the counter to obtain an aspirin. It occurred to me that I was coming at this investigation from an

oblique angle because I really didn't know the policies
and procedures at Mount Prairie, and the place had been
central in Reeves's life. And his death. What I needed
was a good excuse to get back inside and snoop around.
Since Nurse Lavin already knew I wasn't Doctor Sterling, I'd have to find another way.

I clicked on the recorder again and listened to Reeves
as he mentioned the discharge of a patient and a "need to
hire a woman psychiatrist to handle rape and wife abuse
PTSD." Later, he talked about the woman he wanted to
hire, Sandra Whittle. In his opinion, ". . . she's good.
Maybe slide some of Grimhaur's case load her way."

". . . end of the month," he said. "Lavin's files need
some checking. Meeting on the first to hire Whittle. I'll
have to cancel sailing in the regatta with Adam and Alison. It's the shits. I need the break."

Then, there was only blank tape.

I felt the loss once again, deep in my soul. He was dead
but not buried. Weeping wouldn't change that. Neither
would lashing out. But Reeves, or his memory, deserved
answers. Then he can rest in peace in . . . his urn, I remembered. It occurred to me that he'd given the job of
scattering his ashes to Nick and me for a good reason.
He'd known that both of us had seen enough death to
hone our avoidance skills to a razor edge. Spreading his
ashes ourselves might restore the illusion of control, of
finality.

I was beginning to think like a shrink. I wondered
what a shrink would have thought about that.

Reeves couldn't have known that his death was coming so soon. No doubt, he'd imagined me and Nick as
grizzled old codgers, hauling his urn and our wrinkled
butts up some obscure mountain we thought he'd mentioned. We'd throw his ashes off the top and have simul-
taneous coronaries.

I hoped Nick had some good ideas about what to do

with the ashes because I couldn't keep my mind away from Grimhaur and Kurt Schmidt. I opened the file drawer beside the desk. A hanging folder, labeled "Correspondence, Personal," held a sheaf of letters, some with envelopes attached and the responses Reeves had sent. Glancing through, I saw that the file went all the way back to New Year's Day of this year when Reeves had, apparently, responded to Christmas card greetings.

I told myself that I wasn't just snooping, but investigating, when I paused to read a letter he'd written to a mutual friend. Reeves mentioned that I was doing very well with my art and had a beautiful girlfriend.

"He should marry the lady," Reeves had said. "About time Adam settled down. You think?"

The advice, given second-hand, made me feel anything but settled. Marry Alison? I slid the letter back into the file.

There was another file with bills, all paid up. As far as I could tell, Reeves's finances were in order. He lived well, but he could afford it. Blackmail or extortion were too remote to be seriously considered as motives for murder.

But I still thought money was a primary motive. "What about Noble? Could the trail lead back to him?"

Reeves would have said, "Hell, yes. Noble wants his property back, and I'm pissing on the wheels of progress."

Not to mention that Mount Prairie wasn't exactly the sort of institute that Noble Heights-ites were fond of claiming as their own. Margot, for one, would have preferred Ye Olde Betty Ford Clinic instead of an institution for the likes of Abe, Martin and Jerry.

Using the phone on the desk, I checked in at my house, using the prearranged code. Call, let the phone ring once, then hang up. Then, call back. I had my doubts about the functionality of such a system but, as in so many other situations where the Squad is concerned, it was easier to play along.

"Yes," Jerry hissed. "Who's this?"

I didn't bother to tell him that his phone manners could use work. "It's Adam. How are things going?"

"All clear, man. Nothing unusual to report. Over."

"What are you maniacs up to?"

"Abe is fishing off the dock with Binky, Marty is in the studio drawing stuff and I'm watching MTV." He paused. "Did you know tomorrow is the Fourth of July? Over."

"Yup."

"I love Independence Day. Sprinklers, fireworks exploding. Over."

"And parades," I said, glumly. Sitting on a reviewing stand could be a particular waste of time . . . unless I could use the time to sweat Grimhaur. "Do you men have enough beans, blankets and bandages to hold down the perimeter for the night? Over."

"We're A-okay, man. Over."

I gave him Alison's phone number in case they needed to reach me. "And tomorrow morning, I'm going to the Noble Heights parade at ten o'clock, I mean O-ten-hundred. I'll be home by early afternoon-hundred. Over."

"Everything's cool," Jerry said. "Don't worry about a thing. Over and out."

Too late for that, I thought as I hung up the phone. I slid out from behind the desk as the office door opened and the unlikely twosome of Grimhaur and Randell stepped inside.

". . . thoroughly inappropriate," Grimhaur said to the young man. "Randell, you've got to behave more—"

They both turned and stared at me.

I waved, "Don't mind me."

Predictably, Randell said, "Yo, what's up?"

The sky, the moon, the top of Mount Hood, my blood

pressure. I knew that Reeves and Felicia had spent large bucks on private schools for both their kids. Randell had been given the best of everything, all the advantages, and he was throwing it back in his mother's face. "Yo, nothing."

Grimhaur frowned. His lower lip stuck out like a diving board. His styling gel had long since lost the battle. His hair stood up like the crest of a woodpecker. "It's lucky you're here. Randell seems to have the idea that his father was murdered, and he has hinted that you—"

"That's what my man, Adam, said." Randell pointed at me. "Murder. You said it."

"That's right." I nodded.

"Well, Mr. McCleet," Grimhaur said with thinly disguised disgust, "we all process our grief in different ways, and I suppose it's natural for you to avoid accepting the death of your friend with some delusional behavior. It's important to remember, however, that illusion is not truth. Isn't that right, Randell?"

"Oh, man, forget that shit." Randell grabbed his crotch. "Illusion this. My man, Adam says my father was murdered and I want to know what's up with that."

This angry young man was nothing like the eight-year-old kid I remembered. He'd been so cute he made the Care Bears look like Satanists. I remembered when Randell, Reeves and I went to a baseball game together and the little boy had eaten enough popcorn and hotdogs to choke a small horse. He'd wanted to be the next Daryl Strawberry.

Randell, the teenager, had lost every trace of cuteness.

"How about this, Randell?" I offered. "Leave it up to me."

"I don't think so, man. He was my daddy." Randell took a swipe at the corner of his eyes. "I'm going to find out who killed him, and I'm going to make it right."

"Let's calm down," Grimhaur said. He patted Randell's forearm in a gesture that should have been placating.

The young man reacted as if he'd been poked with a branding iron. "Don't touch me. Don't you never touch me."

"I'm sorry. I didn't mean to invade your personal space, but I—"

"You're so full of shit." He pulled back his shoulders and stuck out his chest. It was a pose. "I'll take care of this."

I came out from behind the desk and went to where the two of them stood. The three of us formed a triangle. Randell's attitude—his 'tude—bothered me. He was a pseudo-punk, which was a lot worse than a kid with real street smarts who would have known when to back off.

"How are you going to take care of this?" I asked, dreading what I expected would come next.

"Somebody murdered my father, I find him and bust a cap in his face. That's on the real side."

The real side of stupid.

"Randell, please," Grimhaur said. "Try to be reasonable. This is a memorial service for your father. It's not the time or the—"

"This is a white man's show," Randell said. I thought he had a point. Though I hadn't been counting, there were very few African Americans in attendance at Reeves's service in Noble Heights.

"Whitey ain't doin' shit."

"Let's talk about this issue," Grimhaur suggested.

"No talk!" Randell dug into the spacious pocket of his baggy trousers and pulled out a small .25 caliber handgun. "I'll let this do the rest of my talking."

Grimhaur went even whiter. "I hear you, Randell. You are enraged."

"Damn right."

"You are seeking retribution on a primal level. However, you must take into account—"

"Shut up!" He waved the gun in Grimhaur's direction.

I'd had enough. Both of Grimhaur and of Randell. I could see a green dot on the side of the pistol. The safety was still locked. Trying not to telegraph my movement, I reached out and snapped the weapon from his hand. "Give me that! What the hell is wrong with you? You think Reeves would want you to pull this shit?"

"He was my father, and—"

"And he wanted you to go to school, to make something of yourself."

"Gimme my piece."

I pressed a lever on the side of the grip and a full clip dropped onto the floor. As I pulled back the slide to make the gun safe, a bullet ejected from the chamber and bounced off Grimhaur's forehead. I stuck the pistol in my pocket, wondering how the boy had managed to arm himself during the brief time he'd been in Portland. There was no way he'd gotten his "piece" onto a plane from Denver. "When you're ready to act like a man, call me. Your mother has my phone number."

I left Reeves's office, said my good-byes to Nick and to Felicia, mentioning that if Randell wanted to talk I would be at Alison's or at my home number. With Alison on my arm, I headed for the door.

"You're staying at my place tonight?" she asked.

"If it's okay with you."

"Of course it's okay. But it might be nice if you asked instead of assuming. I might have other plans, you know."

Grimhaur probably would have told me that I should acknowledge her feelings and we ought to do some kind of processing ritual. But I was processed out. "Do you? Have other plans?"

"I might. You know, Adam, I could. There's no legitimate reason that I couldn't."

I climbed into the passenger side of her car and waited for Alison to finish her thought.

She revved the engine. "I'd appreciate if you didn't take me for granted."

"I don't," I said honestly. "Alison, here's the true story. I love you. Adore you, in fact. You are the most exciting woman I've ever known."

I hesitated, hearing Reeves's advice echoing in the back of my head. *Marry her. What are you waiting for?*

"Alison," I said, "I want you to mmmmm . . ." The word stuck in my throat. "Make love to me tonight."

"Fine. Terrific. I don't want to argue."

I knew I was tiptoeing at the edge of a volcano, and I tried to step clear of the eruption. "Maybe you should drop me off at my place."

"I don't think you should be alone," she said.

"Is Eric still staying with you?"

"He never did. We talked for a while, then he went back to his own place."

Her concern for Eric had distracted her from further discussion of my shortcomings. Grateful for the respite, I pursued the topic of Eric's mental health. "How do you think he's doing?"

"Great! He's himself again. Easy-going, gentle, sweet. I don't think much of Grimhaur, but he seems to have done his job as a psychiatrist."

Or a murderer. I thought it, but didn't make the accusation aloud. I didn't have to. Alison knew me well enough to read my mind. She said, "You think Grimhaur had something to do with Reeves's death, don't you?"

"The thought may have crossed my mind."

She was taking the route toward her house in Portland. "I wish you'd drop the investigating, Adam. It's not going to bring Reeves back."

"Kurt Schmidt was on something," I said, dogged as Binky pursuing a tennis ball. "I want to know who gave him the drugs."

"Denial," she diagnosed. "You want to believe this was some kind of complex murder scheme because you're in denial about Reeves's death."

"You're really getting into this stuff, aren't you?"

"More than you know." She braked for a stop sign and turned to me. Her green eyes looked troubled. "Adam, I've been seeing a psychiatrist for the past three months."

"What?" Alison was the most in-control person I'd ever known, the woman least likely to need a shrink.

"You heard me. I've been in group therapy."

Group therapy? I gulped back the derisive noises that rose instinctively in my throat. If Alison, the woman I admittedly adored and trusted, had been disturbed enough to seek the help of a therapist, why hadn't I picked up on it? Why had she kept it from me? "Was there something specific bothering you? Or was this general angst?"

"Maybe a tiny bit of depression. I mean, I'm not at the Prozac level or anything, but it was a tough year. Especially with what happened in Seattle."

The episode in Seattle had been my fault. I'd started out looking for my missing brother-in-law and ended up chasing bad guys, getting drugged by a whacko and facing a ruthless murderer, the Yuppie Ripper. Alison had, unfortunately, gotten caught in the middle of the mayhem.

"People died," she said, reducing the disaster to its simplest form. "I kept thinking about my dad, and how I never really dealt with his death. Anyway, I figured that a few visits to a psychologist might be good for me."

First Eric. Then, Nick. Now, Alison. Was I the only person in America who wasn't seeing a shrink?

She merged into traffic with a casual ease that I admired. "Anyway, I started in this group of women, talking about my father. Now, it's . . . Well, I guess, I'm talking about us, Adam. About you."

I really didn't like the sound of this. It was one thing to have Reeves and Nick tell me that I ought to marry Alison, but I hated the idea of a strange group of females dissecting my problems.

"Adam, would you like to know what my group thinks?"

I envisioned a coven of crones, cackling around a boiling cauldron, urging her to take a bite from the poisoned apple. "Sure," I said. "Let me have it."

"Everybody, including the psychologist, pretty much agrees that we'll never get married because you're terrified."

"Terrified?" I had, as Jonathan Noble had discovered, a wheelbarrow full of citations for valor. "Your group is wrong, Alison. I'm not scared."

"Of commitment," she said. "You're afraid to make promises. You know that's true, Adam. You can hardly make plans for one weekend ahead, much less for a lifetime."

I'd always thought of that particular character trait as charming spontaneity. "So, what does this coven of yours tell you to do?"

"Coven? That's so sexist, Adam."

I remembered her earlier pig comments about Captain Jack, and I didn't like being dumped in the same category. I pointed out, "There's nothing sexist about calling a group a coven. Witches don't have to be female."

"I know what you meant," she said.

"Is that one of those things you learn in group? Mind reading?"

"To answer your question, what the group advises is this: It's up to me. You won't change. So, I need to decide if I'm willing to settle for an uncommitted relationship."

"I see." I could have left it right there, but the whole idea irritated me like an itchy scab that I just couldn't leave alone. I had to keep picking until I drew blood. "Have I met any of these women, or are they basing this brilliant advice on their general ignorance of the inner workings of the male psyche?"

"Adam, you don't need to get defensive."

Whenever I hear that statement, I feel the need to protect my groin. "Of course not. You're only talking about ending our relationship. It's perfectly reasonable to seek out the advice of uninformed third parties on such matters." Though I felt like yelling, I made a conscious effort to keep my volume down. "Did you plan to talk to me about any of this?"

"Isn't that what I'm doing, now?"

"Yeh, well . . . Are you?"

"Am I what?"

"Willing to settle?"

She sucked in a big sigh and blew it out. "I don't know."

This sounded like dangerous territory to me, and I declared a personal moratorium on the subject, limiting myself to nods and "uh-huh" noises. My restraint lasted all the way through dinner when she told me more about the group of professional women, much like herself, and their many relationship issues.

I kept my mouth shut that night, when I shared her bed and we made love. But the next morning, when I wakened to Alison saying, "Men who have fear of commitment usually have unresolved issues with their mothers. Maybe you transferred those feelings to Margot, and that's why the two of you don't get along."

"Civility," I said, rubbing the sleep from my eyes.

"What do you mean?"

"I have it, Margot doesn't." I staggered toward the

bathroom, hoping to drown out the psycho-babble in a long hot shower, but Alison followed me.

"Really, Adam. I'm serious about this. You could learn something. It might be good for you to keep an eye on your relationship with your sister."

"I always keep an eye on Margot." Unwatched, she might take it into her twisted mind to rip out my clavicle and use it for a toothpick. I turned on the water in the shower, waiting for the hot. "Alison, you can't believe that Margot is a sane and logical human being. She goes through husbands the way most women go through lipstick. She's completely wrapped up in herself, and she's vicious to people who get in her way."

"Then why did she recommend you for the Noble Heights sculpture?"

"Because it would make her look good. And she had the hots for Reeves." I stepped into the shower, trying to regain the safety of my former disinvolvement. "But I'll try to do what you're saying. Margot is also going to be on the reviewing stand at the parade. I will try to interact with her as if she were sane. Will that make you happy?"

Over the thrumming of the shower, I heard her issue forth with another of those deep sighs.

Chapter
Twelve

Though I begged her to join me, Alison opted to drop me off at the parade and head back to the relative calm of the Brooks Art Gallery in the Pearl district. She said she needed to check on things. But I knew, by the angle of her wrist as she waved good-bye, she was headed for the nearest phone. The women in her group would have further advice on how to thread a male camel through the eye of a matrimonial needle.

I had always known, in the back of my cluttered mind, the time would come when I would have to make a decision about Alison and marriage. But at the moment, I had the Noble Heights Independence Day parade and Grimhaur to think about.

The whole town had turned out for the grand event, and there must have been a tacit agreement among them to wear red, white and blue. In my black shirt and khaki trousers—part of my wardrobe that had found its way to Alison's—I stood out like Johnny Cash at an Up With People revival.

The Independence Day revelers were absurdly well-behaved. Along the parade route, which circled Ye Olde Town Square, there were no alcoholic beverages and no smoking. I didn't see any signs, but I was pretty sure spitting and cursing were out, too. I suspected the bratwursts were low-fat and the cotton candy was made from a soy-bean substitute. My nostrils detected the sickening sweet smell of granola in the air. I supposed it made sense that when people reached a certain elevated income level they would be concerned about their health. After all, what else could go wrong?

Locating the reviewing stand amid this mass of red, white and blue wasn't easy. I felt like I'd fallen into a "where's Waldo?" picture. Finally, at the south end of the square, I spied a section of red, white and blue bleachers, draped with red, white and blue bunting, occupied by people dressed in red, white and blue. When I was close enough to the stands to separate the shapes, I had no trouble spotting Margot in her white toga-style sundress. Her earrings were blood red, as was her lipstick.

I tried to follow Alison's advice and analyze my relationship with my sister. My immediate reaction was caution, honed by experience. I'd known my younger sister all her life, and I still had no idea of how she would react in any given situation. She might be into mourning Reeves. Might have found another sucker. Might be done with men forever and have joined a therapy group.

When we were face to face on the risers of the viewing stand, a good four feet above the neatly groomed heads of the happy Noble Heights-ites, I asked, "When was the last time you saw a psychiatrist, Margot?"

"My second, no, third husband was a shrink," she reminded me. "And, of course, I was going to him before we got married. I haven't been to any other shrinks, not after he took a flying leap out of the eighteenth-floor window of that hotel in Vegas wearing a red cape and nothing else."

I nodded. "So, tell me about the parade."

"Reeves was a psychiatrist," she said.

"So he was." I didn't want to open this can of worms. "Didn't you organize this parade?"

"In my small way, I contributed." Across her chest, there was a banner that said: Parade Committee. "Of course, dear little Raven would probably tell you differently."

"Why's that?"

"She thinks she's some big expert on the Fourth of July because she was a history major in college before she went into law school. What that means is that the little snit wouldn't let me be George Washington on the Garden Club float."

I didn't think it took a history major to know that George Washington was a man. "What about Martha?"

"What about her?" Margot snapped.

"I was just thinking that—"

"Speaking of George and Martha, here come the Schmidts. They have their nerve."

The Schmidts wore matching navy blue jackets. The white of Martha's pleated ankle-length dress was the same shade as George's trousers. They marched through the crowd, looking neither right nor left. It was hard for me to imagine how they must feel. They'd lost one son in Vietnam. Now, the other son was under arrest for murder. Martha's face was puffy. George looked as stern and hard as a statue on Mount Rushmore.

"Tacky people," Margot said under her breath. "Apple farmers." Then she beamed at them. "If it isn't the Schmidts! Lovely to see you both. So sorry about the tragedy. Really I am."

Martha's fragile composure shattered and she wept softly into a hanky.

"Dear me," Margot said, resting her scarlet fingernails above her breast. "Is it something I said?"

"Shut up, Margot." I turned to George. "You don't have to do any of this. Why don't you take Martha home?"

"We said we would be here." He mounted the steps to

the reviewing stand. "And we will honor our commitments."

Apparently, he didn't have any unresolved issues involving his mother. They sat at the far end of the stand, quiet and solid as a pair of German bricks. I considered telling them that I didn't believe Kurt was responsible for his actions, that he'd been drugged. But they didn't need my intrusion any more than they needed Margot's phony commiseration.

Raven Parducci was the next to join us on the stand. In her red vest, white shirt and jeans skirt, she almost looked casual. As I watched her, I wondered how an eight-year-old Italian girl had come to know Reeves in Vietnam. Figuring that one loose end was as good as another, I took a seat beside her. After the "Hello, nice day if you're not the Schmidts" small talk, I said, "So, Raven, I understand you're a history buff."

"Study of American history was required by immigration, and I became interested."

Immigration? "You're not a natural-born citizen?"

She cocked an eyebrow. "I was born Vietnamese."

Clearly, she was waiting for a response, and there wasn't a damn thing I could say that didn't sound stupid. She didn't look Vietnamese. Didn't have an accent. Her last name was Parducci not Nguyen. If I'd been a politically correct kind of guy, I would have let the matter drop.

"Don't be too uncomfortable," she said. "I know you're a veteran, but I don't bear a grudge against the American troops that killed my mother, brother and sister."

I could hardly believe my ears. "When did you get out?"

"I left Saigon just before the fall, and I was adopted right away. Probably because I don't particularly look Vietnamese."

"No," I concurred. "You don't."

"My grandfather was French, so my mother was French-Vietnamese. My father was an American G.I. who I never knew."

"Reeves?" I guessed.

"I don't look black, either," she pointed out. "I never did know my father's name. I never cared to know."

The crash of cymbals announced the beginning of the parade. Two high-stepping drum majorettes in skimpy outfits sashayed down the center of the street, pausing occasionally to fling their silver batons skyward and almost catch them. Behind the twirlers, two other glowing young ladies of Noble Heights carried a banner that said: Jonathan Noble—Parade Grand Marshall.

Noble sat in the rear of a convertible draped in bunting. He grinned and nodded as if every person in the crowd was a personal buddy. Every few minutes, he raised his arm above his head and did a semaphore wave.

Raven and I applauded politely.

While the clowns from the local branch of the Shriners came past, I turned toward her, "You mentioned that you'd met Reeves in Vietnam. How did you know him?"

"I remembered his face. He treated me more kindly than any of the others," she said. "When I came to Noble Heights and learned of his background, I put the pieces together."

"Hell of a coincidence," I said.

Marion Grimhaur raced across the street, just ahead of the Noble Heights High School marching band in their snappy uniforms of white and gold. The band looked a lot better than they played, but it might have been the choice of music—a John Philip Sousa beat applied to the Whitney Houston ballad, "I Will Always Love You."

Grimhaur joined us, spewing apologies. He took the last seat, the one between Margot and myself. Though Grimhaur was still my number one suspect, I didn't slap him with questions right away. The conversation with Raven had given me something to chew on. Reeves must have been in some sort of combined action unit, helping orphaned children or something. The fact that she'd bumped into him was remarkable. That she'd managed to recall him and make the connection was even more amazing.

The first float rolled onto the street, causing wild cheers. It was from the Garden Club. Made entirely from red, white and blue carnations, the float depicted Washington crossing the Delaware. The person portraying George himself was a small man whose glasses kept slipping down his nose. He sweated profusely in his heavy, wool costume and the steadily rising heat of the day.

Margot reached around Grimhaur to grab at my arm. "See what I mean. He's a little nerd. I mean, look at my profile and look at his. I would have made a better George. Don't you think?"

Grimhaur nodded politely.

"I would," she insisted. She squished her boobs beneath her hands. "I could have bound my breasts."

I'd have paid a thousand dollars for someone to bind her mouth. More, if the procedure were irreversible.

After the Toledo Boomers High School marching band filed past, there was a lull along the route. At the end of the block, we could see a guy, dressed like an American colonist, struggling to get his horse under control. I turned to Grimhaur. Might as well jump right in, I figured. "How's the lawsuit going?"

"What?"

"The malpractice thing? Reeves told me all about it."

"I'm terribly sorry, Adam, but this isn't—"

"Don't tell me it's not the time or the place. I want to get some answers from you."

"Make an appointment."

"Now is fine with me."

The colonist raced past on his runaway mount. His three-cornered hat had blown off, and his powdered wig had slipped over his eyes. "One if by land, two if by sea," he screamed in a frantic, high-pitched voice.

I leaned close to Grimhaur. "Look, I know there's something funny going on with the drugs at Mount Prairie. You can talk to me about it. Or you can talk to the cops."

"You don't know what you're talking about." He was getting huffy. "Clearly, Adam, you are delusional. I suggest you seek long-term therapy."

I was about to tell him what to do with his therapy when I saw a ragtag band of Vietnam veterans wearing camouflage rainhats and jackets with unit patches sewn on the sleeves. They straggled by with no attempt at marching in step or formation. Out of phase with place and time. I felt compelled to stand.

"You're as confused as they are," Grimhaur said, nodding toward the gaggle of aging heroes. "You think you've been cheated, and you want everyone else to feel bad about it. But the battle is lost. The only thing you can change is your acceptance, or lack thereof."

"You're talking about a war. I'm talking about murder."

"What's the difference?" he said glumly.

Grimhaur was keeping me on my intellectual toes. When he wasn't psychoanalyzing, he waxed philosophic. As I glanced up the parade route, a clever reply formed in my mind, but the words that came out of my mouth were, "My car!"

Turning the corner behind the Daughters of the American Revolution Mounted Posse, was my Mustang, painted in tiger-stripe camouflage of green and brown, with an occasional patch of the original red showing through. Jerry was behind the wheel. Abe and Martin sat in the back seat, waving to the crowd as if they were royalty.

"Well, shit," I said.

Grimhaur stared as well. "Isn't that the Death Squad?"

"None other," I said with some chagrin.

"They should be back at the Institute," he said, still staring straight ahead. "They'll never assimilate on—"

Grimhaur's forehead exploded like a ripe melon. His body stiffened for an instant in a shock reflex, then slumped to the floor of the reviewing stand, a lifeless heap.

I could hear my own heart pounding inside my chest, but I hadn't heard the gunshot that turned Marion Grimhaur's head into an unrecognizable puddle of chunky soup. My initial instinct was to hit the deck, but I'd learned the hard way in similar situations that the worst thing I could possibly do was to allow myself to be pinned down. Besides, no one else had noticed that we were under fire.

"Margot," I yelled, "get down." But the racket from the marching band that followed the Death Squad drowned out my voice.

My sister was busy retouching her lipstick in her pocket mirror. I yelled again and Margot looked away from her own reflected face long enough to notice the scarlet stains splattered across the front of her white dress.

"What is this shit?" Margot screeched. "Someone is going to pay—"

I grabbed her by the shoulders and pushed her to the floor.

"Adam, have you lost your freaking mind?"

My stomach was in my throat but I did my best to remain in control. "Please shut up and listen, Margot.

Someone is shooting at us. We've got to get everybody off this platform fast, without causing a panic."

Margot was furious. "And just why the hell are we being shot at, Adam? Did you beat up on someone on your way to the parade this—"

A sustained, piercing scream—like a police car siren, only louder—issued from the small but powerful lungs of Raven Parducci. She'd spotted the mess that once was Marion Grimhaur. As Raven stared and continued her horrific scream, people began to turn and see what the hell the screaming was all about, then stared and screamed in kind.

Time always seems to stand still when I'm being shot at. Seconds turn into hours and hours to eternities. Though it seemed like forever had passed between the time Grimhaur fell and when Raven began to scream, in actuality, only seconds had elapsed. In another second, everybody in town was staring and screaming, but nobody was moving. No one except the Schmidts. George wove through the stunned onlookers as nimbly as a point guard for the Portland Trailblazers—with Martha close on his heels.

Margot screamed into my ear through cupped hands. "So much for not causing a panic. Now what?"

Another bullet passed through Margot's handbag and punched an oblong hole the size of a bottle cap in the aluminum bench a few inches from her head. I still hadn't heard a shot, but I was getting a feel for the trajectory.

Margot studied the smoking hole in her purse and screamed louder than all the others, "Run! Run for your lives!" She was on her feet and moving. Raven, who continued to stand and stare like a deer in the headlights of an eighteen-wheeler blocked my sister's retreat. Margot appeared to take a certain amount of pleasure from slapping the shocked attorney into reality and pushing her along.

Panic spread like wildfire. Marching bands tossed their trombones and snare drums aside as they scattered across the square. Horses bolted from under their riders. Mothers shielded their children's eyes from the gruesome sight on the reviewing stand. People of all sizes, shapes and ethnic origins stampeded like cattle, shoving, pushing, falling down and climbing over. Two men tried to jump over the side of the reviewing stand only to become entangled in the bunting and fall to the asphalt, where they were immediately trampled.

I imagined a line passing through the hole in the bench and a point in space where Margot's purse had been. My focus was directed to the only likely site for a sniper, a four-story brick building on the east side of the square. Ye Olde Book Repository?

The few cops I could see were caught up in the frenzy of the crowd. I vaulted over the railing at the edge of the reviewing stand, taking care to clear the bunting and land on my feet. I hit the ground running, or trying to run. But the crowd had bottlenecked between building fronts and abandoned floats. My own frustration rose to a maddening level. I wanted the sniper in the worst possible way and I couldn't move. I craned my neck to see a way out. Down the parade route the crowd seemed to be breaking up, separating. I pushed in that direction but the freaked-out crowd wouldn't cooperate.

I managed to work my way a few more feet in the right direction and broke into a small opening. I heard a car horn, some shrieks, and the opening grew larger as my convertible with its brand-new camouflage paint job backed through the crowd and stopped a few feet from where I stood. I vaulted into the passenger seat. Jerry's eyes bulged like marbles and his mouth gaped.

"Over there." I yelled, pointing at the four-story building. "The sniper's over there. Let's go!"

Jerry dumped the clutch and burned rubber as we

broke ranks with the disintegrating Noble Heights Independence Day parade. We bashed over the curb. Jerry had chosen the shortest distance between two points—a straight line. We plowed directly through the town square where, someday, there might be an original Adam McCleet sculpture. Right now, there was nothing to stop us but trees, trash cans, flowers and an occasional park bench. Jerry crashed over everything that was less than two feet in height. A bed of crysanthemums flattened beneath the Michelins. A wire trash basket went flying. We hit a lemonade stand and picked up additional decoration—crepe paper streamers fluttered across the windshield like red, white and blue spaghetti.

"Watch out for mines!" Abe yelled.

"Your what?" Jerry yelled back.

"Minefields, you weenie! Mines. Like boom, boom."

"No flashbacks," I ordered. "Come on, fellas. We got to get this guy."

"Yeah! Right!" Abe backed me up. "What guy?"

"A sniper. Just killed Grimhaur."

"Dr. Grimhaur?" Marty questioned. "Our Dr. Grimhaur?"

"It was Fran Lavin," Abe deduced. "Death to Lavin!"

"Woof," said Binky.

"What?" I whipped around in my seat and came face to drool with my neighbor's wolfhound who had apparently been given honorary membership in the Death Squad. He sat in the back seat between Abe and Marty as if he belonged there. He wore a camouflage scarf instead of a collar. He swung his big head from left to right, spraying us all with dog slobber.

Jerry rocketed across the square on a winding course, miraculously avoiding pedestrians. Most of them moved pretty fast. These Noble-ites were in fine physical condition, capable of jogging at a moment's notice, even in

Birkenstocks. They scattered like well-dressed chickens as the camouflaged Mustang roared toward them.

We reached the four-story building. At this point in the parade, we were at the Garden Club float. George Washington jumped up and down in his carnation boat and Paul Revere cantered in lopsided circles on his ill-mannered pony. A Harley Davidson motorcycle parked on the street beside the building looked out of place, with its black saddlebags, extended front forks and high-rise handlebars. It was a major hog with a chromed engine capable of powering one of the parade floats. Not the sort of machine that I expected a Noble Heights resident to be riding.

The guy who ran toward it was dressed in black leather pants, tight as a second skin, and a Grateful Dead T-shirt. His helmet had orange flames painted on the sides. I stood up in my seat and pointed. "That's our man!"

I almost flew over the windshield when Jerry came to an abrupt halt, inches away from a hysterical baton twirler in a shiny silver bathing suit with silver fringe and white boots with little silver tassels. "I saw him! I saw him!" she screeched. "Like, oh my God!"

I waved her out of the way. The Harley rider was mounting up, and we were losing the little momentum we had. I wished that I hadn't hidden Randell's pistol in a corner of Alison's garage. But when I left her house this morning, I hadn't been planning on a shootout.

The majorette wouldn't budge.

I did what I had to do. We needed to go forward. And if she'd seen the shooter with the gun, she'd make a great witness. I ran from the car, grabbed the girl, flung her into the front seat between Jerry and myself and pointed to the departing motorcycle. "Follow that hog!"

"Pigs? Is there livestock?"

Sometimes the Death Squad was so literal it ached. "The Harley," I clarified.

On our way past George crossing the Delaware, we sideswiped the float. The bumper hooked into chicken wire and carnations spewed over us. The baton twirler, perched between the bucket seats gave a little yelp. "Like, what's going on? Am I, like, a hostage or something?"

"What's your name?" I asked, just in case she really was a witness.

"Well, it's Diana, but my friends call me Duffy."

"What did you see, Duffy?"

"That guy on the motorcycle. Like, he came running out of that building, really fast, and he had on these black gloves but it's really hot today so I thought that was weird, you know? Oh, and he had this, like, thing, you know. This great big long rifle kind of thing."

"A gun," I clarified, keeping my eyes riveted on the Harley. "You saw the gun."

"Absolutely, for sure. And I started really screaming, really loud, you know." She tossed her head, sending shimmers through her bouncy blond hair. Every time she moved, her silvery fringe danced and rippled around her breasts. "And then, he went running back inside the building."

Jerry had negotiated his way onto the sidestreet in time to see the Harley turn left on a road that would only lead him back to the town square. Jerry did his best to keep the shooter in sight, but the chopper was far more maneuverable than my jungle combat Mustang, and we soon lost him in another turn.

"No problem," I said. There were only a few good routes in and out of Noble Heights. I advised Jerry on the shortest course to the highway entrance. I figured we could wait there for the hog to roll past.

I glanced at Duffy who was busily bestowing beauty queen grins on Abe, Marty and Binky in the back seat.

The guys, I realized, had not only destroyed the paint job on my Mustang, which was probably karmic retribution for the peace sign on the door of Captain Jack's bubba-mobile, but the Death Squad had fashioned costumes for themselves. Camouflage fatigues of rip-stop nylon and jungle boots. "Where'd you get the clothes?"

"They're ours," Abe said defensively.

"You went back to the Institute," I said.

"Well, everybody was at the funeral yesterday. So, we just zipped in and out quick."

"I told you guys to stay at my house."

"We had to do some reconnaissance. Jerry hot-wired the car, and we—"

"Jerry," I interrupted. "Have you got a driver's license?"

"Hell, yes."

"What year?"

"Maybe sixty-nine."

I nodded. "So, maybe I better drive. Listen, Duffy, my girl. Give me your last name, and we'll let you out of the car."

"Like, why should I do that? I don't even know you, and I don't think I want to give you my phone number. My parents get really, really mad if I pick up guys."

"This isn't a pickup," I explained. "It's a murder. And if you really saw the guy with the gun—"

"I did! Really! He didn't have the gun the second time he came out of the building so he must have hidden it or something."

I felt a furry head on my shoulder and a cold nose pressed against my jaw. "Get back, Binky."

"He's got to stick his head out the window," Abe explained. "Or else he gets carsick."

I didn't ask them why they'd brought the dog. I didn't want to know. At the turn-off to the highway, there was no sight of the Harley. Either we'd lost him altogether. Or he was going to come roaring past at any moment.

He had to be a paid killer. At the parade, I'd seen all my major suspects, except for Birkenshaw, so none of them had actually pulled the trigger. They all had an alibi. Besides, Grimhaur's death had been carried through in a professional manner with a professional long-range weapon. If I was going after a pro assassin, I needed to lose the Death Squad, Binky and Duffy. "Everybody out of the car," I ordered.

"I don't think so," Duffy said, fluffing her curls. "I mean, what am I supposed to do? Hitchhike?"

"Woof," Binky said, probably in support of Duffy's view.

"Bad plan," Abe said. "You can't go it alone, Adam. With more of us, we can spread out, tail the guy."

Further discussion was cut short when the assassin roared past, taking the highway toward Portland as I had suspected. Jerry eased onto the highway behind him, actually doing a nice job of following in traffic, staying a few cars back and to the left of the Harley.

"So, like, what's going on," Duffy said haughtily. "I mean, listen here, somebody has their hand on my bottom."

Marty leaned his head forward to the front seat. "You're the most beautiful woman I've ever seen."

"Thank you, I'm sure. Now, keep your hands to yourself." She emphasized her request by boinking him on the head with her baton.

"I mean it," Marty said. "We're going into combat, Duffy. I don't know if I'm coming back. It would help a lot if you told me you'd be here for me."

"Like I don't know. You're kind of not in my age group. I'm only nineteen, and you've got to be—"

"What does age matter when we're so right for each other?"

Yeah, I thought, both crazy as bedbugs.

I kept my eye on the Harley while Marty droned through every cliché in the book, and Duffy fell for every word he said. The Portland skyline was clearly in view when he said, "I don't even know your last name, Diana. But will you marry me."

"Just like that?" I snapped. "Just like that you ask somebody to m-m-marry you?"

"We could be in love," Marty said quietly. "What have I got to lose?"

Abe put in his two cents. "Ignore him, Marty. Adam has a problem with commitment."

Damn, everybody's an analyst! "How would you know about me and commitment, anyway?"

"I've been around shrinks most of my life. I've picked up a couple of things."

I hated myself for asking, "Such as?"

"You got this amazing female, Alison, hanging around and you haven't asked her to get hitched. Now, I'm pretty sure you aren't queer, so what else could it be?"

"How about this? How about I don't see any reason to mess up a perfectly good relationship by getting married?"

The Harley took an abrupt right, exiting highway twenty-six. He was headed north, toward downtown. Jerry whipped across two lanes of traffic to follow. This part was going to be tricky. On the highway, the chopper wasn't difficult to follow, but in town he'd be able to weave through the city traffic and lose us. In town, a camouflaged convertible Mustang with soldiers, a large dog and a majorette was fairly obvious. "If you see a cop," I advised Jerry, "Try to attract his attention. We could use some backup."

"Got it," he said, speeding up to catch an amber light before it changed to red.

We skirted the edge of downtown and trailed the Harley down inconveniently deserted streets. There was no way the guy hadn't spotted us, especially since Binky spied a dog-walker and began howling his furry heart out.

A few blocks from Union Station, I spotted three police cars in the parking lot of an Ethiopian restaurant. "Stop," I yelled.

Jerry stood on the brake pedal and the car skidded to a stop. I could see four uniformed officers sitting in the window of the eatery. I reached in front of Duffy and laid on the horn.

When the cops looked up and saw us, I motioned for them to come outside. They waved.

In a desperate attempt to get them off their dark-blue upholstered butts, I flipped them the bird. They flipped it back.

"Okay, Jerry. The cops aren't coming. Catch up with him again."

It was no use, the chopper was out of sight, lost among the alleys and side streets of downtown.

"What now?" Jerry said morosely.

"Pull over." I pointed to a phone booth at a gas station.

I telephoned Nick. He was, luckily, at home. I gave him the license plate number. "It's a Harley, big hog. The guy is a pro assassin. He just killed Doctor Grimhaur at a Fourth of July parade in Noble Heights."

"Jesus Christ! Okay, I'm on it, Adam."

I hung up and turned to find Binky right behind me, sniffing my butt and spilling a puddle of drool on the asphalt. The guys were fueling the Mustang and had gotten out to stretch. Jerry paced and frowned. Marty made goo-goo eyes at Duffy who fluffed her hair while idly twirling her baton.

"Everybody back in the car," I ordered, wondering how I had become commander of this bizarre squadron.

"We're going to cruise the area. See if we can spot the Harley."

We ranged up and down the streets, passed a number of coffeehouses and vendors selling flowers on the street corners. We stopped right beside one of them, and I stuck my head out the window. "Pardon me, but . . ."

"Do I have any Gray Poupon? Ha-ha," the guy said. "Very goddamned funny. You know how many times a day I hear that joke? A lot, that's how many."

"What I wanted to ask was: Have you seen a Harley?"

"Big hog? Guy wearing leather pants?"

"That's the one."

"Want to buy some roses for the lady?"

"Sure." I tossed him a ten.

"The Harley went straight down this street. Away from the city."

"Thanks. Keep the flowers."

"But I want them," Duffy said.

Marty grabbed the roses and presented them to her. "They're nowhere near as beautiful as you are."

"Well, like, I hope not. These are all wilted and grody."

We circled the general area several times before Abe yelled. "Thar she blows. Harley on the left."

The big bike was parked at the entrance to an alley between two five-story buildings. There was a liquor store on the corner. Though it was midday, the setup reminded me of that time with Nick when I faced the kid in the alley.

I had a bad feeling about this. I considered going into the liquor store and calling Nick, giving him my location and requesting cop backup. But there was the meantime to worry about. If this professional shooter came out of the alley with guns blazing, we'd all be dead before the police arrived.

"Jerry, pull around the corner and park. Marty, go

into the liquor store and call this number. Ask for Nick, tell him where we are and that we've got the shooter in an alley."

"What about you?" Abe questioned.

"I'm going to look around."

I borrowed Duffy's baton to use as a weapon and strolled up to the alley's entrance. It was shadowed between the buildings with iron fire escape stairs attached to one brick wall. The acrid scent of urine and decomposing garbage emanated from a dumpster.

I blinked hard. Visions of the past were rising up to overtake me. I imagined darkness, with moonlight reflecting off puddles of rain water. But this time, I didn't have a gun. I had a twirler's baton with silver streamers attached to both ends. I walked slowly, cautiously into the alley but after three steps, I was overcome by something which felt very much like common sense. I backed out. I'd wait for the cops.

Then, Binky came frolicking up beside me.

"Go back," I whispered. "Go away, Binky."

"Woof."

He bounded into the depths of the alley. Dumb-ass dog! If he got himself shot, he'd have no one to blame but himself, but I followed anyway. "Here, Binky," I called. "Come on, boy."

No one fired on the beast, and I certainly would have if I'd had a gun. I went in after him.

At the back of the alley, behind a dumpster, Binky nosed at the crotch of black leather pants.

The assassin lay flat on his back, a clean bullet hole through the center of his dark helmet.

Chapter Thirteen

A motorcycle guy with a bullet through his helmet, an alley that smelled like the site of a bed-wetters' convention and a corner store with advertised specials on Ripple Wine did not represent Portland, Oregon at its finest. In most parts of the city you couldn't throw a cat without it landing in a park of some kind, but every urban environment has a seamy side, and I have a decided talent for sniffing out the waxy yellow build-up in the corners. I felt right at home. On the other hand, I was pretty sure that this was the first time Duffy the Majorette had been this far from the Gap, but she was handling the situation with enthusiastic aplomb.

While waiting for the cops to come speeding to the scene of our life-and-death emergency call, Duffy proceeded to entertain an assortment of derelicts and local winos with baton tricks. Abe had retrieved his wheelchair from the trunk of the Mustang, and Duffy recruited him into her act, standing with her feet, in their little white boots with silver tassels, braced on the arms of his chair and her crotch just above Abe's head, she announced to the watching throng, "Okay, you guys, I call this the Statue of Liberty."

Saluting with her left hand and twirling with her right, she balanced while Abe whizzed along the sidewalk.

When she leapt down, her silver fringe sparkled and she high-stepped to the corner, with Binky at her heels. Duffy flipped her baton fifteen feet in the air and caught it without missing a beat.

"Ta-da!" she said simply.

The applause, though not deafening, was raucous, punctuated by wild shouts from Marty, "Marry me, marry me."

A gang on the sidewalk agreed that this was the best Fourth of July ever. One greasy-haired, toothless bag lady who wore a faded pink tank top and baggy men's trousers of an indeterminate green shoved her grocery cart of belongings toward me and approached the Duffster. "Can I give it a shot?"

"I'm, like, sure you can," Duffy said brightly.

When the faded bag lady grasped the baton, she was transformed. She tossed her head proudly, threw back her scrawny shoulders and marched back and forth in front of the arriving cop cars. When she twirled, the baton became a silver blur, and she tossed it high, end over end, then spun it under one arm, then the other. She ended her routine doing the splits with the baton whizzing above her head like a helicopter rotor.

"Like, oh my God." Duffy bounced up to her, clearly impressed because she repeated "oh my God" at least five times. "Like, how did you learn how to do that?"

"I used to be your age." She wheezed a chuckle. "Hell, I used to be you. Listen, girlie, we're not all what we seem to be. That bald guy on the corner—" She pointed. "Give him a tux and he might be Ed MacMahon. With a bath and a shower, that character over there might be Clint Eastwood. And me? Hell, sweetie, I just might be Shirley Temple."

"Wow! So, like, what are you all doing here?"

It was a good question, but one that the bag lady

didn't have time to answer because the police joined us, scanning the group for a leader. I stepped forward.

"What's the problem?" the cop asked.

"Dead guy in the alley," I said. "Want to see?"

Two of them fell into line behind me, muttering about how much they hated the Fourth of July. I remembered the sentiment from my days as a cop. Other people looked forward with good cheer toward the holidays. For a cop, Independence Day meant that neighborhoods all over Portland would erupt with cherry bombs and rockets' red glare. Come nightfall, the city would be a mess and the emergency wards at the city hospitals would be full.

I pointed out the dead guy in the motorcycle helmet and offered a brief explanation about how we had come to find his body. They quickly deduced that this was, in fact, homicide and the investigation, coordinating with Noble Heights, would be a major pain in the butt.

Nick arrived midway through our preliminary explanations. He wore a Hawaiian shirt and still had traces of barbeque sauce around his mouth. Though he didn't personally know the officers on the scene, they recognized him and were glad when he verified, "Adam used to be a cop. You can trust what he says."

"What about those guys?" The officer gestured toward the Death Squad who had, thus far, refused to divulge anything but name, rank and serial number.

"Try to ignore them," I suggested.

Nick frowned, "Come on, Adam, you know we can't do that. They're witnesses."

But they were as useless as the three proverbial monkeys: hear no, see no, and speak no evil.

Nick and I tried to reason with them.

"Come on, Abe," I said, "these are the cops. They're the good guys. We want to help them."

He rolled his eyes. "Don't you get it, Adam. They're

spies, cleverly disguised." To the other two, he said, "Don't tell them our position. That's key, men."

"They're staying at my house," I informed the officer who was taking notes.

"Why?"

"I don't know. It seemed like a good plan at the time."

But now? Things were more serious now. I had gotten myself smack in the middle of three ongoing murder investigations.

"Two dead shrinks?" The officer raised his eyebrows. "You got something against the psychology profession?"

"As a matter of fact—"

"He doesn't," Nick said. His seniority and reputation on the force were the only thing keeping the officers from arresting the whole bunch of us, including Binky and Duffy who, unlike the Death Squad, was delighted to babble on at great length and to punctuate her statements with baton tricks.

While the red tape continued to unfurl, Nick and I stole a couple of private minutes in his car, a beat-up station wagon that I had often teased him about. It was his turn to gloat. "Too bad about your Mustang," he said unsympathetically.

"Nothing a little sand-blasting and a gallon of red lacquer won't fix." Recalling the outrageous estimate that Captain Jack had gotten from Daddy Bud's Custom Shop, I added, "Of course my insurance company will cancel my policy."

"So, what do you think, Adam? Is all this shit related to Reeves's murder?"

I nodded. "Grimhaur was connected. Maybe he didn't give Kurt Schmidt the drug that made him violent, but he knew something about it."

"And that's why he got shot. Why at the parade? There had to be a more convenient place."

"Alibis. Everybody in Noble Heights was there."

"But now? Here? You think one of them Noble Heights people came into town and executed the assassin?"

"Makes sense," I said. "Whoever hired the assassin probably arranged to meet here at a predetermined time so they could make payment. If you investigate their checking and savings accounts, maybe you'll find that one of them has a big withdrawal."

"But they didn't need money," Nick pointed out. "They killed him instead of paying off."

"Right." Hire a shooter. Then shoot the shooter. Cold-blooded but clean.

Plus, the alibis after the parade would be impossible to trace. Everybody could claim that they were so upset they went home to bed.

"Who are we talking about in the way of suspects?" Nick asked. "In addition to Birkenshaw. Oh, by the way, I did get some information on him. He's got a police record."

"Which is?"

"Two arrests for possession with intent to sell. That was in San Francisco during the glory years of Haight-Asbury. Since, he's accumulated a slew of DUI's. Right now, his driver's license is suspended."

"So, what do you think, Nick? Could he have set up Reeves?"

"My gut feeling?" He patted his ample belly. "I don't think so. Birkenshaw's record is the portrait of a punk. He might have slipped something to Kurt Schmidt on account of they were buddies in the old days. But none of the popular recreational drugs showed up in Kurt Schmidt's samples. There were some weird imbalances in brain chemicals . . ."

"Brain chemicals?"

"Stuff that the brain makes naturally. Seratonin and

adreneline. Or noradrenaline. I don't know, Adam. The main thing was: no evidence of foreign substances."

I was surprised.

"As far as the lab technicians can tell, there's nothing. That's why they made particular note of the brain chemicals. There are plenty of drugs that absorb quickly and wouldn't show a trace. Kurt wasn't tested until several hours after the murder."

"No evidence." I was left with no proof other than my own impression that Kurt Schmidt had been high when he attacked Reeves. No tangible evidence. "Are the cops going to drop the whole thing?"

Nick didn't see it that way. "There's going to be more investigation. Now that we've got this guy in the alley and the other doc. There are too many dead guys not to."

"But it's all dead end," I said. "Literally, dead. Grimhaur was your best suspect."

"Come on, Adam, we've solved more complicated stuff with less to go on. Tell me about your suspects. I know you favor Birkenshaw and his benefactor, Jonathan Noble. Anybody else?"

Basically, it was everybody on the memorial committee and Nurse Fran Lavin at Mount Prairie. "Raven Parducci," I said.

"Reeves's attorney?"

"She's part Vietnamese and claims to have known Reeves in Vietnam."

"Doesn't look Vietnamese," Nick muttered.

"So, maybe you can check out her background. But why would she lie?"

He dug into his glove compartment and made a note on a receipt from a gasoline credit card. "Okay, who else?"

Reluctantly, I mentioned the Schmidts. "They're the parents of Kurt. Maybe if they found out that Grimhaur had given their son drugs that caused him to go crazy and

attack Reeves, they would have hired an assassin for revenge. They're the people who run Schmidt Apples."

"Big bucks," Nick said. "That's a high-class crowd
you're running with."

"You know whose fault this is?"

"Margot?" he guessed.

"Damn right, it's Margot. If she hadn't dragged me
into their meeting to mess with the statue, I wouldn't
have gotten into the middle of this thing."

"And you're surprised? I keep telling you, Adam, the
woman's a she-devil. Has she ever been anything but
trouble for you?"

"Maybe when we were kids . . ." Even then, Margot
had been prone to instigating problems. I vividly recalled
a playground incident where I got duped into defending
her dubious honor and had the shit beat out of me.

"What about Alison's brother?" Nick asked.

"He's fine, now."

"But he had some kind of outburst, didn't he?"

"What's your point?"

"Is he on some kind of drug?"

"I don't think so," I said. "Eric is the kind of guy
whose body is his temple. I guess there's a possibility of
steroids."

I stared through the windshield, watching the street
drama of cops and winos and a majorette. As far as I
could tell, dead end was the most accurate summary of
the situation. No traceable drugs in Kurt Schmidt's system. The assassin had been executed. And Grimhaur
. . . somehow, Grimhaur was tied up in this, as was
Mount Prairie Institute. With two shrinks violently deceased, that elegant front for the post-traumatically
stressed was steeped in murder. "I have an idea," I said.

"I hate it when you say that," Nick grumbled. "This is
going to be something off the wall, something crazy."

"Crazy just about describes it." I grinned maniacally. "That's what I am. I should be committed."

"To what?"

"Mount Prairie. If I'm a patient, I can move around easier, scrape some poop off the inside, hold it up to the light and see what's crawling around in it."

"Nice image," Nick said.

"Put me in for a forty-eight-hour observation or something. Hey, I'm single-white-male, Vietnam vet, ex-cop. I might have any number of psychological maladies. I might have PTSD."

"Might have." But Nick wasn't laughing.

Later that afternoon when we had finished giving statements to half a dozen different cops, the Squad and I drove back to Noble Heights. Duffy was in the back seat, next to Marty, whose devotion to her had not flagged. I was driving. Jerry and Binky sat in the passenger's seat, both with their heads hanging out of the car, catching mouthfuls of wind.

I followed Duffy's directions with Marty interpreting her finger-pointing and "that way, no, this way" into actual rights and lefts until we finally located her parent's mansion in Noble Heights. With tall white pillars and balconies, the place looked like something out of *Gone With the Wind.* I asked, "Duffy, what does your father do for a living?"

"It's like, I don't know, something boring at a bank."

"Like, owning it?"

"Kind of." She climbed out of the Mustang, flashed her best majorette smile and waved. "Okay. Bye-bye."

She took two steps up the curving sidewalk, then scampered back to the Mustang and planted a tiny kiss on Marty's forehead. "I really, really had a good time."

Then, she skipped up the walk and paused at the doorway. After a final bounce of her silver fringe, she went inside.

"I can't let her go," Marty said. He was halfway out of the car.

"Get back here," I ordered. "We don't have time."

He stood outside the car with fists stuffed in the pockets of his camouflage trousers. "You don't get it, Adam. This is the girl I've been waiting for all my life."

He straightened his shoulders, ran a hand over his hair and marched up the sidewalk.

Confronting Duffy's parents would be certain trauma, and I'd grown kind of attached to these guys. I followed, for emotional support.

He stood at the door and pressed the bell.

The large man who answered had that indefinable aura of wealth. It wasn't necessarily the silver streaks in the hair at his temples or the fact that his fingernails were manicured or that his teeth were perfectly capped. There's just a certain stink about rich people.

"Excuse us," I said, "we wanted to make sure Duffy got inside all right and to apologize for the inconvenience—"

"She telephoned earlier," he said with an indulgent chuckle. "Our Duffy is quite a kidder. She said she was at an inner city liquor store, and there was a dead person, and she would be home after she spoke with the police."

"What a sense of humor!" I chuckled, too.

"Thank you for bringing her home." He smiled as he swung the door closed.

Marty braced his combat boot against the doorjamb and blurted, "Sir, I am deeply in love with Duffy and want to ask for her hand in matrimony."

"She's only nineteen." The only outward sign that he was annoyed was a slight quaver in his baritone voice. "And it appears to me that you are closer to my age than to hers."

"But I love her."

Duffy's father stepped onto the porch and closed the door behind him. "Look around you," he said. "This is a nice home, nice area. We are nice people. We expect nice things for our children. To be quite frank, you don't fit."

"I'm sorry, sir," Marty said, "But you don't know anything about me."

Thank God, I thought.

"What's to know?" asked Duffy's father.

Marty whipped out a pen and a three-by-five-inch spiral notebook from his rear pocket. He thought for a moment, then scribbled down a few words and a number, then held out the scrap of paper. "I'll be in touch," he said.

I followed him down the sidewalk, fairly impressed by his composure. Apart from the fact that most guys don't make matrimonial pronouncements after knowing a woman for less than eight minutes, Marty had behaved in a relatively normal manner. "So?" I asked him. "What did you write down on the paper?"

"The number for my Swiss bank account."

I smiled. *Scratch normal.*

By the time we got back to my house, I had informed the guys that I would be spending a few days at Mount Prairie. "For a rest," I said.

Nick and I had decided not to let them in on the undercover scheme. They'd want in on it. The Daughters of the American Revolution in mounted posse would be less conspicuous.

The Squad didn't protest. Jerry said they had the phone number, and they'd call if there was any trouble at the house. Marty wandered into my studio where he began drawing sketches of Duffy. I was rather disturbed by their calm acceptance that I might need hospitalization for psychiatric care.

"A bit of advice," Abe offered. "Don't eat the food. It's got saltpeter."

The words were still ringing in my ears when Nick marched me up to the desk to face Nurse Fran Lavin. The big clock behind her head said it was seven forty-five, and I began counting the minutes.

"Forty-eight hour evaluation," Nick said. "Here's the paperwork from the Veterans' Administration."

"I see." She glared through her cat's-eye glasses at me. "Name? And don't try to tell me it's Doctor Sterling."

"Frances Farmer," I said.

"Try again."

"Jack Nicholson." I winked. "Me and the boys would like to watch the world series?"

Her smile went from cold to frigid. "Perhaps we need to use restraints with this patient. Or a straitjacket."

"Adam McCleet," Nick said.

He pulled her aside. If I strained my ears, I could just hear what he was saying to Nurse Lavin. "As I'm sure you know, Nurse, Adam was there when his friend, Reeves, was killed. He was standing beside Grimhaur when he was shot. And he just found another body in Portland. All the violence must have triggered a flashback. We found him curled up in a ball, whimpering about Vietnam and . . ."

Well, shit! I wanted to be a happy whacko, not a whiner.

". . . in any case," Nick continued, "I contacted the VA and they arranged for this evaluation. We all thought he might feel better being here where he's familiar with the set-up."

"I don't mind telling you," she said, "McCleet is a troublemaker. He came in here, impersonated a doctor and sneaked out with four of our patients."

"Obviously disturbed," Nick said. "I think we may have gotten him here just in time. Thank you, Nurse."

"This is difficult," she complained. "After Dr. Washington and Dr. Grimhaur . . . Well, we're a little short-handed."

"I'm sure you can handle it."

He passed her the paperwork, and she went through procedures while I stood there, trying to look crazy.

Lavin was joined at the counter by the short, sweet-faced nurse who had been there the first time we'd brought Eric in to see Grimhaur. She gave me a perky, professional smile and said, "How nice to see you, again."

Lavin whispered something to her, and she whispered back at length, probably telling Lavin about how I had been running around half-naked in a lab coat, demanding aspirin. When she turned back toward me, her smile did not waver, but she leaned slightly away, as if I had acquired an unpleasant odor.

I informed her, "I'm not really crazy, you know."

"Whatever you say, Mr. McCleet."

"I mean, really."

"Of course."

At least she sounded sympathetic. Behind my back, I could hear Nick chuckling quietly.

Nurse Lavin shoved a wire basket toward me. "Empty your pockets. I also want your belt and wristwatch."

I rolled my eyes at Nick. "Do I have to do this?"

"Don't talk to your friend," Lavin ordered briskly. "In case you've forgotten, McCleet, this is a hospital for PTSD. We have a number of depressed patients, and we must always consider the possibility of suicide."

"How about if I promise not to kill myself?"

"Put your possessions in the basket, McCleet. You'll get them back when you check out."

"Okay," I said, "but I'm keeping my navel lint. I need it. To talk to. When I get lonesome." Still muttering under my breath, I did as she asked.

"Hold out your arm," she said.

"Why? What are you going to do?"

"Are we a tiny bit paranoid, McCleet?"

"Why the hell does everyone think I'm crazy?" I stuck out my left arm, figuring that if part of the procedure was to lop off a body part, I'd rather lose the left than the right hand.

She clipped a plastic bracelet around my wrist.

"No drugs," she said, glancing over at the other nurse and raising her eyebrows. "We know all about you, McCleet. Don't even try to get into the supply."

The sweet-faced little nurse picked up my manila folder and escorted me through the main building and onto the grounds, giving a guided tour as we went. "The dining hall is behind the big house and breakfast is at seven o'clock in the morning. You'll be staying in one of the men's wards. After nine o'clock at night, you are not allowed to leave your ward building."

"Why is that?"

"We have both men's and women's wards. Fraternization is not permitted."

For the sake of argument, I asked, "What if both parties are consenting adults?"

Her eyebrows drew into a scowl. "I wouldn't try it. Many of the women patients are rape victims, and some of them are militant in their dislike of the male gender."

"How militant?" I pressed.

"Does the word 'Bobbit' ring any bells?"

I fought the urge to cover my genitals as she marched me into the far building on the east side of the grounds. "You won't be having a roommate tonight," she said. "But if you get lonely, there is always someone on duty. There's a television in the lounge area, but it's lights out at eleven o'clock. Any questions?"

How many more minutes until forty-eight hours were up? "No, I'll be just dandy. I have my lint."

"The doctor will be in to see you at eight-thirty, for a preliminary interview." She glanced at my chart. "Oh dear, this is such a shame. But I guess it can't be helped. We just don't have enough doctors and—"

"What?" I interrupted. "What's wrong?"

"Nothing. You've been assigned to Dr. Whittle."

She left me alone, and I sank down on the too-hard mattress of the bed. Dr. Whittle? The name sounded familiar. I searched my brain and came up with a connection. On the tape in Reeves's office, he'd mentioned that he was going to hire a new doctor, someone who specialized in the treatment of rape and abuse patients. Dr. Sandra Whittle.

In spite of what the little nurse thought, this was a stroke of luck. Dr. Whittle had just started working at Mount Prairie. There was no way she could be involved in the murders.

I welcomed her with open arms when, half an hour later, she gently rapped at the closed door of my room. I put on my most sane expression as I shook hands with this small-statured, gray-haired woman who wore gold-frame granny glasses. "You're probably not going to believe this," I said, "but I'm not really here for a forty-eight-hour evaluation."

"Then why are you here, Mr. McCleet?"

"This is a kind of undercover assignment."

"For the police?" she asked in a gentle, British accent. "Are you a policeman?"

"Not anymore, but I used to be."

"Did you really?" She'd taken a seat at a small table beside the window. "That is so very interesting. How long were you a policeman?"

I'd given her the dates, my promotional record on the Portland police force and had begun talking about the time when Internal Affairs investigated me before I realized that she was listening with a professional ear and taking down my history. "Reeves was right," I said. "You're good."

She didn't bother to deny it. "And so are you, Adam. One would hardly suspect that you have any chinks in that armor of glib toughness."

"Do I?"

"You tell me."

"Here's the deal." I was enjoying our exchange. "I'll tell you something, then you answer a question for me. Okay? I start."

She raised her eyebrows and waited for me to speak.

"Brain chemicals," I said, thinking of what Nick had told me earlier. "What are seratonin and noradrenaline?"

"Seratonin inhibits violent behavior. Noradrenaline pumps you up." She portrayed the corresponding balances with her small hands, elevating one palm and holding the other low. "One goes down. The other goes up."

"And?"

"If the seratonin production is suppressed and the noradrenaline goes up, the result may be a sudden, unpredictable outburst of violent behavior."

"Is there—"

"Wait, Adam. It's my turn." She folded her hands and asked, "Have you ever been married?"

"No," I said quickly. "Now, tell me if there's a drug that suppresses seratonin and accelerates the production of noradrenaline."

"I am not familiar with a drug designed to do that. However, there is always experimentation with drugs that work on brain chemicals." She smiled. "Now, Adam, tell me how you feel about your mother."

Chapter Fourteen

So, we talked about Mom and about Dad and the sibs.

"Not much to say." I shrugged. "I think we were pretty much your normal dysfunctional family. Nobody was too whacked out. Nobody too sane."

"I hear the word 'except' in that statement, Adam. Who aren't you telling me about?"

"I have a sister. Margot."

I had been avoiding Margot. If I wanted to keep Dr. Whittle thinking that I was on the sunny side of sane, I didn't want to start frothing at the mouth or shrieking uncontrollably, which was my usual response whenever the subject of Margot the Maniacal arose. "Listen, Doctor, I'm not saying that I couldn't use a bit-o-therapy, but that's not why I'm here. Reeves Washington was a friend of mine. I witnessed his death, and I know it wasn't an accident. The guy who killed him, Kurt Schmidt, was high to the max. I'm reasonably certain that somebody doped him, knowing he'd snap under therapy."

"Ah," she said. "Hence your probing inquiries regarding the properties of noradrenaline and seratonin."

"Yeah, hence. And that's what I want to talk about. Not the lumps in my Mom's gravy or the first time I had sex or any other psychoanalytical crap."

She glanced at the oversized numerals on her extralarge wristwatch. "I have only ten more minutes with you, Adam. Shall we talk about the death of Dr. Washington?"

"Good." Now we were getting somewhere.

"I, too, was quite fond of Reeves Washington." Behind the granny glasses, her blue eyes blinked once. "I share your grief."

I believed her. Her few words held more sincerity than all of Marion Grimhaur's issue-processing psychologue.

"Your suspects?" she said.

"My first pick was Dr. Grimhaur. But he's dead."

"Quite."

It occurred to me that she had access to a lot of the Mount Prairie records. "Reeves told me that Grimhaur was in a malpractice lawsuit involving inappropriate use of drugs. I'd like to know more about that. Maybe you would, too. Maybe the Institute is liable."

She murmured and made a note. "And the others?"

"Then I've got to go with the members of the Noble Heights Memorial Statue Committee." I listed them. When I came to the end, I added with reluctance. "And Margot."

"Your sister?"

"But she's not a suspect. Though Margot is adept at driving other people to acts of mayhem, she's not a murderess."

"We only have a few more minutes, Adam. Give me a thumbnail sketch of these people."

"The Schmidts. Kindly, stolid people. They look like Bavarian salt and pepper shakers with their caps screwed on a little too tight. Parents of Kurt Schmidt, the guy who killed Reeves."

I was very aware of time passing and the need to spill all this information into Dr. Whittle's little lap. "There's

Birkenshaw," I said, "Drug pusher and user, stuck in his glory years as a protestor in the sixties."

"When you were in Vietnam?"

"That's right. Anyway, Frank Birkenshaw is an old buddy of Kurt Schmidt. Runs around town painting peace signs on trucks. And there's Raven Parducci, a local attorney. She claims to be Vietnamese but doesn't look Asian."

I told her about Raven's assertion that she'd known Reeves in Vietnam. "Which seems bizarrely coincidental to me."

"Who else?"

I mentioned Jonathan Noble and his lofty standing in the community. "He likes to do nude wood carvings of his ancestors. I watched him perform a radical mastectomy on his great-grandmother with a chain saw."

"Did you now?"

"On a sculpture."

She leaned forward. "And Margot. Describe her."

This clever little doc had gotten me back to square one.

"Describe Margot?" I sorted through a number of possible descriptions, two-faced, evil, treacherous, hateful. The words that spilled out of my mouth were: "Malicious self-involvement."

That was all I intended to say on the subject. "I also have reason to suspect, in a casual way, Nurse Fran Lavin."

Dr. Whittle stood. The effort made her barely taller than when she was sitting. "I will see you tomorrow in my office at nine o'clock sharp, Adam."

"And?"

"We'll continue this discussion." She twinkled a smile. "By the by, Adam, I seriously doubt that you are in the throes of any sort of trauma or post-traumatic anxiety. I suspect however, given the events in your life over the past week, you are a very tired man. Use these two days to rest. I'm not quite sure what you think you're going to learn in here, but I'll try to help you find some answers. Please don't do anything stupid, like breaking into the drug supply closet."

She was a mind reader. "Me? You think I would—"

"Don't do it, Adam. There have been quite enough disruptions here."

"Believe me, I would never—"

"Have I mentioned that after these forty-eight hour observations, the attending physician—myself—can insist upon further treatment if she believes the patient poses a physical risk to himself or others?" She was still twinkly, but stern. "Keep that in mind."

When she pulled open the door to my room, Nurse Lavin was standing there in all her radiant, neo-Nazi glory.

"Nurse," said Sandra Whittle, "were you eavesdropping?"

"Certainly not." She whipped a giant syringe out from behind her back. "I'm here to give McCleet his B-12 shot."

"Very well. Carry on." She turned back to me with a final admonishment. "I suggest you practice cooperation."

Friendly Dr. Whittle left me in the hands of the Nurse from Hell. Fran Lavin approached slowly, relentlessly. "Okay, McCleet," she said with what I thought was undue relish. "Drop trou." The look in her eyes told me this would be more than a harmless little injection. She intended to inflict great pain.

I knew whining wouldn't stop her. I could have taken her out with a quick karate chop to the throat, but Sandra Whittle had made her point, and I was not ready for her version of long-term commitment.

Nick and I had played the system to get me in here, and now I was stuck, or about to be. If I wanted a recommendation that would set me free in two days, I had to cooperate.

"Drop 'em," Lavin said. "This won't hurt a bit."

The hell it wouldn't. The gleam in her eye told me she wasn't here because she was excited about getting a look at my milky white butt. In the course of a given day, this woman saw more butts than a high-paid call girl.

I bared my ass and tried to relax, but the cold alcohol swab caused my muscles to tense involuntarily.

She stabbed hard and plunged the transparent pink liquid under my skin all at once. The pain registered a solid point six-five magnitude on the sphincter scale.

"Okay," I said through gritted teeth as I pulled up my pants. I could feel a golf-ball-sized lump on my hip. "So, Fran, how often will we be sharing this intimacy?"

She cackled. "All the patients get B-12 at least once a week, but you look particularly run-down. I think, for you, twice a day."

By the time I got out of Mount Prairie, my bottom would look like an eggplant. "Anything else I should know?"

"Television off at ten. Before Letterman because he makes everybody crazy. Lights out at eleven. Breakfast at seven."

She slammed the door when she left.

I sat on the bed. Crossed my legs and wiggled my toes. It felt like I was in solitary confinement with nothing to consider but my past sins and the hours until morning. Outside my door, I heard the sounds of shuffling feet and chatter, but I wasn't here to win friends and influence people. I was here to find out what had really happened to Reeves.

Where to start? There was no possibility of slipping out and checking the grounds until after the inmates had settled in for the night. I glanced at my wrist for the time, but there was only the plastic hospital I.D. where my watch had been.

Television until ten, Lavin had mentioned. A little escape into the boob tube might have been nice, but I was tired. It had been a long and unusually eventful day. Dead psychiatrist, dead assassin, camouflaged Mustang, serious relationship negotiations with Alison. I needed to think—to organize my disjointed thoughts into some kind of action plan.

I picked up the controller to the standard issue, hard-as-a-brick hospital bed and lay back. The bed made an electric hum as I held down one of the buttons on the controller and elevated my feet. Another button raised my head. I played with the controller until I found the ideal thinking position. It was very similar to my concept of the ideal sleeping position.

Lying on the bed, I could see my own distorted reflection in the unbreakable-plastic mirror, mounted on the wall over the stainless metal dresser. It looked like the two-way job in Reeves's office, but I knew the room on the other side of the wall was my bathroom. None the less, it made me nervous. I climbed off the bed and wandered into the bathroom, just to ease my mind that no one was observing me from some secret place.

The bathroom was as ordinary and sterile as the rest of the room. Another plastic mirror was bolted to the wall over the stainless metal sink, opposite the stainless metal toilet, next to the stainless metal tub and shower. Except for the yellow rubber duck, non-slip appliqués on the bottom of the tub, the room was as clinical and ordinary as they come. No secret hiding places, trap doors or revolving bookcases.

Determined to finish the job of exploring my surroundings. I checked the closet, just outside the bathroom—empty. I got on my hands and knees and looked under the bed—nothing. I pulled open the drawers of the dresser and found a pair of pajamas, blue cotton with red piping on the collar and cuffs—my size. Good disguise, I thought. In my official Mount Prairie pajamas, I'd look just like one of the patients. Then I caught a look of myself in the cheap mirror, the purple bruise with yellow edges radiating from the ouchless bandage on my forehead. The swollen jaw from Schmidt's wild roundhouse punch. The dark bags under my red eyes from too many hours of lost sleep. I realized, I was a patient. No disguise necessary. I needed rest. I slipped into the pajamas.

In the drawer of the nightstand next to the bed, I found several back issues of *Gray Matters,* the psychiatric magazine Reeves had mentioned. I shuffled through them until I found the one with the article he'd written. I flipped past the definitive study of "Women Who Sleep with Their Shoes and the Men Who Love Them." The women or the shoes? A moot point. There were a bunch of drug-related articles, indicating the current trends. On the page opposite Reeves's article about the applications of hypno-therapy in the treatment of PTSD, there was a piece on "Effects of Early Parenting on Verbal Conduct." A study of potty mouth? I glanced through it, discovering that in a massive number of statistical studies, children adopt their parents' ethnic dialectic intonations, accents, in the first ten months of infancy.

"No shit?" I muttered.

The article went on to say that speech patterns formed early in life are very difficult to change. I thought of Reeves's wife, Felicia, and her perfectly honed anchorwoman's voice. Who had she been talking to for the first ten months of her life?

The article answered me. The television, of course. That was one place kids could pick up a variety of accents. However, it went on to state, babies in secluded or rural environments never lose their accent. They were marked for life.

I turned to Reeves's article. As I read, I could almost hear his assured baritone voice. "A subject of PTSD is likely to become agitated when pressed on the specific details of a traumatic episode."

A statement worthy of page one in the book of understatements.

I'd planned to slip out during the night and do some more snooping, but I could feel my eyelids trying to slam shut. Maybe tomorrow.

Before I fell asleep, I wondered if Lavin had slipped a sedative into the B-12. I wondered if it was safe to sleep.

The next morning, I might have slept through breakfast, but the ward was a hive of activity. In the hallway, doors slammed, voices echoed and a heavy-duty vacuum cleaner crashed repeatedly into my door as it roared past. I remembered why I had come to hate the military. There was no consideration for personal privacy in a building full of men. If there'd been showers on the wards instead of private bathrooms, I would have expected towel snapping.

Like a good little inmate, I showered quickly and followed the herd out of the men's ward toward the smell of breakfast in the main building. But I veered off before the final turn into a huge dining hall. Since Lavin had been working late last night, she couldn't possibly be on duty now.

Without my morning caffeine, it was hard to radiate good cheer, but I managed a grin for the nurse at the front desk. "I'm supposed to see Dr. Whittle."

"Not now. It's breakfast time," she chirped.

"No, really. She told me to wait for her. Which way is her office?" Hopefully, I pointed down the hall where Grimhaur had left Alison and me waiting. I would have liked to sift through his office, find out something about his malpractice suit. "It's down there, isn't it?"

I started walking, following my own pointing finger. I

got just far enough to read the brass placard on the closest door. Rolanski. Dr. Rolanski.

The nurse caught up with me, chided me for being a naughty boy, told me Dr. Whittle was upstairs and sent me on my way to breakfast.

I would try again later, using Rolanski as my reason for going down the hall. The dining room was filled with men and women, all talking at once but not together. Men on one end of the room and women on the other. The food they ate didn't look as bad as Abe had warned. I grabbed a cantaloupe slice and a bowl of oatmeal. The coffee was decaf only, but I filled a cup anyway.

I was trying to decide where to sit, when I saw Jerry, of Death Squad fame, enter the room. Since I was the only person standing, he spotted me at once and made a beeline.

"What are you doing here?" I demanded, disregarding the obvious reason that he was crazy and he belonged here.

"We talked it over."

"We? Meaning the Death Squad?"

"And we decided that you are in way over your head. I'm going to show you the ropes."

"The ropes?"

"Yeh," Jerry said. "You know. Things like who's cool and who's not, how to get around the nurses, who'll give you pound cake for ham and lima beans."

"Who?"

"No one."

Jerry filled me in on a lot more worthless information as I picked at my oatmeal, but some of the stuff was useful. Like, the times of the nurses' breaks, who does and does not pay attention to the patients and how to get extra ice cream at dinner to smuggle back to your room.

After breakfast, Jerry showed me around the grounds and brought me up to date on Marty and Duffy. "They take turns calling each other, every half hour or so. It's spooky, man. Old Marty's got it pretty bad."

"What's Abe doing?"

"When I left your place this morning, he said he was going to set some antipersonnel devices around the perimeter."

Visions of punji pits, trip mines and civil suits flashed in my head. "He wouldn't do anything that my neighbors could get hurt on, would he?"

"No way, man. You know Abe. He wouldn't hurt a flea. Why do you think he makes his traps out of yellow rope? He just likes to keep busy."

By nine o'clock, Jerry had introduced me to all of the day staff worth knowing, and several of the other patients. "We'll rap more later," he said, heading for the men's ward. He reminded me of a college kid on his way to nude figure drawing class.

I went upstairs to Whittle's office. The receptionist recognized me and I thought, for a moment, she was going to burst into tears. "Whittle," I said.

"That way." Snuffling into a lace-edged hanky, she pointed.

Sandra Whittle's door was open, and I recognized the gruff voice of her visitor. Jonathan Noble. I sat in an upholstered chair, just outside the door and out of their view. I couldn't help overhearing every word. Pleasantries aside, they were both pretty much all business. Noble wanted his property back, and he wanted Sandra Whittle's help.

". . . You know, Sandra," Noble was saying. "May I call you Sandra?"

"I prefer Dr. Whittle."

I smiled. Perfect. Make the old fart sweat.

"Dr. Whittle then," Noble said. "I've offered your board of directors a very generous cash incentive to surrender the Mount Prairie lease. When I heard you'd been appointed chief of staff, I thought, finally some one with the maturity and wisdom to recognize a golden opportunity . . ."

Noble was spreading it on thick, but Whittle remained true to her style.

"Really, Mr. Noble. I was only appointed acting chief of staff this morning. The position is temporary, I assure you. Only until a suitable replacement can be found. I'm afraid you've greatly overestimated my scope of influence with the directors. Actually, I haven't as yet, had the pleasure to meet them all."

"No worry," Noble said. "They will all be charmed, as am I. May I take a few more minutes of your time to explain the details of—"

"I'm sorry, Mr. Noble. I have a nine o'clock appointment. He should be here any second. Perhaps another time."

That was my cue. I stepped into the frame of the open door. "Hi. Hope I'm not too late."

"No, Adam," Whittle said as she stepped around her desk. "You are very prompt. Mr. Noble was just leaving. I believe you two know each other."

"Sure. How you doing, Jonathan? You must be pretty upset about the tragic death of your friend, Marion," I said sympathetically.

"Yeh," Noble grumbled as he stepped around me and headed for the door. "I guess you won't be coming to the meeting."

I'd forgotten about the scheduled meeting of the memorial committee. "Guess I won't."

He turned back to Whittle and smiled graciously. "You should come downstairs with me and meet the other members of the committee."

Whittle started to decline but I interrupted. "By all means, Doctor. You really must meet these people. They are Noble Heights at its best."

Jonathan Noble himself confirmed my assessment of his neighbors with a nod.

Reluctantly, she agreed. "Only for a minute. Would you like to come down with us, Adam? There is no reason you shouldn't attend the meeting. We can reschedule our session for later."

"I don't think so. As you said, I need the rest." I dropped into the chair in front of her desk and tried to look exhausted. "If you don't mind, I'll just sit and wait for you here."

"I would prefer if you would wait in the reception area," Whittle said.

I pulled myself out of the chair and followed them to the top of the stairs where I said good-bye to Noble.

"I will be back in five minutes," Sandra Whittle said, descending the stairs.

"I'll be right here. Please say hi to my sister, Margot, for me."

As soon as they were out of sight, I turned to the receptionist and said, "The doctor wanted me to wait in her office."

She sniffled and wiped at her red nose with her hanky. "Okay."

Sandra Whittle's office was similar to Reeves's. Same kind of desk and chairs. The mirror behind her desk was also a two-way. Six cardboard boxes were stacked in the corner next to the empty bookshelves. She hadn't even unpacked and Noble was already in her face about his precious real estate.

The only personal touch, the only hint of the real Sandra Whittle was an antique, silver-lace picture frame housing an eight-by-ten-inch, color photo of Dr. Joyce Brothers. The inscription was simple, "Your pal, J.B."

I pulled open the drawers of her desk. All five were empty, except for a Mount Prairie Policy and Procedure manual, which jumped into my hands. I fanned the pages. No pictures. But on the inside of the back cover, a four-digit number was written in pencil, four-seven-six-one. Could be her employee number or her locker combination at the YWCA. Could be the code to the drug room. There was a very good chance the number meant nothing, but I repeated it a few times in my head, just in case.

Without tearing into her unopened shipping boxes, there was little else to be learned in Dr. Whittle's office. I returned the manual to the drawer and myself to the reception area to wait for Joyce Brothers's pal, Sandra.

The receptionist gave me a curious look when I sat down on the leather bench near the staircase.

"I was lonely," I said. "Would it be okay if I wait out here?"

Before the teary-eyed woman could answer, Whittle appeared at the top of the stairs, slightly out of breath.

"I'm sorry, Adam." Her tone seemed overly dramatic. Her eyes looked at once vacant and horrified, as if she'd just witnessed the apocalyptic swarm of locusts.

"Why?"

"I . . . I simply had no idea."

"You met my sister."

Chapter
Fifteen

Margot had that mind-numbing effect on people. I patted Dr. Whittle's small shoulders. "Would you like to sit down?"

She tottered behind her desk and flopped into the chair. Her little legs didn't quite reach the floor. "Your sister, Margot, was dressed in black—tight black—and stiletto heels. Mourning. She wept without tears. Claimed that she and Reeves and Dr. Grimhaur had all been so close. It sounded rather like a sick love triangle. Does she actually sleep with every man she meets?"

"Only the ones she intends to marry." I found myself making excuses. "She's shopping for a new husband."

"Quite," said Sandra Whittle. "Her hat sported a black veil that fell dramatically to her knees. Come to think of it, she rather resembled a bride. The bride of—"

"Dracula?" I suggested. "Satan?"

"Frightening woman." Whittle shuddered.

"What about the rest of the committee?"

"They pale in comparison." She visibly pulled herself together. "I found your descriptions to be accurate. Ms. Raven Parducci interests me. Does she have a history of abuse?"

"Not unless you call coming of age in Vietnam and watching your family get killed abuse. Why do you ask?"

"There are symptomatic indications. I work mainly with abused women so I am, perhaps, more aware than most people. It's her dogged obsessiveness that I find worrisome. She was so utterly focused on their agenda that she hardly took notice of Margot's posturing and the poor, sad Schmidts, weeping and mourning."

"What about Birkenshaw?"

"Thoroughly unlikeable." She looked around the office as if she might have made a mistake in coming here. "The same description applies to Jonathan Noble. Are they truly representative of the community?"

I nodded.

"Oh, dear."

"We could reschedule this appointment for later," I said. "If you'd like some time to pull yourself together."

"Thank you, Adam."

Who was the shrink here, anyway? I headed toward the door of her office, but before I stepped into the hall, she called out a reminder. "Adam, despite your sister, I will not excuse extreme behavior. You must not take the law into your own hands. Are we clear on this point?"

"You bet."

Though I tried to sneak past the receptionist without causing a new outburst of tears from her, it was physically impossible. Every time she caught sight of me, she started to sniffle, and I couldn't make myself invisible. I left her weeping behind her desk at the top of the staircase. But hey, that's the kind of guy I am, spreading joy wherever I go.

I liked Sandra Whittle. Maybe, after we'd hung out for a while and swapped neuroses, she might even help me get into the drug cabinet to investigate. But I couldn't wait. The wheels were turning too slowly. I was in this place for forty-eight hours, and I'd already used up twelve of them. I needed to make some progress.

When I approached the front desk and sighted Nurse

Fran Lavin, I knew my ploy to visit Dr. Rolanski near the drug cabinet was futile. Nurse Lavin leered and gloated and looked down her long nose past her hairy lip. As an inmate at Mount Prairie, I was beginning to understand the hostility of the Death Squad.

"McCleet," she said.

"Lavin," I responded.

There was no way around her. No way I was getting near the drugs while she was acting watchdog. Clearly, I needed a distraction.

That was where Jerry came in. I found him easily enough. He was patrolling the perimeter of the center courtyard.

"How'd it go?" he asked.

"I got a problem. A nurse problem."

"Lavin?" His eyes lit with a wild, enthusiastic flame. "Nurse Fran Lavin?"

"I need to get her away from the front desk so I can go down the hallway to the drug cabinet."

"Piece of cake." He cackled. "Stand by, man. I got just the thing."

Jerry rushed into the men's unit and, before I could say paranoid schizophrenic, he dashed back out with something concealed under his camouflage T-shirt.

"Scope this out, man." Jerry lifted his shirt and produced an object that looked suspiciously like a turd, plump and shiny brown, about six inches in length. He cradled it gently in his hands, like a proud father.

"Is that what I think it is?"

"Yeh," Jerry beamed. "Ain't it great? It was Abe's idea. I only made it."

"You're being too modest," I said. "It appears you've made a very healthy poop."

"It's rubber."

I was relieved to hear that, but none the less puzzled.

"Can you tell me how you intend to distract Lavin with rubber poop?"

"Oh, man, this isn't your average rubber poop." Jerry pulled a wooden stick from his shirt pocket, about the size of a cocktail swizzle stick. To one end, a rectangular card with a peace sign was fastened. He stabbed the stick into the phony feces and placed the assembled unit on the sidewalk. When he let go, the turd took off under its own power, parading the peace sign along the walk. It rolled fast until it bumped into the curb then turned around and rolled until it bumped into Jerry's foot.

"Ain't that groovy," Jerry said. "It's a peace movement."

"I see. That's extremely clever, Jerry, but I'm still having a problem understanding how—"

"It explodes."

"Now we're talking distractions."

With Jerry's assurance that the explosion would not be large enough to do any real damage, I returned to the main building and waited for the rubber shit to hit the fan.

Lavin was still at her station. I took up position nearby and flipped through another issue of *Gray Matters*. I was just getting into an article entitled "Me and My Neurosis: A Practical Guide to Self-Analysis," when I heard a manly shriek.

I looked up to see Fran Lavin moving quickly from behind her desk to pursue the deadly dump as it rolled down the hall, away from the infirmary. When she caught up with it, she reached for it with her hands, but then it must have looked too real, because she recoiled. "Ick."

The toy turd gained a slight lead then bumped into a wall, turned and headed straight at Lavin. "Oh, my God," she gasped and ran back toward her desk as the peace movement bounced off another wall and reversed direction again.

This time the rolling rubber poop made it all the way to the end of the hall and disappeared under a utility cart, heaped with dirty linen. A harmless bang and a puff of white smoke issued from under the cart, which burst into flames.

While Lavin was busy beating out the flames from the explosion with her clipboard, I dodged down the hallway past Rolanski's office and went to the door marked "Infirmary." I'd only opened it a crack when I heard the sound of people talking. A couple of the staff were actually in the infirmary. I eased the door closed and reconsidered my options.

Having gone to such ridiculous lengths to gain access, I wasn't willing to give it up. I proceeded down the hall to an office I knew would be empty. Grimhaur's office.

There wasn't a need to turn on the overhead light because there was a whole wall of arched windows, shedding sunlight on a fairly impressive array of clutter. It looked like a bachelor's office with papers and office junk tossed carelessly on the desk. The chairs and coffee table arrangement, probably the place where he'd done his counseling, were fairly tidy. And the padded leather upholstery looked comfortable.

I understood completely. The ordered disorder was a guy thing. If you've got a comfortable chair where you can settle your butt, the rest of the mess doesn't seem all that important.

Ignoring the desk litter, I went to the file cabinets and yanked open drawers until I found what appeared to be personal correspondence. In a section tabbed "Legal," a fat folder took up most of the space. It was the malpractice suit. I took the folder to the counseling area to read. To skim, actually. In spite of my background as a cop, I have never been legally inclined. The wherefores and heretofores and notwithstandings annoyed the hell out of me, and I never comprehended why lawyers couldn't come right out and use the word because.

The very first thing I noticed in the papers was that R. Parducci was the attorney of record for the defendants, Marion Grimhaur and Mount Prairie Institute. I shouldn't have been surprised. Reeves had said she represented half of Noble Heights. At the time, I'd thought he was exaggerating, but she did seem to have her hands in a lot of legal pies. I wondered how Raven might profit if the Institute closed down. If Noble was one of her clients there would certainly be a conflict of interest on her part. Noble was the kind of man who wouldn't hesitate to slip a ringer onto the Mount Prairie team.

The suit, filed on behalf of Walter Strom, alleged that Grimhaur had administered an experimental drug called Neurozak to Strom without explaining possible side effects or adverse reactions. Under the influence of the drug, Strom flew into an uncharacteristic fit of rage, and one of his arms was broken when some of the Institute staff attempted to restrain him. Just like Eric Brooks and Kurt Schmidt.

I couldn't make it through more than four or five motions before my eyeballs were crossed. I shoved the papers in a briefcase sitting beside the desk. Later, I would go over this stuff. Right now, I wanted to try the code number I'd found in Whittle's office.

I heard a shuffling noise in the hall, as if feet had stopped right outside this doorway. There wasn't time to hide, so I prepared to brazen it out. I could always throw a minor fit and say that I was in here processing my post-traumatic Grimhaur grief.

The door pushed inward and Birkenshaw followed. He spotted me immediately. "What the hell are you doing here?"

I might have asked the same question. I found it real

interesting that Birkenshaw had, once again, used the occasion of a Memorial Statuary meeting to roam the grounds of the Institute. "What happened to your meeting?"

"It's bullshit, man. Margot is holding forth and everybody else is thinking up excuses to leave the room before they either vomit or slap her."

"Everybody?" I questioned. "Or just you?"

"Raven's been to the bathroom twice. Noble had to check on something in his car. Even the Schmidts decided they needed to take a break and drink some cider or something. Hell, man, you know what Margot's like. She insists that we come to a decision today, and we're not going to break up the meeting until we do. Problem is, with Washington dead, we have an even number of people and every time we vote on something, it comes out a tie."

She had them all gripped in her iron claw. After a few hours of enforced Margot time, the committee would agree to anything. But that wasn't my problem. Birkenshaw was. After Grimhaur's death, he should have graduated to the position of number one suspect. But I really couldn't see him being clever enough to hire the motorcycle sniper then shoot him. Birkenshaw would have speechified the guy to death.

"You seem to like wandering the grounds here." I plunged right ahead. "Was there anybody else, besides Kurt Schmidt, who you were supplying with drugs?"

His eyes darted to Grimhaur's desk. "Hey, man, I don't know what the hell you're talking about."

"Grimhaur?" I guessed. "You were supplying Grimhaur? Or were you buying from him?"

"Don't get in my face, McCleet. I'm clean."

"I've seen your record. Maybe you're clean right now, but—"

"Long time ago," he said, "I used to move a little

doobage. Maybe some coke once in a while. But I'm finished with that. People change. I'm clean, baby."

He didn't look it. I was growing tired of dancing around with this freak. "You're stoned now."

"Am not."

"Then how come your eyes are so red and your nose is always running?"

He looked shocked. "Is that why you think I'm stoned? You ever heard of allergies, man? Do you have any idea how much freakin' pollen is in the air in Oregon this time of year?"

I did. Reeves had made note of his own allergy, on his pocket recorder. Still, if Birkenshaw was so straight, why did he always seem to be hiding something? I decided that he would not be leaving the room until I'd asked all the questions, even if all the answers were lies. "What do you do for Jonathan Noble?"

Birkenshaw shrugged his drooping shoulders. "Stuff. Why?"

I leaned closer and looked him hard in the eyes. "Because I'm about to accuse you of conspiracy to commit murder. And unless you can convince me otherwise, I'm going to place a call to one of my cop friends and dump on you. I want to know your relationship with Noble."

"I read to him."

"You read to him? Why?"

"Because he can't read, man. He pays me to live at his place and read whatever he needs read. I'm teaching him whenever he has time, but he's a pretty busy guy. He's also very sensitive about it. So don't tell him I told you this."

How sensitive was he, I wondered? "Who else knows he can't read?"

Birkenshaw shrugged again. "I don't know, a few people I guess."

"Did Reeves Washington know?"

"Maybe."

"Did Grimhaur know?"

"Definitely. He ordered a book for me on learning disorders. That's what I came in here for." He gestured toward the desk. "It's probably in there."

I moved around the desk and pulled open the top drawer. There was a book, *Teaching the Functionally Illiterate Adult.* Was Noble killing everyone who knew he couldn't read?

I handed the book to Birkenshaw. "Why you?"

"Why not me? I have a Master's Degree in language arts, and an Oregon Teacher's Certificate."

This, too, would be easy to check. "Where were you when Grimhaur was killed?"

"I was at the parade, man. Not important enough to sit in the reviewing stand like you, but I was there. I'm surprised you didn't see me. I was wearing red, white and blue."

"Who can verify that?"

"Apparently, everybody but you. Ask your sister. She was so freaked after Grimhaur got shot, I wound up driving her home in her car." He checked his watch. "Shit, man. I have to get back to the meeting before Margot asks Noble to read something."

I nodded. "By all means. Go."

I waited for him to storm down the hall before I grabbed the briefcase full of Grimhaur's legal history, made my exit and went tiptoeing down the linoleum in the corridor. There wasn't a soul in sight, but I had a sense that somebody was watching, a kind of prickling on the hairs at the back of my neck.

This time, the infirmary was empty.

Ignoring the oversanitized medicinal smell, I went straight to the heavy metal door with the lever handle. Beside the handle was the code box with a little red light blinking on top. If I screwed up and punched in the wrong numbers, I fully expected screaming sirens and a computer voice advising me, "Move away from the door."

Wouldn't be prudent to try and screw up. But I had to try. I was right here with an itchy button punching finger. I tapped the buttons. Four-seven-six-one. I stepped back, gritted teeth and waited for the sirens. Nothing. The red light had stopped blinking.

"Fer sure," I said as I turned the handle and stepped inside.

I flipped on the light switch beside the door. The drug cabinet wasn't really a cabinet, but a room that was about eight by twelve. There was a sink with cabinets hung above it. On the countertop beside it was the computer, printer and a notebook.

The notebook looked less daunting than the high technology screen and keyboard, so I studied it first. The notations were arranged in neat rows. This was record of dispensary for B-12 which was apparently taken out in large sections and kept on the wards. Every shot. They logged every shot which seemed overly obsessive to me. B-12 was so harmless I couldn't figure any reason why they kept track at all, but then I remembered that Grimhaur had been required to make note of the aspirin he gave to me.

After punching a few buttons on the computer and getting nothing other than indecipherable requests for code and control and log, I decided that I might need Whittle's help after all. For a moment, I considered asking Jerry to plug into the system, but dismissed the thought. Sledgehammer mentality wasn't going to help with finding the magic numbers to get a printout of the drug withdrawals on the day Reeves was killed and on the day that Eric went crazy on the boat.

"Shit."

Unwilling to accept the fact that I'd gone to all this

trouble to discover nothing new, I explored the room, hoping to find the steaming pharmaceutical concoction that would turn mildmannered Dr. Jeckyll into the evil Mr. Hyde.

There were two tall glass cabinets, full of neatly labeled amber bottles. I scanned the labels for the words, Neurozak or Experimental, but there were none. A double-door refrigerator filled with liquid substances, likewise contained nothing that bore the Neurozak label. I also didn't find any popsicles or Häagen-Dazs which would have been a pleasant and welcome surprise.

I was poking through the cabinets on the far wall when I heard the click of the door handle. I turned, but not fast enough. Whoever opened the door had hit the light switch as soon as they entered. This room was windowless, darker than pitch.

My first thought was to yell something, like "Halt, who goes there. Friend or foe."

Then my brain kicked in. Whoever had entered was not my friend. And I wasn't supposed to be here.

I hit the floor when the first gunshot exploded.

Chapter Sixteen

The gunfire, blasting repeatedly in a square sealed room, was deafening. Thunderous echoes overlapped and redoubled. I rolled across the floor. If I couldn't see the shooter, they couldn't see me. Ricocheting bullets, bouncing at high velocity off the walls and metal cabinets, compounded the seriousness of the situation. Even if the shooter never got close, I could still wind up dead.

I heard the shatter of the glass drug cabinets and felt the rain of slivers and shards. I fought the impulse to curl up in a fetal position and take my chances. If I kept moving, rolling and dodging, the shooter couldn't draw a bead on the sound of my frantic breathing. I dove across the floor and somersaulted into a far corner. I felt like a duck in a shooting gallery, hoping the gunman would come up empty.

The rapid fire burst came from a semiautomatic. By the size of the muzzle flashes and the way the bullets pinged off the metal walls instead of tearing straight through, I guessed small caliber.

One of the cabinets had burst open, flinging the metal door against the wall. My hand found a box of small bottles. I tossed them in a far corner. The shooter fired three quick rounds at the sound. That was my best chance, get him to use up his bullets then rush him. Or rush him while he's shooting in the wrong direction.

There was an electrical flash, a hum and I heard the computer printer rachet to life.

With no real cover, it was only a matter of time and odds before I was hit. Then I remembered the refrigerator. It had a light. If I could make it to the door and pull it open.

Another three-round-burst kept me pinned down.

I tossed another box full of bottles at the far wall and made a break for the refrigerator. Two more shots and I recognized the metallic snap of the slide locking back as the last spent shell ejected from the gun. I scrambled to my feet but smashed the top of my head into a low shelf as I stood. I jarred my brain, jammed my neck and bit my tongue. As I slid down the wall beside the refrigerator, the door opened and closed with a thud and a click. The shooter was gone.

I slipped open the refrigerator door, and the glow of the light inside sparkled on what looked like a billion shards of glass.

I sat on the floor, letting the cool refrigerator draft chill the dampness I could feel on my skin. I hoped it was sweat, not blood. But it was a few minutes before I dared to pick up my hands and hold them in front of my eyes.

Apart from dozens of superficial scratches, there was only one injury that worried me. A large, knife-shaped shard had embedded in the fleshy part of my palm. I didn't feel a thing. I was in shock, and as I pulled the glass from my palm, I decided that shock was my friend. As soon as my sense of touch came back, this gash was going to hurt like hell.

Stumbling to my feet, I felt around my legs and torso, patted my aching butt. There didn't seem to be any permanent damage. Amazing though it seemed, considering the number of bullets that had been fired, I had not taken a direct hit.

When I turned on the overhead light and surveyed the damage that had turned the orderly room into chaos, I took a moment and offered thanks to St. Jude, patron saint of lost causes and my personal favorite among the higher powers. Somebody had been looking out for me on this one. Not only had I escaped serious physical damage, but the computer had printed out a fat ream of papers. Apparently, the correct access code was: Print or Die.

I gathered up the green and white striped pages of computer printout. The heading indicated that this was the record for drug entry and release, but those were the only decipherable words on the page. Everything else was code. It appeared to be an abbreviation for the name of the drug and the company that manufactured it, then a listing of dosage and a number that might be a patient number. And dates. I could figure out the dates. What I had here was a listing that went back three months.

Figuring that it was going to take some time to break these codes, I filed the pages in the briefcase, along with Grimhaur's legal history, and reached for the door handle. It seemed a little strange that nobody had come in response to the sounds of an eruption the size of Mount St. Helen's, but I guessed the room must have been soundproofed.

The door handle wouldn't turn. Using my right hand, the lesser injured of the two, I yanked. The door was locked.

I was beginning to get a little ticked off. The fact that there was an armed homicidal maniac roaming the grounds of Mount Anal Retentive seemed like a major breach of security.

The worst part, I realized, was that I was probably going to get blamed for it.

There was a telephone hanging on the wall, probably there in case of just such an occurrence, somebody getting locked in. However the phone had fallen prey to a wild bullet. It was dead.

I had some choices. I could sit here and bleed to death waiting for someone to get a headache and come looking for aspirin. I could mix together the drugs, take a big dose and forget about everything. I could throw my body against the door until I had dislocated both shoulders because the door opened in, not out.

Or I could make some more noise.

I took one of the bottles from the refrigerator. A nice, heavy full bottle and hurled it against the door. It smashed, and a nice ooze of some potentially lethal drug substance dribbled down the door like an original Jackson Pollack. I imagined Fran Lavin's face on the next bottle.

I kicked away a pile of broken glass and soggy cardboard in a far corner, looking for something else fun to throw—and I found the gun. It was an American Arms PK-22, about six inches long, double action, blue finish. On the force, we called these guns "pocket automatics." No doubt if I ever got out of here I could turn it over to the Portland police, they could run ballistics tests and link this weapon to the death of the guy on the motorcycle.

The handle on the door clicked.

I prepared my alibi. "Oh, hi there," I'd say to whomever opened. "I was looking for the bathroom and accidentally got locked in here." Or maybe the ever popular amnesia alibi.

As the door opened, I said, "Oh, hi there."

It was Jerry. He stood in the doorway like a liberating hero, then he saw the mess. "Whoa, Adam, you're in deep shit."

"I didn't do this."

He nodded. "So, who did?"

"You didn't see? Why'd you open the door if you didn't see somebody lock me in here?"

"I didn't know you were in here. I just knew you wanted inside, and I figured we could short-circuit the lock fairly easy."

"Is that what you did?" I was honestly impressed. Outsmarting a computer lock required some pretty intense reasoning for someone who invented the peace movement. "Some kind of short-circuit?"

"Didn't need to."

He held out a scrap of heavy gray linen paper lined at the edge with red. The code number was scribbled in the center.

Jerry kicked his way into the room, then eyed me warily. "Did you flip out?"

"Somebody else did this."

"Yeh, sure. Whatever you say."

If Jerry didn't believe me, nobody would. It was like when I was a kid and told my teacher that I would have brought in my homework but an eight-foot-tall Sasquatch jumped out of the bushes and knocked me down, grabbed the homework out of my hand and ate it in one bite.

The teachers had never believed me. And I didn't think Fran Lavin was more gullible.

But somebody had broken into the drug room and sprayed it with bullets. I didn't know exactly who, but I had a fair idea where I could find them.

I passed the briefcase to Jerry. "Guard this with your life."

I was done with being subtle. Being shot at does that to me. I stormed past the nurses' station without even looking at Lavin.

She saw me, though. "What happened to you, McCleet?"

I kept going.

"McCleet?" she yelled after me. "Hold it right there, mister. You can't go into that meeting."

The hell I couldn't.

I threw open the doors guarding the Noble Heights Memorial Statuary Committee meeting, immediately garnering the attention of the assemblage. Covered with scratches and oozing blood from several pores, I must have been stunning because they all looked shocked, mouths agape. Except for Margot, of course.

She adjusted her veil. "Well, Adam, it's about time. Why don't you sit down so we can take a vote."

Why not? I pulled out a chair and tossed the pocket automatic into the center of the polished oak table. "One of you left this behind."

Margot said, "All in favor?"

Timidly the Schmidts and Margot raised their hands. And so did I.

"Good," Margot said. "We've finally got a decision. Congratulations, Adam, you'll be doing the sculpture and it will be a veterans' memorial."

There were murmurs of relief and they all stood. The Schmidts started toward the door.

I was out of the chair, blocking their way. "Nobody gets out of here until I find out which one of you assholes tried to kill me."

Martha Schmidt cowered against her sturdy husband. If I'd been in a more forgiving mood, I would have felt bad. But I'd had enough of Noble Heights and all the phony bullshit. "Who left the room?" I turned toward my sister, hoping that for once in her life, she would be helpful. "Margot, who left the room?"

She pulled the black veil away from her face. "Who didn't? Honestly, it was all I could do to get them to sit down so I could take attendance."

I stared past Birkenshaw at Noble. "Was it you?"

"Settle down, McCleet. You're making a scene."

"This?" I went to the silver coffee and tea service on the table in the corner. "This isn't a scene, Noble."

I overturned the tray. "Now, that's a scene."

The crash of silver and the spewing dregs of coffee were slightly satisfying, but not enough. I grabbed the front of a bookshelf and pulled it over, spilling a set of leather-bound reference books onto the floor. "That's a scene."

But not enough. I had a point to make here.

I picked up one of the padded conference chairs, flipped it upside down and crashed the legs against the long antique table.

Raven, Noble and Birkenshaw scattered.

I continued to hammer at the table until the legs came off the chair and I flung the pieces through the beveled glass of the front window.

"Jesus, that feels good."

Days of frustration, weeks of holding back, years of suppressing all the bullshit exploded at once, and I was cleansed. "Jesus Christ," I repeated.

The committee watched through frightened eyes. Couldn't say that I blamed them.

Birkenshaw stuck out his chest. "What the hell are you doing, McCleet? Who the hell do you think you are?"

"I'll show you who I am you ridiculous little geek."

When I started toward him, he danced across the room and ducked behind the Schmidts.

Lavin and her orderlies crashed into the room like the cavalry coming over the hill to rescue the pathetic wagon train.

I tried to tell them that I was fine and would come along quietly, but nobody listened. The orderlies grabbed my arms. Lavin stabbed with a syringe. "Get him out of here," she ordered.

They propelled me, quite efficiently, through the big house and into the courtyard where Jerry stood at attention, saluting as I went by. Whatever Lavin had in the syringe started to affect me by the time I got to my ward. I was aware that we'd entered my room, then I went blank.

When I woke up, my vision was fuzzy. There was sunlight coming through the bars across the window in my room, glinting off the metal furniture. The first thing I was aware of was pain. In my head. My neck. My lower back. My hands. There was one spot below my left eye that felt okay, but pretty much everything else hurt.

And I couldn't move. I was lying on my back in bed, wearing the standard issue Mount Prairie jammies. My wrists were fastened to the hospital bed rail with passive restraints, fleece-lined cuffs of heavy canvas. My ankles got the same treatment at the foot of the bed.

And Nick was sitting beside me. Except he wasn't the old battle-weary Nick I knew. He was eighteen years old, wearing camouflage fatigues and an optimistic grin. "I'm from Oregon, too," he said. "Long way from home, huh?"

There was a girl behind him. Long black hair. Satiny blouse with a Mandarin collar. The young Raven Parducci. She bobbed her head and moved away, unsmiling.

"What's this?" My speech was slurred. I had to be dreaming. "It's not Halloween."

"Reeves is dead," he said.

"Yeh, I know."

As I watched, Nick's head swiveled, seeing something beyond my line of vision. He raised his M-16, but too late.

I tried to reach him, but I couldn't move.

Nick took a bullet in the throat.

I kept watching him, staring. Before he fell, his fatigues

changed to the uniform of a rookie cop. Nobody gets away forever.

I closed my eyes again. On top of the other pain, I was crying.

"Adam."

I heard a voice that seemed faraway. A familiar, raspy voice that sounded like gravel sliding off a tin roof.

"Adam, wake up."

My eyelids forced themselves awake. "Nick, are you okay?"

"A lot better than you."

He was the present-day Nick in his polyester slacks and JC Penney's plaid cotton shirt. There was a spaghetti sauce stain on his beige necktie. He patted my arm. "How're you doing, buddy?"

"I've been better." I tried to move but the restraints held fast. "Get this shit off me."

"Can't do it. You had a major flip-out."

All I did was smash up some furniture. "Not in the drug cabinet. Somebody was shooting at me."

"That's not the story I'm hearing. They say you got a gun, locked yourself in there and went nuts."

"They're lying."

"I believe you."

But I could tell that he had doubts. I had pieces that would fit into the puzzle of Reeves's death, but I couldn't remember clearly. "Grimhaur," I said. "He had a drug. Neurozak. Makes people go crazy. He's getting sued. His lawyer is Raven Parducci." I paused, waiting for some kind of logic. "Weren't you going to find out something about Raven?"

"Not much to tell. She was adopted."

"From Vietnam?"

"That I don't know. I talked to her adoptive mother on the phone. Foul-tempered woman. She got Raven from some kind of agency, but wouldn't say what or who. The mother hasn't seen Raven in years. She ran away from home when she was eighteen. There was some history of abuse from her father. He's dead now."

Whittle had been right. Abuse in the family.

"You rest," Nick said. "We'll figure this out tomorrow."

Would we? I remembered Sandra Whittle telling me that I wouldn't get out of here without her recommendation. There was a good possibility that I was about to become the fourth horseman on the Death Squad. "I'm not crazy."

"Hell, no. Nobody says you are."

"Get me out of here."

"Tomorrow. Okay? You need rest. I shouldn't have let you get involved in this shit in the first place."

"A little late to think of that."

"Go back to sleep, Adam."

"What else am I going to do? Jog? Go for a sail?"

I closed my eyes. For lack of anything better to do, I slept.

I had a pretty good idea of who my next visitor would be. It was either the Ghost of Christmas Past or Reeves. He looked pissed off, as annoyed as he ever got. He said, "Haven't you got it, yet?"

"Tell me."

"Doesn't work that way, Adam. You've got to figure it out. Make a commitment to figuring it out."

At the mention of the magical word—commitment— Alison popped up behind him. From out of nowhere, there was wind that rustled in her hair and brought a blush to her cheeks. Goddamn, she was pretty. I tried to say her name, but my tongue was stuck on the roof of my mouth.

She rested her hand on Reeves's shoulder. "Is he going to be all right?"

"Adam? He'll be fine if I don't kill him."

"He's got all the answers." She gazed at me appraisingly, as if I were a piece of art. "How long do you think it'll take for him to put it together?"

"Clue," I finally managed to spit out. "Gimme a clue."

She grinned at me. "Let's see now, we're in a psychiatric facility. Could it be—I don't know—but could it be psychological?"

"A psycho?"

"You know, Adam, when I was talking about commitment, I didn't mean this kind of commitment."

"Alison, let me up, hon. I'm not crazy."

Reeves shimmered and disappeared. Alison came forward and squeezed my hand. "Of course you're not. You just need rest."

She had all the answers. I could see it in her wise green eyes. "Who killed Reeves?"

"Kurt Schmidt," she said simply. "The real question, Adam my love, is who drugged Kurt and why?"

"Why?"

"Hate." Her lip curled and she shuddered. "Who hates Kurt Schmidt?"

"I dunno." From the little I knew about him, Kurt Schmidt was a good guy. Likeable and easy-going.

"And who hated Eric?" she pressed.

This was a mental stretch I was incapable of making. Kurt and Eric seemed completely unrelated, except for the obvious fact that they were both here in Mount Prairie. Who could possibly have a reason to hate both of them? It hurt my head to think this hard. "I don't know."

"What do they have in common? Think about it."

"Both vets. Both here."

"And what happens to everybody who's here?"

"Therapy?" And something else. I remembered the drug mentioned in the brief. "Neurozak."

"Adam, sweetheart," she said softly. "Eric already

told us that he wasn't on anything. And Kurt denied it, too."

"Had to be." That was the only thing that made sense. They'd both gotten a dose of Neurozak from Grimhaur.

She kissed my forehead. "You just rest. We'll talk tomorrow."

I tugged at the restraints. "There's a killer loose in this hospital. Tried to kill me. You've got to get me out of here."

"I don't think so." She smiled.

"Come on, Alison, please. I'll do anything you want?"

"Marry me?"

Oh, shit, that wasn't fair. Somewhere in my head, I knew this was only a fantasy Alison. But she was acting a lot like the real thing. When her hand descended and stroked my forehead, it felt like the real thing. She kissed me. I was getting a real erection. "Remind me," I said. "Why was it I'm not marrying you?"

"I don't take it personally." Her hand caressed and soothed. "You can't say the M word without sputtering."

"I love you. Does that count?"

"Usually." She took a step back. "I'll be waiting."

"Don't go."

But she had already started to shimmer and disappear. In her place, I could feel the cold hard edges of reality forming. The aches and pains were coming back. The inside of my head felt like a woodpecker convention.

The next voice I heard was Margot.

"You're pathetic," she snapped.

There was sunlight coming in the windows. I felt the restraints on my wrists and ankles. My left hand, where I'd stabbed myself on the glass, throbbed.

"Margot," I said. It seemed appropriate that now, while I felt like hell, I would be visited by a she-devil.

She whipped the mourning hat off her head and tossed

it in the corner of my room. "Do you know how embarrassing this is? Do you, Adam? To have my brother committed to a nuthouse?"

Sensitivity was never her strong suit.

"People are going to talk," she said. "Whenever it's a family member, they think it's genetic. People are going to think I'm crazy, too."

And people were going to be right.

"You're so selfish, Adam. If you had one ounce of common decency, you wouldn't be here. Think about me for a change." She looked down at me as if she wanted to rip my throat out. It was an expression I was familiar with. "There's a lot to be said for the good old days," she snarled.

"What good old days?"

"When they used to take the family embarrassment and lock him in the castle tower. God, you're a mess."

"So, spring me, Margot."

She was unfastening the restraints. I didn't think I was imagining this. Margot was actually loosening the straps. "What are you doing?" I asked.

"Saving my reputation. Stop moving. You're making this stuff tighter."

"What time is it?"

"How should I know and why should you care? Almost five, I think."

I tried to remember the schedule. It seemed quiet in the hallway outside my room. The inmates, I thought, were at dinner. "Good timing," I complimented my sister.

"Shut up, Adam."

But I was free. I sat up on the bed, tried to shrug off the pain. It didn't work. I was stiff and sore all over, but I forced my body off the bed and staggered to the closet.

"What are you doing?" she demanded.

"Looking for my clothes. You don't want your

brother running around town wearing Mount Prairie pajamas, do you?"

She turned her back. "Hurry up and change."

As sensation returned to my extremities, I began to function. But my sense of balance wasn't too hot. I almost fell over while pulling on my pants.

"I haven't got all day," Margot said.

The semblance of a plan was forming in the back of my head. First thing I needed to do was find Jerry and the briefcase of information. There were answers in there. If I could check the record of drug withdrawals from the cabinet, I was sure that I'd find that Grimhaur had taken out a shot of Neurozak on the day Eric went nuts and on the day Kurt Schmidt killed Reeves.

The fact that Grimhaur was now dead didn't alter the issue. Somebody had killed him to shut him up. Probably Noble.

"Okay, Margot, I'm ready."

The door to my bedroom crashed open. Nurse Lavin was standing there with a dripping syringe of transparent pink B-12 in her fist.

Chapter Seventeen

Lavin squared off with Margot. Looked to me like a battle of the titans.

"What are you doing here?" Lavin snapped at her. "It's past visiting hours."

"Don't quote rules at me."

Lavin stared at me through her beady little eyes. "What's he doing out of bed?"

"Leaving," Margot replied. "He's my brother and, quite obviously, he's been confined here by mistake. We don't have looneys in our family."

"Looneys?" Nurse Lavin's face went scarlet. The coarse hairs under her nose stood at attention.

"Well, that's what this place is," continued Margot the Misanthrope. "A looney bin."

"I've never heard such a thing. How could you possibly come in here and—"

"Step aside," Margot ordered. "We're leaving."

Frothing at the mouth like a mad pit bull, Lavin tossed aside the syringe of B-12 and braced herself like a sumo wrestler. "Try it. Just try to get past me."

For a second, I thought Margot might deck her, but she turned to me. "Adam, would you take care of this creature. I don't want to mess up my manicure."

When Fran Lavin charged at her, I barely had time to

step forward. Using Nurse Lavin's considerable forward
momentum, I flipped her off balance. She turned a midair
somersault and landed on the bed, gasping for breath.

There seemed only one thing to do. Before she recovered, I fastened the passive restraints on her wrists and
thick ankles. By the time I'd finished, she was fully alert
and struggling furiously. "You'll never get away with
this, McCleet."

"That's so cliché," Margot said, standing over her.
She'd retrieved her Bride of Satan hat from the corner of
the room and plucked the syringe of B-12 from the folds
of her long veil.

When Lavin opened her mouth to yell, Margo stuffed
a wad of veil in her mouth. Her eyes were wide as headlights, shocked that anybody dared to lay hands on her.

Margot not only dared, she enjoyed it. Her smile at
Lavin was pure evil. "Don't mess with the McCleets,
honey."

She strode to the door. "Come along, Adam."

I trotted behind her, semiobedient. The ward was, indeed, vacant, and I supposed everybody was at dinner. I
wondered if everybody included Jerry. It seemed the
most likely place to find him, but I couldn't very well
stroll in there and ask if Jerry could come out to play.

"Margot, I need your help."

"You need a nice long bath. Maybe a pedicure. Really,
Adam, it's so relaxing to have somebody paint your toes.
After that, I'm sure you'll be just fine."

"I want you to go into the dining hall—"

"Really, Adam, I hate to indulge your delusions."

"If you don't, I'm going to pitch a fit right here and get
myself committed for life. How embarrassing would that
be?"

"Oh, all right."

We crept through the bushes to the window. Actually,
I crept. Margot marched right up as if she had every right

in the world to be doing exactly what she was doing. I pointed to Jerry. "That's the guy. Bring him out here."

"No problem."

While I watched, she sailed into the dining hall, leaving open-mouthed shocked inmates in her wake. She went directly to Jerry. "You!" She pointed at him. "Come with me!"

"Okay, sure."

I was pleased to see that he'd managed to hang onto the briefcase. Matter of fact, he had it handcuffed to his left wrist.

After they'd left the dining hall, Dr. Whittle rose to her small feet and announced, "It's all right, everyone. Let's continue to enjoy our meat loaf, shall we?"

Thus reassured, the troops returned to their feed. Whittle scurried from the hall in pursuit of Margot and Jerry. We all met up at the same time in the courtyard.

Sandra Whittle regarded us with concern, not anger. And she was wise enough to discern that the most sane person in our threesome was me. "Adam," she said, "whatever are you doing?"

"I didn't blast the drug room with a semiautomatic weapon," I said.

"Of course not," she immediately agreed. "But I assume you were in there illegally. Weren't you?"

"Yes." I didn't tell her that I found the code in the book in her office. I wanted her on my side. "Are you familiar with Neurozak?"

"An experimental drug," she said. "Supposedly, its use is to lower inhibition, but it has the same propensity for releasing aggression. I believe it has been recalled to the manufacturer."

"What would you say if I told you that Grimhaur's lawsuit involved Neurozak? And there might be a quantity of that drug here at Mount Prairie."

She sighed. "I'd say we must look into it. I presume you have a plan. Shall we all go to my office?"

With Whittle as an escort, I felt fairly safe in heading through the Institute. But Margot bitched and moaned all the way up the stairs. Since it was after five, the receptionist had gone home, and I didn't have to worry about setting off a new fountain of tears.

In Whittle's office, I handed over the drug printout and gave her the dates to check.

"Why those days?"

"These times coincide with times when two patients at Mount Prairie had uncharacteristic flip-outs."

Margot sank into a chair, pouting. "What am I supposed to do while you people are staring at some dreary computer sheet?"

It occurred to me that she might be useful. "How are you with legal documents?"

She rolled her eyes. "Don't be stupid, Adam. Anybody who has been divorced as many times as I have knows law."

I passed her Grimhaur's file. "Check this for any reference to Neurozak."

While the two expert females perused their respective documents, Jerry and I stood there grinning at each other.

"We're breaking out?" he questioned.

"Guess so."

"Cool, man. I'm calling Abe and Marty to bring the camouflage vehicle."

"My Mustang?"

"Yeh, right."

When he picked up the phone, I didn't stop him. I kind of wanted my own transportation. Margot's threats about locking me up until I stopped being a looney weren't to be taken lightly.

Since everybody else was busy, I settled my butt in one

of Whittle's office chairs. I was glad that I wouldn't be on the receiving end of anymore of Lavin's B-12 shots, glad that I was leaving the Institute, glad that we were making some kind of progress. If we were . . .

I picked up a copy of *Gray Matters*. It was the one with Reeves's article.

"Nothing," Dr. Whittle said. "No mention of Neurozak."

"I've got something," Margot put in. "There are two suits in this folder, one is Walter Strom, hereafter referred to as the party of the first part, suing the Institute, hereafter referred to as the party of the second part and Grimhaur, hereafter referred to as the party of the third part. Whereas the other is Grimhaur and the Institute suing the pharmaceutical company, that manufactured the Neurozak, Wadco."

"Wadco?"

"Western Area Drug Company," Margot clarified. "The drug, hereafter referred to as—"

"Stop," I yelled, grabbing my head. "Skip the hereafters and tell me what the hell it says. Paraphrase."

"Don't bark at me, Adam. If you want my help, don't bark at me."

"Please, Margot."

"It says the drug was transferred to the attorney of record, two months ago, for independent analysis." Her eyes shone with an evil light. "That's little Raven Parducci, isn't it? Oh, I hope she's screwed up. I'd love to see her get her comeuppance after that George Washington incident."

Dr. Whittle flipped back through the computer papers to the date indicated on the legal document for a transfer of evidence. Her cultured British voice held a note of surprise, "Quite right, Adam. There is indication here that an experimental drug, Neurozak, was deleted from the Mount Prairie drug supply on that date."

"Raven's got the Neurozak," I concluded.

"Not necessarily," Sandra Whittle reminded me. "She might have done exactly as indicated and turned it over for analysis."

"So, we need to break into her office and search," I suggested.

Jerry bobbed his head enthusiastically.

Margot was also in favor. "I always hated that little Raven and her whining about growing up Vietnamese. As if anybody cares."

"Vietnamese?" Whittle questioned. "Ms. Parducci claims to be Vietnamese?"

I glanced at *Gray Matters,* and remembered the article about early speech patterning. Raven didn't look Vietnamese. But, more importantly, she didn't *sound* Vietnamese. "Impossible, isn't it? She's got no accent."

"None whatsoever," Whittle said. "She might have been to Vietnam, but she wasn't born and raised there."

"God!" Margot exploded. "Everybody's been feeling sorry for her for no good reason at all. That pig! I hate—"

"Why?" I asked Whittle. "Why would she pretend to be Vietnamese."

"Much as I deplore instant analysis, it would not surprise me. Abused women often invent alternate histories. Their own childhoods are too traumatic, so they assume other identities."

"So, Raven might really believe she's Vietnamese."

"Quite."

And she might want revenge for the deaths of her imaginary mother, brother and sisters at the hand of the American GIs. What better place than Mount Prairie, an institution that specialized in post-traumatic stress disorder, to find vets. And drug them?

"Let's go," I said. Our destination was Raven's office. I allowed Margot and Jerry to precede me out the door and turned back to Sandra Whittle. I felt like hugging her, and telling her that she was finally the shrink I could trust. Instead, I said, "You might want to check on Nurse Lavin. She's in restraints in my former bedroom."

"Former room?" Her eyebrows arched disapprovingly, but her mouth was smiling. "Are you leaving us, Adam?"

"That's correct."

"Come back and see me, anytime."

I had a feeling that I would.

The arrival of Abe, Marty and Duffy in the Mount Prairie parking lot was suitably dramatic. With Marty behind the wheel, they circled the drive. Hot in pursuit was Captain Jack in the bubba-mobile. The first time they passed, I yelled, "What the hell is going on?"

"Blocking the driveway," Abe replied. "He wouldn't let us out."

Captain Jack roared after them. He was, apparently, intent upon inflicting severe and irreparable damage on my rear bumper. He'd outfitted the front of the bubba-mobile with a snowplow.

"Jack," I yelled. "What's the problem? I'll pay for the damn paint job."

"Screw you," he squealed, tossing an empty can of Olympia beer at me.

Fortunately, the snow plow slowed him on the corners. On the next circuit, Jerry and I jumped in. "Bye, Margot."

"I think not." She sniffed. "If that slut Raven is involved in this, I'm—"

Her words were lost as we whipped out of the parking lot.

Duffy, turned in the front seat, flipped her hair and

said, "Like you guys are so much fun. I mean, really more funner than my friends."

"Show him," Marty said.

She flashed an engagement ring with a diamond the size of a .45 caliber slug. It had to be from a bubble gum machine. "You're not engaged," I said.

"Oh, but, like we are. Mumsey and Daddy don't know yet. But, we are."

I gave directions to Raven's Ye Olde Law Office in Noble Heights. It was only six-thirty and still light. The cover of darkness would have been nice for a break-in, but I had the sense that speed was of the essence. If Raven had, in fact, managed to dose both Eric and Kurt with Neurozac, triggering their superviolent reactions, she was legally responsible. I wasn't sure exactly how, but it had to be actionable. Otherwise, why would she have hired the sniper to kill Grimhaur? Why would she have trapped me in the drug closet and blasted away like there was no tomorrow. The woman was getting desperate.

Behind us, Captain Jack jammed on his horn and treated us to the discordant *ooo-ga, ooo-ga.*

Abe and Jerry simultaneously gave him the finger.

"Don't do that," I admonished them. "Don't tick him off."

"Let me tell you something, Adam," Abe offered. "There are times in this life to sit back and do nothing. Believe me, I've backed off more often than not. But there are times when you got to take the bull by the balls."

"What's his prob?" Jerry demanded, staring at the bubba-mobile with undisguised longing. "That's one fine machine. If I had a truck like that, I'd be a happy camper."

The nose of the snowplow nudged my bumper. I was trying really hard to stay calm. This morning, in the conference room, I'd expelled enough hostility to lower my aggression level to zero.

Marty pulled up at a stoplight and Jack smashed into the back of the car.

Wearily, I said, "Shit."

I climbed out of the back of the convertible Mustang and onto the hood of the bubba-mobile. I stared in the windshield. "Back the hell off, man. This is the last time I'm going to tell you."

"Then what?" he yelled. "You going to spray paint more shit on my truck?"

"I will personally jam a spray paint can down your ignorant throat and write my initials on your spleen."

I dove back into the Mustang as Marty drove away.

Apparently, my threat had given Captain Jack something to think about, because he held back. He was still following us, but at a safe distance.

After we parked in a small lot beside Raven's office, I told Abe, Marty and Duffy to wait. "Protect the vehicle," I instructed.

"What about Jerry?"

"I need him." If there was breaking and entering to be done, I figured Jerry was the expert rock thrower.

We were tapping politely at the front door when Margot's Mercedes squealed onto the sidewalk beside us.

I waved. "You can go away now, Margot. Everything's fine." I turned to Jerry. "What about this lock?"

"The good news is that we can get past it easy. The bad news is that there's a burglar alarm system."

"So we've got to move fast," I concluded. "Okay, Jerry, let's get the lock out of the way."

He was looking around for a suitable rock, then noticed Margot. "Hey," he called out. "How about if you pull up here and drive through the door?"

"Will it mess up my car?"

"Heck, no!"

Of course, it would. There was no way to perform a surgically correct collision with a car and a door without inflicting damage on both. "If I were you, Margot, I wouldn't."

"Well, you aren't."

She backed up slightly and took a run at the door, using her Mercedes as a battering ram. Only in Noble Heights, land of upscale lunatics, could this be happening.

The door crumbled.

Margot backed up. There was surprisingly little damage to her car. Amazingly, she didn't seem to care. She fired a tight smile and cackled. "Don't you love the sound of things breaking?"

"Not particularly."

"I might be good at this, Adam."

"Breaking things?" I picked my way past the rubble of Raven's front door and went into the office.

"No, stupid! I'd be good at sleuthing. I figured out the whole thing with Raven, didn't I?"

As a matter of fact, she didn't. But we didn't have time to argue. I figured the Noble Heights police would be there at any minute, and I really wanted to present them with a completed investigation before they hauled me off to jail.

"We need to find the Neurozak," I said.

"Liquid or pill?" Jerry asked.

I didn't know. I had never actually seen the stuff. "Let's try refrigerated first."

In the employee lounge, we located a refrigerator that was packed with juice and soda pop. The freezer held several packages of frozen yogurt bars, but nothing that looked in the least bit suspicious.

Gleeful shouts from an inner office indicated that Jerry had found a safe. It appeared to be more of a decorative

piece than anything else. An antique design was applied
to the front corners and the top held several plants.

"What do you think?" Jerry asked.

Margot was right there beside him. "What we need,"
she said, "is dynamite."

Jerry concurred.

"How about try the handle," I said. When I did, the
metal door opened. It appeared to be nothing more than
personal storage space for Raven Parducci. There was a
stack of stationery. I noted that it was gray with a red
border, just like the piece of paper Jerry had found with
the code number for the drug closet. I squatted down to
take a better look in the rear of the safe.

There was a shimmer of light against glass. I removed
a tray of glass vials. The markings on the labels indicated
that I had found a quantity of the experimental drug,
Neurozak.

I held it up to the overhead light and studied the clear
pinkish liquid. It looked exactly like B-12.

That was how she'd done it. Raven had gone onto the
wards with her supply of Neurozak and substituted it for
B-12 which would then be administered by the nurses
without anyone suspecting a thing. But how could she be
sure who got the shot? How could she orchestrate the administration of shots? I knew there was the notebook log
in the drug closet. But how could she tell the order in
which the shots would be given?

"What?" Margot demanded. "What are you doing,
Adam? Why are you just sitting there?"

I was sure the police would be there momentarily to
ask the same questions and more. "Let's get out of here."

I tucked the Neurozak under my arm and we made our
exit. As I suspected, the cops had arrived. The only reason they hadn't charged the building with pistols drawn
was Duffy, the banker's daughter. She was standing in
front of the battered down door, lecturing them. "If

you'd been doing your jobs, instead of scarfing donuts which aren't really good for you anyway, we wouldn't have to break down doors and stuff. Like, you know what I mean?"

"Yes, Duffy," said one of the uniformed policemen. "But we really have to—"

"Like these people are my friends. I promise they won't do anything wrong. Okay? Like okay?"

Marty smiled at me. "Isn't she something?"

"Yeh, something."

But I'd seen something a lot more interesting beyond the flashing police lights and my Mustang and the bubba-mobile. I recognized Raven's small face, peering from the driver's side window of a gray BMW that was parked across the street.

She seemed to look directly into my eyes and laugh. She was going to get away with it.

Unfortunately, the vehicle that was the most in the clear was Margot's Mercedes. I remembered that day when Reeves and I had been returning to the marina and Margot had chased us down under the pretense that Reeves had forgotten his pen. She'd been stubborn, hard to shake, a pain in the butt. Actually, she might have a talent for this stuff. I pointed at the BMW. "Margot, let's go. Follow that car."

We were in pursuit.

Margot and I followed Raven.

The traffic jam in front of Ye Olde Law Office must have broken up quickly because I heard a happy tooting of a car horn, turned and saw Marty, Duffy and Abe following us in the Mustang. Then came the bubba-mobile. I couldn't see past that, but I assumed that there was a parade of police cars behind Captain Jack's truck.

Raven was cruising southeast, keeping within the speed limit, staying on narrow double-lane roads.

Margot hunched over the wheel. "I'm going to ram her little Beamer butt."

"Gosh, I really wish you wouldn't."

"Why's that, Adam? Chicken?" She made clucking noises and cackled again. "Don't be a big baby. Little Miss Prissy Raven Parducci is responsible for Reeves's death. Are we going to just let her drive into the sunset?"

"Though I'm sure the idea of law and order is way beyond you, I'll try to explain. When we've fingered a murderer, it's not our job to run them down like a dog and kill them."

"Why not?"

"That's what cops are for."

She was edging up closer and closer to Raven's bumper. "Can I at least run her off the road?"

"No."

Behind us, I heard Duffy and the Death Squad singing along with "Satisfaction" on the radio. Behind them, Captain Jack lurched and hovered, waiting for the proper moment to crash. And then, there had to be a contingent of Noble Heights police cars. I had the feeling that I was riding in a demolition derby parade.

We were headed in the general direction of Oregon City, and I wondered about Raven's destination. "I wish I could talk to her," I mumbled.

"Why not?" Margot said. "I've got her car phone number in my Day-Timer. Use my car phone."

The whole idea was so yuppified that it made me a little ill, but this was Noble Heights, after all. I found the number and dialed.

She answered right away. "This is Raven."

What does one say to a woman who drugged two men and caused the death of a third. Not to mention the cold-blooded killing of the sniper. Or the attack in the drug closet. "This is Adam."

"You think you've got me," she said. "But there's nothing. No evidence."

"Nothing except for your little stash of Neurozak. And the gun. And the notation for the code to the drug closet written on your stationery. Nothing except the fact that I'm pretty damn convinced that you were dosing the B-12 at Mount Prairie with Neurozak."

She muttered a curse. I recognized the language. Vietnamese.

"Why?" I asked. "Why did you pretend to be Vietnamese."

"I am," she insisted. "You bastards killed my family."

"What about your adoptive parents? Somebody talked to your mother."

"My mother is dead."

"And your father?"

"I have no father. There was never a man who meant anything to me. Never! They are all bastards."

It would have been handy to have Sandra Whittle in the car, offering me wisdom and advice in how to handle post-traumatic stress in abused women. But this probably wasn't the ideal condition for therapy.

"Pull over, Raven. We can take care of all this."

"I won't go to jail." She stomped on the gas and shot ahead of us. "You can all go to hell."

Margot tried to keep up, but Raven was flying. And I had a pretty fair idea of where she was headed. I used Margot's phone to call the cops. I wasted valuable minutes explaining that I was part of a high-speed chase involving a BMW, a Mercedes, a Mustang painted in camouflage pattern, a bubba-mobile and several cops. Finally, I got somebody who seemed to understand that what I needed was a police blockade that would force Raven to pull off the road.

It was too late. We were winding along the Willamette,

headed toward a section where there were vertical cliffs with a drop of over a hundred feet.

I dialed Raven again. But she didn't answer.

With Margot at the wheel, we were sailing. The Mercedes was a fine, solid car, capable of hugging difficult roads, but we were still taking the curves on two tires.

At the top of a rise was a bluff. Nothing beyond but blue sky.

Raven's BMW, moving at sixty-five miles per hour, soared off the edge. The car seemed to float for a moment, suspended between earth and sky, then dropped to the bottom of the canyon with a crash.

We all pulled off to park. The front bumpers of our vehicles were poised at the edge of the cliff as if they were looking down. We gathered in quiet little clumps.

Duffy shrieked and collapsed against Marty's chest, sobbing. Jerry had loaded Abe into his chair. They stood looking out at the river. And the cops swarmed, doing their emergency procedure thing and telling us not to leave.

I realized that there was one member of our parade missing. "Where's Captain Jack?"

"Who cares?" Margot said. "Too bad about the Beamer."

"And the lady," Jerry reminded her.

"Sure, too bad." Margot said, studying the finish on her perfect manicure.

I saw the bubba-mobile easing forward quietly, inch by inch, toward the rear bumper of my Mustang. Geez, didn't this guy ever give up. Some people—like Raven— couldn't get revenge out of their systems. Not that I was an expert on forgiving and forgetting, but I wasn't psycho about it.

I started toward Jack. "Hey, let's get this square."

He floored it. The snow plow lurched forward and

made hard contact with my Mustang. I could only hope that Marty had remembered to set the parking brake.

He hadn't. In response to the bubba bump, my Mustang edged over the cliff and plummeted, bouncing end over end.

"Oh my God!" Duffy screeched. She stared over the edge. "So, how come it doesn't explode into flames?"

"Just lucky, I guess."

Chapter Eighteen

About four months after the death of Raven Parducci, I had completed the memorial statue for the Noble Heights town square. Of course, Margot made a big deal of the unveiling, which was to take place on the day before Halloween, which meant that the residents of Noble Heights were colorcoordinated in black and orange.

I hadn't expected a crowd, but it was a Saturday and a community event, so there was a respectable throng. Not as big as the Fourth of July parade and, I hoped, not as bloody.

All my former suspects—except Fran Lavin—were there. Lavin would never forgive me, but the others seem to have found reasons to forget my chair-smashing, window-busting episode. The Schmidts stood side by side. They were even grateful to me. Though Kurt was still convicted of manslaughter, his sentence was mitigated by the fact he'd been drugged. His time for enforced stay in a mental facility was to be reduced. Birkenshaw and Noble would never be my best friends, but we managed to face each other without spitting.

I stood between Nick and Alison, holding hands with her. She was the first to see Dr. Sandra Whittle making her way through the respectable-sized crowd. The doc

was hard to spot. Her little head was level with most people's shoulders. Nonetheless, she found a place beside
Alison and they exchanged greetings before she twinkled
at me, "And how are you feeling, Adam?"

"Fine. Just fine."

"I'm holding your appointment for Wednesday," she
said.

I heard Nick chuckle under his breath and turned my
head in time to see him wipe the smirk off his face.
"Hey," I said, "A little therapy never hurt anybody."

"If Adam ever makes it to one of these appointments,"
Sandra Whittle said. "He's cancelled three. No, make
that four."

Alison leaned toward the doctor and whispered, "He
has this little problem with commitments."

And they giggled. I wasn't sure that I liked the idea of
my girlfriend and my shrink snickering about me. Before
I had a chance to complain, we were joined by Marty and
Duffy who were now officially an engaged couple. Marty
had become totally acceptable after he transferred the
considerable monies in his Swiss bank account to Duffy's
daddy's bank. Who knew that Marty was an heir? Or
that the giant diamond was real?

"Like, hi, you guys." Duffy had her baton with her and
wore orange crepe paper tassels on each shoulder like
epaulettes.

Being unsure of the procedure at statue unveilings in
Noble Heights, I asked, "Are you performing today?"

She batted her long eyelashes at Marty. "I already
did."

"I like when she marches," he said.

As they moved away, Alison murmured, "The perfect
couple. Do you think they'll ever get bored?"

"I don't think they know the meaning of the word."

We were still missing Abe, Jerry and Eric, but I wasn't
too concerned. Alison's brother had a new job, and it was

hard to get away. Abe and Jerry had just opened a novelty store in Portland, and their business was booming. Literally.

Margot stepped onto the platform where my statue was covered with a huge canvas cloth. There was a yellow rope attached to the top of the canvas that would be lifted when the time came.

Margot wore her usual Halloween costume of a business suit and her own charming personality. She tapped on the microphone and did a testing, one, two, three, before starting, "Okay, everybody settle down. This is a solemn occasion."

The crowd stilled slightly, but people were still gathering and chatting.

"That's enough," Margot said. She paused for about three seconds, then screeched over the mike, "All of you. Shut up."

There was silence.

"Okay," she said. "This statue has been constructed after a great deal of effort from our committee." She introduced Noble, Birkenshaw and the Schmidts. "Those are the surviving members."

"A little ominous," Alison remarked.

"The deceased members are: Dr. Marion Grimhaur, who as I'm sure you all remember, was gunned down right here in the square during the Fourth of July parade."

She waited for applause. When there was none, she continued, "And I suppose I have to mention Raven Parducci, who took a header off a cliff in her Beamer while suspected of being at least an accessory to murder."

Instead of applause, there were a couple of groans.

"And Reeves Washington," she said. "He was a brave man and a good friend. This memorial statue is dedicated especially to Reeves's memory."

Most especially. Nick and I had our own special dedication last night. Before the statue got carted off to its permanent place, we had placed the ashes of Reeves Washington in their final resting place in the statue's base. It seemed like a fitting place, linking Reeves forever with the men he did so much to help.

"And now," Margot said, "the color guard."

Jerry, in his camouflage fatigues, marched in front. Eric, in his Desert Storm fatigues, pushed Abe in the wheelchair. Abe held the flag on his lap. Binky the dog brought up the rear with his tail wagging. They performed a snappy halt at the flagpole that stood to the left of the statue. Efficiently, they went through the ritual, fastening the large American flag to shackles and running it slowly up. Red, white and blue unfurled in the October breeze. The three vets saluted and pivoted.

I was touched. They weren't in fancy uniforms, but every step they took was true.

Then, Jerry marched to the far end of the yellow rope that was attached to the cloth covering the statue and I began to worry. Yellow rope usually meant a booby trap.

Jerry gave a sudden pull, and the cloth went flying, releasing half a dozen smoke bombs and a banner that said: Shop at Abe and Jerry's. Fifty Percent Discount on Exploding Turkeys for Thanksgiving.

He grinned at me and pulled up the banner.

I called the memorial statue, *Mortal Remains.* The figure, a steel gladiator, was down on one knee. On his left arm, he wore a round shield. In his right hand, he held a broadsword, and he wore a wide-rimmed helmet. He was constructed almost entirely of parts from my totaled Mustang, chromed and polished.

It had been a challenge to put an expression on the face. I left him looking down, not defeated but contemplating.

Alison squeezed my arm. "I love you, Adam."

It had been a while since she'd made that particular admission, and I was anxious to hear more. I accepted all the congratulations and got her away from there as quickly as I could.

We went to her car, slipped in the front seat and I said, "I'm glad you mentioned love. Because I—"

"It's okay, Adam. I'm happy with things the way they are. And I think I might be even happier after you start seeing Sandra on a regular basis."

I held out a black velvet box, ring-sized. "This is for you."

As soon as she opened it, I started apologizing. "It's not as big as the one Marty got for Duffy, but I did manage to get you a real diamond. Or diamond chip."

"It's beautiful, Adam."

"Will you marry me?"

She closed the lid on the velvet box, turned to me and took my hands in hers. "I'm not ready."

I felt a flood of relief. "Are you sure?"

"Let's just go steady."

PINNACLE BOOKS HAS
SOMETHING FOR EVERYONE—

MAGICIANS, EXPLORERS, WITCHES AND CATS

THE HANDYMAN   (377-3, $3.95/$4.95)
He is a magician who likes hands. He likes their comfortable
shape and weight and size. He likes the portability of the hands
once they are severed from the rest of the ponderous body. Detective Lanark must discover who The Handyman is before more
handless bodies appear.

PASSAGE TO EDEN   (538-5, $4.95/$5.95)
Set in a world of prehistoric beauty, here is the epic story of a
courageous seafarer whose wanderings lead him to the ends of
the old world—and to the discovery of a new world in the rugged,
untamed wilderness of northwestern America.

BLACK BODY   (505-9, $5.95/$6.95)
An extraordinary chronicle, this is the diary of a witch, a journal
of the secrets of her race kept in return for not being burned for
her "sin." It is the story of Alba, that rarest of creatures, a white
witch: beautiful and able to walk in the human world undetected.

THE WHITE PUMA   (532-6, $4.95/NCR)
The white puma has recognized the men who deprived him of his
family. Now, like other predators before him, he has become a
man-hater. This story is a fitting tribute to this magnificent animal that stands for all living creatures that have become, through
man's carelessness, close to disappearing forever from the face of
the earth.

*Available wherever paperbacks are sold, or order direct from the
Publisher. Send cover price plus 50¢ per copy for mailing and
handling to Penguin USA, P.O. Box 999, c/o Dept. 17109,
Bergenfield, NJ 07621. Residents of New York and Tennessee
must include sales tax. DO NOT SEND CASH.*